TSALMOTH

STEVEN BRUST

TOR PUBLISHING GROUP
NEW YORK

TSALMOTH

Copyright © 2023 by Steven Brust

A Tor Book
Published by Tom Doherty Associates / Tor Publishing Group
120 Broadway
New York, NY 10271

www.tor-forge.com

Tor® is a registered trademark of Macmillan Publishing Group, LLC.

The Library of Congress has cataloged the hardcover edition as follows:

Names: Brust, Steven, 1955– author.
Title: Tsalmoth / Steven Brust.
Description: First Edition. | New York : Tor, Tor Publishing Group, 2023. |
Series: Vlad ; 16 Identifiers: LCCN 2022056791 (print) |
LCCN 2022056792 (ebook) | ISBN 9780765382849 (hardcover) |
ISBN 9781466889705 (ebook)
Classification: LCC PS3552.R84 T73 2023 (print) |
LCC PS3552.R84 (ebook) | DDC 813/.54—dc23
LC record available at https://lccn.loc.gov/2022056791
LC ebook record available at https://lccn.loc.gov/2022056792

ISBN 978-0-7653-8285-6 (trade paperback)

Our books may be purchased in bulk for promotional, educational, or business use.
Please contact your local bookseller or the Macmillan Corporate and Premium
Sales Department at 1-800-221-7945, extension 5442, or by email at
MacmillanSpecialMarkets@macmillan.com.

First Tor Paperback Edition: 2024

Printed in the United States of America

0 9 8 7 6 5 4 3 2 1

This one is for Sisi,
with love, and art, and music.

THE CYCLE

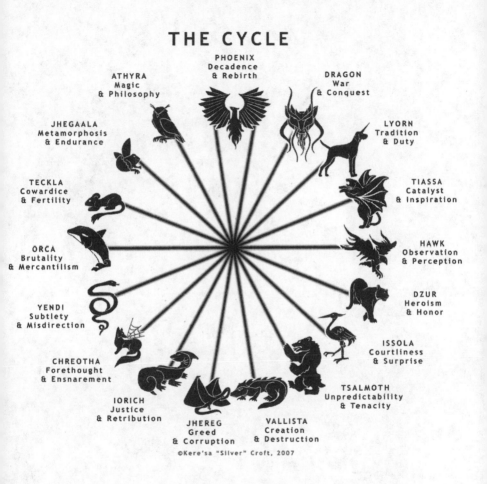

PHOENIX
Decadence
& Rebirth

ATHYRA
Magic
& Philosophy

DRAGON
War
& Conquest

JHEGAALA
Metamorphosis
& Endurance

LYORN
Tradition
& Duty

TECKLA
Cowardice
& Fertility

TIASSA
Catalyst
& Inspiration

ORCA
Brutality
& Mercantilism

HAWK
Observation
& Perception

YENDI
Subtlety
& Misdirection

DZUR
Heroism
& Honor

CHREOTHA
Forethought
& Ensnarement

ISSOLA
Courtliness
& Surprise

IORICH
Justice
& Retribution

TSALMOTH
Unpredictability
& Tenacity

JHEREG
Greed
& Corruption

VALLISTA
Creation
& Destruction

©Kere'sa "Silver" Croft, 2007

PROLOGUE

Have you ever noticed that getting married is like trying to collect a debt from a dead guy?

If you're gonna get married, you gotta decide which traditions to keep, and which ones to throw away, and what to do that's got nothing to do with tradition. And you gotta work it out with someone else—you know, the one you're marrying? That one? Well, you gotta work with that person to get something that's okay for you both.

But if you're living in the Dragaeran Empire, and all your traditions go back to Fenario, where your family came from a few generations ago, then you got a whole 'nother layer of stuff to get through. It's complicated, and it's different for everyone. Just like if some jerk dies owing you money, and you want to get it back, there are a lot of things to consider, and you might start out dealing with it one way, but then change your mind, and you'll have to deal with different sets of customs: one being the Jhereg, that's my House and my organization, where we have policies about loaning money and collecting it, and the other from whatever House the dead guy was in. And then there's the Empire, which exists to make everything more complicated. And sometimes they get all tangled up together, and mixed in with other stuff that you'd think had nothing to do with any of it.

Let's go into detail.

1

INTRODUCTIONS

Most marriages among my people, Easterners, start when you meet someone you're attracted to. I mention that because among the Dragaerans, or at least the high nobility, it usually starts with families arranging things. Sometimes, like with the House of the Phoenix, they arrange for their great-great-grandchildren who don't exist yet to marry each other if the omens are right, or something like that. Not sure how that works, but it isn't my concern.

I also wonder, since they live so much longer than we do, if that makes a difference in how they think about marriage. I'd guess it does, but I don't know in what ways.

Funny thing I've noticed, by the way: anytime marriages are arranged, it's like, between a man and a woman, but among Easterners, and with the Houses where people pick for themselves, you get men marrying men and women marrying women or whatever. You can think about that if it's worth the bother. Me, I've always kind of liked girls. Like Cawti.

I met her on a warm, pleasant day with a nice breeze flowing in from the ocean-sea when she killed me. Nothing personal, she'd been paid. And I got better, didn't I? Death is only permanent if you're unlucky, which makes it the opposite of marriage. But, anyway, that's how we met, and then we hung around together for a while, and we got along pretty good. I mean, that isn't all it takes, but it's a good start, isn't it?

Also, I discovered that she was a kind of amazing kisser, and that never hurts. So we started spending time together, and we found out we both liked to cook. If you get along when it comes to kissing, cooking, and killing, there's a good chance everything else will fall into place, right?

⊰⊱

There are problems that just can't be solved by sticking something pointy into someone. I try to stay away from those kinds of problems, because they get complicated, and I don't like complicated. I'm a simple guy. Ask anyone. "That Vlad," they all say. "He's a simple guy."

"Hey Kragar," I called out to the next room. "I'm a simple guy, right?"

I heard footsteps, and he stuck his head into my office. "What?"

I repeated my question.

His eyebrows did funny Kragar-things, and he came in and sat down across from my desk. "What happened?"

"Why should something have happened?"

He just waited.

I said, "You know that Tsalmoth who went into us for eight and scampered?"

"Bereth. Sure, I put Sticks on it."

"Yeah, Sticks just got back to me."

"And he found him, and got the money, and broke his legs, and everything is fine now, right?"

"Heh," I explained. "Someone killed the son of a bitch."

"Need an address to send flowers?"

"No, I need a way to get my Verra-be-damned money."

"Hmmm. Tricky."

"I know," I said. "Tricky. And I'm a simple guy."

"Can he be revivified? We could add the cost on to what he owes us."

"Sticks says no."

"In that case, Vlad, I would suggest a clever strategy: write off the money."

I felt myself scowling.

"It's not tricky," he added, with his fake innocent smile.

My familiar, Loiosh, arrived in the window about that time, flew over, and landed on my shoulder.

"What's going on, Boss?" he said into my mind.

"Nothing, nothing."

He let it drop.

I said to Kragar—

Wait a minute.

Sethra, Why are you still here? Last time you put me in a room with this box and just left.

Wait, Seriously? You think you can help? But before, you told me—

No, no! I'll take a maybe. Maybe is good. If you can give me a maybe, I'm happy to tell you the whole mess. Get comfortable. Can I get you some wine?

Right. I won't count on anything, I'll just tell it. Only, uh, what happens when you come into it? I mean, do I say, "You did this?" which won't make sense to whoever is going to listen to this, or do I say, "Sethra did this," which is dumb with you sitting there?

Oh, yeah, Sethra. It's so easy to just pretend you don't exist. Heh.

Okay, okay. Where was I? Right. Talking to Kragar. He'd made that remark about, hey, it's not tricky. I said to him, "You see, you might not know this, but I don't like letting money get away. It makes me feel bad."

"Uh huh," he said.

"So, come up with something."

"How," he said, "did I know this was going to end up on my back?"

"On account of that, what's it called? Wisdom."

"Fatalism," said Kragar.

I shrugged. "Let me know what you get."

He left, muttering under his breath. I leaned back and closed my eyes. I checked my link with the Imperial Orb and did deep and powerful sorcery, which it was designed for. Just kidding, I usually leave the deep and powerful sorcery to those who are better at it; I used it to find out what time it was, and discovered that I had a couple of hours to wait until it was time to meet Cawti.

"Aw, Boss," said Loiosh. *"Do you know that every time you think about her—"*

"You can shut up now," I said.

While I waited, maybe I should tell you a bit about myself.

Nah, skip it. That's boring. You'll figure it out.

There was a street singer not far from my window, singing something in a language I didn't know—probably one of the classic disused tongues of the early Empire. I hate listening to songs when I don't know the words.

I still had a few minutes before I felt justified in leaving for the day to meet Cawti when she jumped the bell on me by coming in.

I was up out of the chair in a second, standing there grinning like a Teckla smoking dreamgrass.

Look, I'm telling you what happened, including it all, because that's what you paid for, so there it is. I probably looked like an idiot with that big grin all over my face, so go ahead and laugh. But if you do, I'll track you down and break both your kneecaps, got it?

Uh, I didn't mean you, Sethra. I meant, you know, whoever is going to listen to this.

Right. You aren't here.

All right, so I kissed her, which is as much as you need to know, and then we went out and did some stuff together. We ate and drank and laughed and all that. It was a good time. I asked about Norathar, her partner, or I guess ex-partner, and they'd been in touch, which was good. Then we had an argument about the best kind of pasta to serve with clams and promised to settle it by each doing our own recipe. Then we went home to her flat. She lives a good distance south of me, in a decent neighborhood where she's the only Easterner but where you can smell the ocean-sea, which she likes. And her flat, like mine, has its own kitchen. I mean, a real kitchen, with a stove, an oven, a sink with a pump, cupboards, and countertops. So we hung out there, and decided to find a place in South Adrilankha to have the wedding, and then we did what you do when two people can't keep their hands off each other.

Look, I'm not bragging, I'm just saying how it was, and that feeling that she wanted me was—

Crap, this is hard to talk about with you here, Sethra, and no one's business anyway.

Back to what matters, I finally got around to telling her about the guy who'd had the nerve to go and die when he owed me money.

"Some people," she said.

"I know. Thoughtless."

She stretched like a cat, which made me stupidly proud, as if I'd accomplished something. She put her head on my shoulder and said, "Mmmm. What about his family?"

"Maybe," I said. "I should find out."

She wrapped her leg around me and said, "Maybe." Who can argue with logic like that?

So that's how I decided to check out the guy's family. I still don't think it was that bad an idea, okay? It's not like I have the Dragon treasury; I need the money. And also, once word gets out that people can get away with not paying you, it's gonna keep happening, and eventually you get put out of business. You know, in the big steel thing in your neck way of being put out of business. Not my favorite idea. This time, what with the guy dying, chances are no one would have thought anything except *bad luck*, but I'm still new at this, so I'm not sure and didn't want to take chances. And I wanted my Verra-be-damned money.

I'm just saying this so you'll understand.

Oh, I know. Now you're saying, "He's going after a bunch of innocents, heartless bastard, blah blah blah." That's not how it is, that's not how it was ever going to be. I wanted to see if there was a way to do it clean and easy. I was not going to walk in and start making threats or doing violence to his kids or his grandparents or whatever. For one thing, well, maybe for the only thing, as soon as you cross that line and start messing with families, or with people who aren't involved in the organization, the Phoenix Guard stop being these friendly sorts who greet you with their palms out for their weekly payoff, and turn into mean sons-of-bitches with all sorts of sharp things and no sense of congeniality. And because of that, even if word never reaches the Empire, if the Jhereg thinks you're doing something that might get the Empire involved, then you will end up with a leaky body and a shiny skin. So I don't do that. All I figured on doing was finding out if there were any loose funds there that might be subject to friendly persuasion, by which I mean, this time, *friendly* persuasion. Sometimes you go up to a grieving widow and say, "Sorry for your loss, but he owed me money," and that's all it takes. I had no intention of pushing it any further than that. I didn't. I swear by Verra's extra finger joint I didn't.

The next morning, I told Kragar to find out what he could about the family, which is one of the things Kragar is good at. Some of the other things he's good at are reminding me of unpleasant things I've agreed to do, unintentionally sneaking up on me, and being irritating.

He said, "Don't you want me to tell you what I've come up with?"

"Sure. What have you come up with?"

"Check into his family."

"Good thinking."

"Thanks."

"Get on that, then."

"Already did."

"I suppose you expect a compliment."

"*And* a bonus."

"Good work."

"Thanks. The bonus?"

"Very good work."

"Nice."

"Let's hear about them."

He didn't use notes or anything this time. "Survived by a younger brother, has a fabric shop not far from here, just north of Malak Circle. Unmarried, an occasional lover, a Chreotha named Symik, nothing serious between them though. Parents are both alive, living in Cargo Point, in Guinchen, where they run an inn called Lakeview."

"Financials?"

"Hard to be sure, Vlad. The inn supports them, but not much

more, and there's no signs of wealth. I guess the brother is doing a bit better than the others."

"Then I'll talk to him. Get me his exact addr—Thanks."

Kragar smirked and walked out.

Well, I figured, no time like the present. I stood up, strapped on my blade, and checked the various surprises I keep concealed about my person. Not long before, I wouldn't have left the place without at least two, more likely four bodyguards, but things had quieted down now. That was good, I like quiet. I like things quiet, and simple. Did I mention I'm a simple guy?

So, yeah, a quick stop in front of the mirror to make sure my cloak was hanging right, and off I went. I keep meaning to practice putting on the cloak, you know, with a kind of swirl, like they do in the theater, but I never seem to get around to it, and I don't think the ones in the theater are packed with as much hardware as mine, so it might not be possible. But, hey, since I'm talking about it, let me tell you about my cloak. I love my cloak. It's Jhereg gray, ankle length, and looks good thrown over my shoulder or wrapped around, and it has inside pockets and seams to put things in, and a wide collar for more things to go under. And it looks very good on me; I know because Cawti said so.

Loiosh landed on my shoulder (he says the cloak makes my shoulder less bony, so that's also a plus), and the three of us—me, Loiosh, and my cloak—took a walk through the beautiful streets of Adrilankha. The bright blue and yellow and green clothes of the Teckla were most common, even if a lot of them had become dingy or gotten stained, but there were merchants we walked past as well, and now and then you might catch sight of a Dragonlord or a Tiassa who had business in this part of town.

Malak Circle is built around a fountain, with stalls and carts about the outer edge and streets and alleys shooting off from it. I don't know what magic is used to make the water shoot out from the mouths of the stone dragon and dzur into the cupped hands of the woman in the middle, or how more water sprays in from the sides, or where any of the water goes, but I know I like it, and sometimes I just stand there and watch the water. Not many do that.

There are Teckla in the area, most of them in service, running errands for the more successful merchants or the occasional aristocrat. For the Teckla, just like for the Easterners who live across the river, survival depends on two things: doing what they're told, and never slowing down. They don't have time to stop and look at the sparkling water. I don't blame them for it, it's just the stones they have to play with.

There are merchants around the edge, with carts or stalls: Chreotha, Tsalmoth, Jhegaala. They're much better off than the Teckla, as long as they keep coins coming in and goods going out; if they don't, they can fall even lower than the Teckla, out the bottom, living on scraps and stealing from each other in the Mudtown district, or parts of Little Deathgate. They always know that could happen, and it scares them like Morganti weapons scare me. Talk to one of them sometime. Ask one of them about courtball, and he'll tell you how much sales are better if some local team wins. Ask about the weather, and you'll hear how they can't sell anything when it rains. Ask about rumors of war, and you'll hear about how those rumors make customers stock up on some things and stop buying others. It's always buy and sell, sell and buy, supplying what customers want, and never slowing down to watch the fountain. I don't blame them for it; they, too, have the stones they were given and have to play them as best they can.

The merchants are supplied by the craftsmen: also Chreotha, Tsalmoth, and Jhegaala, and they, too, know what will happen if no one wants to buy what they make, or if someone can make it cheaper, or better. They have to keep the merchants happy the way the merchants have to keep the customers happy. Maybe they aren't told what to do in so many words, but they're told, and they listen, and they don't stop to watch the water because they don't have time, and I don't blame them either, it's just how the game works.

Once in a while, you'll see one of the aristocrats: a Dragon, a

Dzur, a Tiassa noble, an Iorich, a Hawk, an Orca, an Athyra; but even if you put all of them together, there aren't many of them, and even most of those can't support themselves as landlords, so Orca end up on ships, Dragonlords and Dzur in military service, Tiassa as writers or artists, Iorich as advocates, Athyra and Hawks as sorcerers. And all of those might as well be merchants or craftsmen, because someone is telling them what to do, and they're doing it, and if they do it too slow, they, too, will fall out of the bottom, because wishing won't turn a round stone into a flat one.

That's what I can do. I can slow down. I got my income, and my skills to fall back on. If I want more, I can work harder; if I want to take it easy, I can do that too. Yeah, I'm beholden to my boss, but most of the time, I just do what I feel like, just like the landlords, and no one tells me what to do.

That's why the Phoenix Guards hate me, and why some of those I passed in the market who saw my Jhereg colors hated me; I could do what they couldn't. And, worst of all, I was an Easterner—you know, human: short, short-lived, weak; Easterners were supposed to be the next step down from Teckla, and stay there; Easterners should do what they're told, and be quiet, and never slow down.

Some of those I passed knew who I was and what I could do. There are a good number of those in my neighborhood, and in the middle of the day, when the market is busy, they mostly stay out of my way. I'd be lying if I said I didn't get some pleasure out of that. But I got even more pleasure in knowing that no one could tell me what to do, and that I could slow down when I wanted. Because there's one thing we in the organization have in common: we don't like being pushed. People know better than to push us.

Today, I wanted to visit Bereth's brother, but I stopped for a bit on the way there to watch the fountain in the middle of Malak Circle, because I felt like it.

❧

I found the place easy enough; I must have walked past it a hundred times without noticing it. The sort of storefront shop that's pretty common in this part of Adrilankha: a small, permanent brick building with a couple of tables on the street in front of it, and most of the bolts of fabric and skeins of yarn on the tables. This time, however, the tables were in and the door was closed. In mourning for his brother? Probably. I looked up to see if there might be living quarters above it, and there were. I found a clapper and pulled it. I waited about five minutes, then heard footsteps.

He was a tall guy with long dark hair swept back, dressed simply in red and silver except for a white headband of mourning. He had one of those faces where there's like a line from the cheekbones to the chin, but I decided right away not to make any remarks about his having a long face, 'cause it'd only be funny to me and Loiosh and it wouldn't help. As he opened the door the snotty, "we're closed," died on his lips 'cause he recognized me. I didn't recognize him, but that's okay. He said, "I'm sorry, m'lord, we're not trading today."

"Sorry to interrupt your mourning, but can I have a couple minutes of conversation? It's a personal matter."

He looked like he'd rather invite in a dzur with a breath problem, but he nodded, bowed, and stepped aside. Just a few weeks before, I hadn't been getting this kind of respect; just goes to show what a few bodies will do. Though I gotta say, it helps how superstitious most people are. They think it's bad luck to show lack of respect to a guy who leaves knives sticking out of people. I followed him up the stairs. His shoulders brushed against both walls, and mine almost did. Good thing Dragaerans are skinny types, because I've known some fat Easterners who wouldn't have been able to use the stairs at all.

He had a tidy place with a kitchen like mine and a little sitting area, and probably a bed-room around the corner. There were a couple of psiprints on the wall, one of them of ocean waves crashing on rocks that almost looked like it was moving; the other of two guys—a Dzur and a Tiassa—in a seedy pub who looked like they were sharing a private joke. I was pretty sure I'd been in that pub at some point. I had to respect him for having his own kitchen. I did too, and like I told you, so did Cawti, but they're rare. Fact is, it looked a lot like my place, which reminded me I should get a new one now that I was moving up. You gotta look the part, right?

"How can I assist, Lord Taltos?" he said, motioning me to the one comfortable chair.

I took it. "Oh," I said. "You know me?" as if it was a surprise.

He bowed and remained standing.

I said, "Like I said, I hate to impose at a time like this. But your brother."

He nodded and waited.

"He owed me some money."

He didn't look terrified, but he did look wary, like maybe I was gonna start breaking bones or something, which, for reasons I already explained, I wasn't about to do. "It was eight hundred imperials," I said, "which to me is a lot of money. You know, I got a family." Which was true if you counted Loiosh as family. And I was gonna get married, so I'd have a bigger family soon. "So I thought, maybe when you get around to checking the estate, you could see if he had enough to take care of the debt."

"I'll look, my lord," he said, not sounding very convincing.

I thought about it. Eight hundred imperials is a lot of money. It's like half of what I get for putting a shine on someone, and that never comes cheap. In fact, my whole operation doesn't pull down more than a thousand a week, and I got expenses, you know? I don't know who you are, or what you do, but suppose you got some honest job, like, say, you're a journeyman saddler, and you bring in maybe ten imperials a week. Well, how'd you like it if some week you only made two, so you come home for four days stinking of leather and oil and only have a couple of imperials to show for it. Well, that's how I felt about losing this eight hundred, so I was not inclined to let it go.

But like I keep saying, you can't go around messing up the families of people who owe you money, because those are the ones who like to go to the Empire, and the Empire has no sense of humor about that kinda thing. So I stood up and said, "Hey, not to worry. I just felt I should let you know before the estate was settled, otherwise I never would have interfered at a time like this." I gave him a head-bob and turned for his door.

Just as I reached it, he blurted out, "Did you kill him?"

I spun back like I'd heard a sword clear its scabbard. "What?"

He didn't move, but he looked like it was taking an effort not to bolt.

"I asked if you had him killed," he said, and I had to give the guy some respect, you know? I mean, I could see saying this was scaring the heels off his boots, but he went ahead and said it. Tsalmoth are usually craftsmen of some kind, maybe merchants—they do the sorts of things anyone else would get tired of, but they have a reputation for finding different ways to do the same thing, which I guess keeps them from getting bored. Kragar once told me a joke about a Tsalmoth taking twenty years to get from Little Deathgate to the Hook because he had to take every path to decide which one was best. Point is, they aren't known for having guts, so I was impressed with the guy.

"First of all," I said, "I don't do that, you've been listening to too many rumors. I'm just a peaceful guy who runs an herb shop. Second, why would I kill a guy who owed me money? He can't pay when he's dead."

"You could ask his brother," he said.

I blinked. "Okay, you got me there. But no, I didn't do the guy. I was still expecting my money."

"Then who killed him?"

"I got no idea."

"Then do you know why—"

"What I know is that I'm done answering questions now," I said. I took a step toward him. "Did I manage to get that across, or do I need to explain in detail?"

"I understand, my lord."

This pleased me, because I've always felt clear communication is important.

I nodded, turned toward the door, then stopped and turned back. "Why *was* he killed?"

"My lord?"

"I gotta admit, you asked a good question. Who wanted this guy to splash? Uh, sorry," I added, because it's rude to use that kind of slang with the next of kin.

"I don't know, my lord."

"Yeah? Well, you know where to find me. If you hear anything, let me know. 'Cause now I'm curious."

I let myself out and went back to the office.

"*Boss?*"

"Yeah, Loiosh?"

"*What was that?*"

"Curiosity."

"*Uh huh.*"

"*Okay, I'm thinking maybe if this guy was into me, I wasn't the only one. And if someone in the organization puts down my guy, then he's going to assume the debt.*"

"*Think whoever that is will agree?*"

"We'll negotiate."

"*Uh huh.*"

I returned to the herb shop, went back through where a Shereba game was usually running, though right now it was dead. I went up the stairs behind the room and nodded to Melestav, my secretary. "Tell Sticks I want to see him."

He didn't say, "I don't know where he is," because he doesn't say stuff like that. Instead he says, "I'll find him," and then he does. That's how things work in my office.

I gotta tell you about this office. Most guys in the organization don't have an office. They might work out of the back room of an inn, or maybe rent a place above a tinker's shop, or set aside a room in a brothel, or maybe have some other legitimate business where they work. The bosses, the big bosses, don't even have that—they just sit in their manors all day and dispense orders psychically or by messenger. But I like things organized, and I like to know where my people are, and I like things to be neat. So I got a desk for Melestav to sit behind. That way, anyone who comes to see me meets someone sitting at a desk looking like the guy who takes care of shipping manifests. That Melestav has done "work" at least three times, and will cut your heart out of your chest without a quiver isn't something they see. When a customer comes in asking for a loan, or some Jhereg wants to open a business in my area, Melestav is the one they meet first. That's not how most Jhereg do things, but it's how I like it, okay?

Also, I should explain that I mean two different things when I say "my office." I mean, there's the place up above the herb shop that has a front room, a storage room for bodies (I'm kidding about that, okay?), a space for Kragar to hang his stuff, and a place where I sit. So when I talk about my office, I might mean the whole place above the herb shop, or just my own spot in it. I have a desk that's right by the door, facing it, so the door only opens until it hits the desk. I got three chairs in front of it, and one behind. I hired a good cabinet-maker to make that desk, so it's got a lot of drawers, and even a few concealed compartments, because who doesn't want those?

To the left of my desk, the room extends another ten feet and ends in a window that faces east, so the whole thing looks kind of narrow. The walls are dark, thin paneling I had laid down because I didn't like looking at plaster. The north wall has shelves, where I keep some spare cutlery. The south wall has a wardrobe so I can hang my cloak, and where I keep a spare jerkin and the dress cloak that I never use.

It took about ten minutes for Sticks to show up. You know how some guys, just from how they walk and how they carry themselves, look dangerous? Well, Sticks always looks like he's out on a stroll without a care in the world. He came in, sat down in front of my desk in the chair Kragar doesn't use, and stretched out his legs. "What's up, Vlad?"

"The crime of murder," I told him.

"That's terrible," he said. "You want to hear about an old one, or do you want a new one?"

"The first of those."

"Our friend Bereth."

"Yeah. Did you see the body, or just hear about it?"

"I saw it."

"Good. So, how did he get to become dead?"

"A garrote."

"Really? People use those?"

"Some."

"Huh. I've been carrying one around with me ever since Ta— ever since I got taught how to use it, but I've never seen why you'd want to."

"No blood," said Sticks. "Or, at least, not much."

"I guess. Point is, it was a pro."

He nodded.

I could have asked him who used a garrote, and maybe he'd have known, and maybe he'd have been able to find out. But either way, it would have gotten me fuck-all. I didn't care who killed him, I wanted to know who ordered it. I said, "Okay, sniff around a bit and see who might have wanted him shiny." I dug around in my desk and found a purse that felt like it had around ten imperials in it, and tossed it to him.

He caught it, stood, and went to work.

While he did that, I turned my attention to another matter, namely, what Bereth had borrowed the money for in the first place. At the time, I hadn't asked him; what do I care? I looked at his clothes and rings and figured he could afford to pay me back. So I'd told him the thousand he wanted would cost one hundred a month until it was paid back, and if he couldn't afford to pay back any of the principal, he still owed the hundred. He'd made two payments of two hundred and two more of just the hundred, and the next month he was gone.

"Kragar!" I yelled. Then I watched the door, because he has a way of sort of having been there without my noticing him, and that irritates me. This time, I saw him; he came in and took a seat.

"I'll bet you want to know something," he said.

"Uh huh."

"Is it something I already know? Because that's easier than going and finding things out."

"Maybe. Our dead Tsalmoth, Bereth. How did he get his living?"

"A few things. He had a small holding around Thasic worked by half a dozen Teckla that brought him a bit from rents. He was also a driller, which brought him something. And he was an alchemist, so he made some compounding perfumes."

"Legal, or illegal?"

"Mostly legal."

"'Mostly.' But some of it on our side of the street?"

"Some."

"That might be it."

"Might be what, Vlad?"

"Might be what he needed the money for. An alchemist doing perfumes, he's got some experience on working with the Jhereg for the illegal stuff, and now he wants to set up on his own. He probably doesn't have property enough for a money-tender to give him a loan, so he comes to me. It's a quick turn-around business, so he figures he can clear the debt in a month or four weeks."

"I can ask around, see if anyone heard of him planning a business or renting a place."

"Do that."

Now you're probably wondering what the organization has to do with perfume. I don't know, do you buy perfume? You might have put a little money into my purse, or the purse of someone like me. The reason is pretty much the same as anything we make money at: the Empire passed a law that invented a business for us. I gotta explain this a little. There's this thing called hishi that's sort of halfway between sponge and seaweed that grows on the bottom of shallow water near the coast. I've seen drawings, and, let me tell you, if I met something that looked like that in an alley, I'd run the other way. Also, I'm told you can't eat it, but if you've seen it, you wouldn't want to try. But what it is good for, for reasons I don't get, is as a base for perfumes. A little goes a long way, which makes it valuable. But here's the thing: the very best stuff grows off the north coast of Elde Island, and I guess the good people of that island, about whom I know nothing, don't use perfume. So that would mean it's free to grab, right?

Wrong. Anything coming in from outside the Empire is subject to import duties. Well, when you say import duties, I think smuggling.

People think the easiest thing to smuggle is gemstones, on account of how much they're worth for the size, but that's just not the case. All through the Eastern Mountains you got Imperial Sorcerers checking mountain passes, and they have spells that erupt like a lightning storm in their heads whenever they're pointing at anything with a crystalline structure. In case you weren't aware of it, gemstone are crystals. Teleport? Don't even think about it. I don't know how they do it, but I know that the border guards can tell the instant a diamond or a sapphire appears in the Empire that wasn't there before, and they'll be on you before you can say "amortization." (To be fair, it took me a long time to learn to say amortization, and I still don't know what it means except that it has to do with interest, but you get my point.) The result is, smuggling precious stones is risky business. Now, I know it happens, because I've been involved in a few transactions of this type, but it's not something for amateurs to get involved in. The beauty of hishi is that it's got a high return for the amount of risk involved.

Here's how the business works: You teleport to Ridgly and rent a small boat for like ten imperials, which includes a few Orca to crew it, then you cross over to Salute on Elde and you hire a couple of divers for maybe another five. You follow the coast east and then north about twenty miles—and remember, this is Elde Island waters, so even if they know what you're doing, the Empire can't touch you—till you get to Sailor's Bay and the divers go to work. If they're good, they can come up with maybe five pounds of the stuff in one day of diving. You take that, maybe buy the divers a beer and tip them another imperial, and then teleport back to the mainland, anywhere you want. You've just broken the law, but unless you're stupid enough to teleport into a customs office, there's no chance you'll be caught. Maybe someday the Empire will come up with a way to detect hishi like they do gems, but until then, there's no need to be clever.

Once you got this hishi, you bring it to an alchemist who will turn that five pounds into just under a pint of a clear liquid that's got all sorts of properties you want in perfume. You pay the alchemist about twenty gold, he hands you a jar of the stuff, which you then proceed to sell to perfumers for—get this—about forty imperials for a liquid ounce. Or maybe you sell the whole pint to someone for a thousand gold, and this guy does the distribution. Either way, you've just made what in my world we call a nice return.

Now, here's where it gets tricky. There's no chance you'll be caught smuggling, but you can be caught in possession, or selling the stuff, or at any point up until the perfume is made, and it's possible—not easy, but possible—to detect the processing. That means you need someone like me to pay off the local imperial guards so you won't be bothered. For this, you're going to cut me in on the profits. In exchange, I'm going to make sure you have the chance to do some honest dishonest work without interference. Out of each thousand gold, I might get a hundred, of which I'll spread around forty to various Imperial officials. Good deal for you, because you're still making nine hundred imperials on an investment of less than a hundred, and a good deal for me, because I'm making sixty for doing nothing. That's how the hishi smuggling business works, and, let me tell you, I've made good money at it. And not only that, but it makes people smell nice; who can complain about that?

Now, you ask, if this turns out to be true, why does this matter? I'll tell you why: Because maybe he'd taken that money and put it into supplies, and if I could find those, I could get some of my money back. Or there might even be a case or two of expensive perfume I could pick up and unload. I've had things like that happen.

Yeah, this was when I still thought I could maybe get my eight hundred back easy. That would have been nice.

In the meantime, I did my best to put the whole thing out of my mind and got back to work running my vast criminal enterprise, an enterprise so huge that eight hundred imperials was a big deal.

Point is, I still had no idea how complicated it was all going to get.

2

THE COURTSHIP

Before you can even think about getting married—I mean, for us humans—you got to get to know the person. You talk, you have drinks and food, you maybe kill a few people together, that kind of thing. Makes me wonder if Dragonlords ever court on the battlefield, but I think they don't, I think they're one of those Houses where things are arranged ahead of time. If you ask me, that's kind of sad. That time when you're falling for someone more and more, and you get that tension of, "does she like me as much as I like her?" and all that; well, it's good.

Of course, the main part of our courtship involved exposing a plot inside the House of the Dragon that was directed against Cawti's partner, so the question of whether we'd live through it sort of took over from a lot of the romantic stuff. Fact is, I wouldn't have traded it for a more normal courtship. And it did the same thing: gave us time to get more and more drawn into each other. From what I hear, it's like getting hooked on feridine—the deeper you go, the harder it is to get out, and the less you want to.

꒦꒷

A couple hours later I was going over the ledger of one of my brothels when Kragar said, "Hey, Vlad." I jumped a little and scowled at him, then said, "What'd you find?"

"Not much in the way of collateral. Legit guys wouldn't touch him, so you were right about that part at least."

"Good work. Okay, so now we find out if he was setting up as his own perfumer, and maybe stepped on someone's cloak."

"Yeah, or the other two possibilities."

"Two?"

"Might have something to do with him being a driller."

"New gear or something. Yeah. And the other?"

He shrugged. "Something else. Gambling debts, he wanted a vacation, I don't know."

"Right. Unlikely to have anything to do with his land if it's as small as you say."

"Yeah."

"Okay, you check into the driller possibility, I'll check and see if there are any Jhereg dealings."

"What, Vlad? You're going to go out and do something?"

I made an unkind suggestion; he snickered as he headed out.

Oh, right. Driller. Nothing complicated. That's the term for a guy who goes and uses magic or equipment or whatever to figure out where to find stuff in the ground, like ore maybe. Most of the ones I've met have been Tsalmoth, because who else has the patience for something like that?

Anyway, yeah, I decided to go see my boss.

I put on my cloak, checked my weapons, and, Loiosh on my shoulder, headed out onto the street to visit Toronnan. This was the guy who ran a chunk of Adrilankha, including mine. He let me run my area, or, well, he pretty much said, "Yeah, keep as much as you're tough enough to hold," and in exchange for this kindness, I paid him a cut of everything I earned from my operations. Toronnan had a paranoid streak, which led him to do all sorts of things, like keep a sorcerer around him all the time, and pay off some Phoenix Guards just to keep him informed of barracks gossip, and he kept changing where he worked from. In the time I'd known him, which wasn't that long, he'd worked out of a baize-room, a shiner-shop, and two different taverns. At the moment, he had a room above a stable, and it smelt just about how you'd think.

There were two guys playing cards, probably Shereba but I didn't look close enough to be sure. They gazed up with the bored expression guys like that get. If you ever see that bored expression, don't let it fool you; they're ready to cut your neck in a second.

I said, "I wanna see the boss."

One of them said, "He's busy."

"Okay," I said, and turned around to walk out.

"Hey," said the guy. "Where you going?"

I turned back. "You said he was busy."

"Whatdayawanna see him about?"

"I'm selling psiprints of toughguys with their heads up their asses, but I guess he don't need any."

"You looking to get opened up, whiskers?"

"No, I'm looking to see the boss."

They glanced at each other and shrugged. It wasn't like they'd never seen me before. One of them said, "I'll let him know you're here."

I figured to quit while I was ahead, and just nodded. *"Good thinking, Boss."*

"Glad you approve."

A minute later the guy came out and nodded me in. He didn't even stick his foot out to trip me as I went by, which I'd half expected; sometimes our massive and sophisticated criminal organization operates at the level of a pre-adolescent street punk.

I kept the door open, because shutting it might have made people nervous, and people do stupid things when they're nervous. Toronnan, who was always dressed like he was about to take in a concert in the Tiassa Wing of the Palace, and whose desk was always better arranged than my kitchen, gave me a barely polite nod and said, "What is it?"

"A Tsalmoth named Bereth. Was he into anybody for anything?"

He knew the name; I could see it register in the corners of his eyes and how fast he tried to cover it up.

"How would I know?" he said.

"No reason. But he died owing me, so I wanna know if it's okay for me to ask some questions, so if he was into anyone, maybe I can find something of his I could turn into money."

"How much?"

"Eight hundred."

He thought it over. I figured he had a, what do you call it, dilemma. Like, he wanted to tell me to just let it go, and, hey, he was the boss, so he could do that. But if he did, it'd be like saying he knew something about the guy, and it was pretty clear he didn't want to do that. He finally made a sort of a grunt and said, "Go ahead."

"Thanks," I said.

I smiled pleasantly to my two new friends outside his door and strolled back to the office, taking my time.

Now, in case you missed it, this was not something that happens a lot: this Tsalmoth was involved in something, for which he'd needed to borrow eight hundred gold, and which also involved someone else in the organization, and, for whatever reason, Toronnan didn't want me knowing about it. It was puzzling, and with eight hundred of my imperials at stake— well, eight hundred and ten with what I'd given Sticks—I don't so much enjoy puzzles.

"*Hey, Boss. Just how much do you think he wants you to not know about it?*"

"*Yeah, good question. Stay alert.*"

"*I always do.*"

I had the feeling that things were going to get complicated.

I hate complicated.

What I wanted to do was find Cawti and just hang out with her, maybe buy her lunch and talk about wedding plans. I didn't because I had work to do, and I got a sense of responsibility, and because I didn't know where to find her. I might have gone looking if Sticks hadn't come strolling in.

Yeah, he strolls. Once I saw him knock an obnoxious drunk on the head, then cross five steps and do the same to his buddy who was trying to draw a knife, and even then he looked like he was strolling.

When he'd strolled as far as a chair he sat himself down.

"Well?" I said.

"Nothing."

"Nothing?"

"Not a hint, not a whisper."

"Huh," I said. "That's annoying."

He nodded. "Well, I should add, a couple of people heard that he'd borrowed money from you."

"Figures."

He waited to see if there was anything else I wanted from him, while I tried to decide if it meant anything that there was no noise. Probably not.

But what made it odd is that Bereth wasn't a Jhereg. Maybe you didn't know this, but it's unusual—very unusual—for us to kill anyone outside the organization. I won't say it never happens, but there's always a good reason for it when it does, like some poor slob trying to get out of his debts by going to the Empire, or hiring mercenaries to protect him and thinking that means he doesn't have to do what he agreed to do, or, occasionally, someone who saw something he shouldn't have seen and refuses to be convinced of the virtues of silence.

But from what Sticks described, the guy was taken down by a professional, and, not to put too fine a point on it, we're the only professionals. It just seemed kind of weird that we were involved in killing a civilian—an unusual thing—and yet no one had heard of this guy having any connection to anyone but me. That's the sort of thing you can put too much emphasis on, because it isn't like we have all this communication going on among us. But it was worth noting at least.

It hit me suddenly that this could be aimed at me, but no, that didn't hold up. No one was that mad at me right now, and, if anyone was, this would be a stupidly over-complicated way to get at me. I had, uh, let's say, heard of something that complicated once, but it turned out to be a Yendi behind it, not a Jhereg, and there aren't that many Yendi around.

At some point I realized Sticks was still sitting there, and I grunted an apology and said, "Did you talk to Leggy?"

"Who's Leggy?"

"Tsk," I said. "You don't gamble enough."

He shrugged. "No future in it."

"True. Okay, thanks. I'll get hold of you if I need anything else."

"*So, I take it we're going out, Boss?*"

"*What would you expect?*"

"*I wouldn't expect you to show any sense by letting the whole thing drop, so, sure.*"

I gave my, "I'll be gone for a while, so mind the store" nod to Melestav, who gave me his "don't worry, I got this," nod in return. We got nods for all occasions. We should start selling them.

Then it was back out onto the street and down to a tiny little tavern near the edge of my area called the Dancing Biscuit. It was a single long room, with a polished bar all the way down one side and a single row of small tables, three chairs each, on the other. Behind the bar were a pretty good variety of wine, a couple of beer kegs, and two bottles of overpriced Eastern oishka up on a top shelf by themselves like they were something special. For some reason, the place always had a faint citrus smell; I can't think what would cause that unless the owner does it on purpose because he likes it. There was a guy sort of slopping all over a chair at a table all the way in the back, where he pretty much always is. He's called Leggy, and by trade, he handles betting. He'll handle any wager you want. In addition to the carts and the fights and squareball, he'll take action on when a ship will come in, how many duels will be fought next month, or which of two birds will shit first. He'll take any amount of action, but prefers small, and he's got a lot of regulars because they know he'll play straight and pay off without making them wait, and that when the Empire picks him up and puts him through it for not having a license, they won't learn who his customers are, and no records will be lost, because it's all in his memory. He's pretty remarkable like that. And he's good enough at setting odds that he makes money for himself, which means for me.

There's another thing he's good at. While he sits there at his table, customers and friends come up, sit down, maybe make a bet, maybe just have a drink, and wander off, and as a result, he hears things. He hears lots of things. Sometimes it seems like he hears everything there is to hear. He also drinks everything there is to drink without getting drunk. He might use sorcery for that, but I think it's just how he is. I'd bet on that, but who'd take my action?

I sat down at a table near the door and waited until the Teckla he was talking to finished her drink and wandered away, then I joined him at his table.

"Hey, Vlad," he said. "Checking up on me?"

"Forgotten any bets?"

"Ha. What are you drinking?"

"Clear and clear."

He signaled the host over, tapped his beer, and asked for a clear and clear for me. We didn't speak till the guy came back with a mug for him and a cup of watered white wine for me. We drank.

"So," said Leggy. "What is it?"

"A guy named Bereth, Tsalmoth. Heard anything about him?"

"Yeah. Somebody put a shine on him."

"That part I knew. Any idea whose cloak he stepped on?"

"I thought it might be yours. Word is he was into you for a fair sum."

"Yeah, I wish it was me, that'd save me a lot of work figuring out who it was."

"Sorry."

"What, nothing? Leggy, I'm disappointed in you."

He shrugged.

On impulse, I said, "Heard anything about a hishi deal?"

"Huh," he said. "That was Bereth?"

Ding goes the bell.

"So you did hear something?"

"Not a deal exactly. Was Bereth the guy with the hishi?"

"What guy with what hishi?" I was swinging blindfolded. I just had an idea Bereth might have been involved with the stuff, but I don't even know that for sure. "If you've heard something, I want it."

"There might be someone who knows."

"I'm listening."

"A few days ago a guy named Tuppi, a Hawk, comes in to make his weekly squareball bet. We're sitting around gabbing, and he says something about a Tsalmoth who just got robbed of about ten pounds of hishi that I guess he was carrying around with him like an idiot."

"Still listening," I said.

"That's about all I know, but it was about a Tsalmoth, and ten pounds of hishi is a lot."

"Any idea if his operation was protected?"

"I don't know, but if it was, that'd explain why he felt safe carrying it around."

"Yeah," I said. "But then it makes me wonder who had the nerve to lighten him of it." And why there was no noise about it, and how that might have played into him being put away, but I didn't say that aloud. I said, "Where can I find this Tuppi?"

"Not sure. I don't see him unless he comes in here."

"He must know other people you talk to."

"Let me think. Uh, yeah. He sometimes hangs out with another Hawk, a guy named Sojin."

"Tuppi. Real name, or nickname?"

"Nickname, I think, but I don't know his real name. Sojin might."

"Where do I find Sojin?"

"Pamlar, Department of Magical History, which probably means in the library next to the department building most of the time. I don't know what it's called."

I stood up. "Thanks," I said, and tossed him an imperial. I drained my wine, tapped the cup on the table in farewell, and walked out. I headed back to my office and called for Kragar.

I sat down at my desk, and he came in. "Nothing new," he said. "You?"

"Maybe. Get me a map of the city and mark Pamlar University, the library next to the Department of Magical History."

He put on the smirk that meant he was about to emit a witty remark, probably something about my education. "Shut up," I said. "Just get it."

He smirked even more, then went out.

"You know, Boss, it wouldn't hurt you to enroll in—"

"*You can shut up too.*"

He snickered into my mind.

Kragar returned shortly. I took the map, studied it, then stood up.

"Heading over there?"

"Yeah."

"Want company?"

"Sure. Just like the old days."

"The old days," he repeated. "You mean, like, last year?"

"Whatever."

"In the old days, no one wanted to kill you."

"In the old days, everyone wanted to kill me, but it wasn't personal."

The campus of Pamlar University is on and around a big knoll not far from the Imperial Palace, just past the Dragon Wing. I could have teleported, but I'm bad at it, and paying for one doesn't come cheap, and I was doing this to recover money, so I wasn't interested in throwing gold around. Some parts of the city had pedicabs, some of the nobles had horses, and there were even coaches for people who wanted tours or some such, but other than that, if you want to get around in Adrilankha, you teleport or you walk.

"Let's take a walk," I said.

It was a long walk, compared to what I'm used to. No one tried to hurt me as we passed the Dragon Wing of the Palace. Kragar kept up a stream of what he calls conversation and you'd call banter and I call Kragar talk. I enjoyed it, but don't tell him that. Loiosh mostly stayed on my shoulder, taking off to fly around every now and then. Just past the House of the Dragon (where no one attacked me either, just for the record), we turned left, climbed a hill, and a bit later were officially on the grounds of Pamlar University.

They tell me that the old Imperial Palace was never planned, that it just sort of happened, a piece at a time, and from the paintings and psiprints I've seen, I believe it. Wherever they found building designers—what's the word? Right, architects. Wherever they found the architects to do that, they went back to the same place for Pamlar University. Look, I don't pretend to know about building des—about architecturing, or whatever it is, but I got eyes, and when you walk into that big park with the grass they always seem to be cutting, and you stand in the middle, and you look around, you see the big dome that looks like a mushroom, and the long, low red brick thing, and another place that seems to have pieces sticking out in all directions, and right next to it a big white cube. They don't look like they belong together, and they don't look good. I don't know, but if they'd asked me, I could have done it better.

We went past the big cube and just behind it was an eight-sided, four-story structure with more glass windows than you could find in the rest of the city. Okay, so I'm exaggerating. Anyway, that was the library next to the Department of Magical History, so that's where we went, scholar Vlad and scholar Kragar. Oh, and let's not forget scholar Loiosh. We walked in like we had every right to be there, and acted like we didn't notice the looks we got. I think ours may have been the only two swords in the place. Tell you the truth, being around so many unarmed people made me a little uncomfortable.

There was an older Lyorn standing behind a counter near the entrance. We walked up to him and I said, "Know a guy named Sojin?"

I was reaching for a couple of orb to slide him, but before I could, he said, "You'll find him on the third floor, west side."

I don't know how things work in these places.

The stairs were metal covered in some rough thing, I guess so scholars wouldn't slip, and the steps had no backs, but I suppose they weren't worried about anyone slipping through them. Each story was two flights. We climbed. *"I'm turned around. Which way is west?"*

"That way."

I went that way, and Kragar never suspected anything. Damn, I'm good.

We found him at a long wooden table, with an open book in front of him, three closed ones next to him, and a notepad and a pencil. There were only a couple other people at nearby tables; Kragar found a place where he could keep an eye on them. He's good at that. I'm good at noticing when he does.

"Sojin?" I asked.

He looked up, took in our Jhereg colors—gray and black—frowned, and said, "Yes?"

"Just a quick question. Where do we find Tuppi?"

He frowned again, and stood up. He was shorter than Kragar, taller than me, dressed in black, and seemed kind of frail.

"Why?"

"I'm thinking about asking a girl to marry me," I said, "and I want him to stand for me."

"You do?"

I guess sarcasm doesn't fall under magical history, so I shouldn't have expected him to recognize it.

"No," I said. "Not really. I just want to talk to him."

He frowned again. I thought I'd maybe warn him that if he kept doing that, his brows might freeze in that position, but I was afraid it would just puzzle him, and then he'd frown.

He looked at us again, pausing at Loiosh—who was, I have to say, on his best behavior.

"I'm sorry," said Sojin. "I would like to help you, but I cannot."

"Why is that?"

"Tuppi is a friend. I don't know what you want of him, but I can't help you find him."

"Poor guy," said Kragar. "He wants to help you, but he just can't."

"Yeah, no doubt he feels terrible about it."

"You could beat him up to help give him catharsis."

"Good idea. I'm all about helping people get cathasis."

"Catharsis."

"Yeah, that. What is it, anyway?"

He stopped and looked puzzled.

The Hawk said, "It's an emotional release," as if Kragar hadn't just threatened him.

"Emotional release," I repeated.

"For example if your heart is broken, hearing a sad song might permit you to let the pain out, so you'll feel better."

"There's a word for that?"

He nodded.

"Well, thanks for explaining," I said.

"You're welcome."

"So, would you like some carthis?"

"Catharsis," said Kragar.

"Whatever. Would you like some, Sojin? I mean, if I were to break both of your thumbs, do you think you would feel better? Because we can do that. We're all about helping people."

I think it finally went into his head that we were actually threatening to hurt him. He looked at the nearby tables, but if anyone had been doing anything except ignoring us, Kragar would have said something.

"I—" said Sojin.

We waited.

"His real name is Kassier, and he lives just north of Little Deathgate."

"Where exactly?"

"I don't know. I usually see him at a place called the Stolen Boat off Undauntra near—"

"I know it," said Kragar.

"Good," I said. "Tell me something, Kragar. What would happen to this guy if Tuppi, or Kassier, or whatever, was warned that two Jhereg were looking for him?"

"He'd get catharsis," said Kragar.

I nodded, and so did Sojin.

I patted his cheek. "I hope your studies go well," I said.

Loiosh hissed, because he just likes to do that.

We went back the way we'd come.

We walked more. That's all you need to hear. The Stolen Boat turned out to be a big, square place that looked like it had once been some kind of hang-out for the nobility: a lot of gilding on the fixtures, polished floors, expensive chandeliers. I don't know much about rugs; the ones on the floor were thick and patterned in red and black and looked expensive. All in all, the house was still in good shape. The bar was in the middle, and a quick glance said they had a big choice of wine, including some expensive ones. There were tables on each side of the bar, which was a long rectangle, and, best of all, they had booths along one side, just like a lot of Eastern restaurants. Big, high-backed booths of stuffed leather. Kragar said it was owned by a guy named Gerifin who was one of us, and that there was s'yang-stones in the back and a small brothel upstairs. I looked around and realized that all four "customers" were tags waiting for business, and there wasn't yet any business, which meant there was no Tuppi.

"Wait, or come back?" said Kragar just as I was about to ask him the same question.

"Do they have anything worth eating?"

"Whatever that bird is on the spit smells good."

"Yeah, it does. Okay, we wait," I said.

We found a table near the back. The tags looked us over the way Loiosh looks over a dead teckla, then shrugged and went back to being bored. The host came over and we ordered a bottle of decent wine. I said, "Know a guy named Tuppi?"

"Maybe."

I flipped him half an imperial.

"Yeah," he said.

"Give me a nod when he comes in?"

"Gonna kill him?"

"If I was gonna kill him, do you think I'd make you such a perfect witness?"

He shrugged, like maybe he didn't wanna assume I was that smart. "Gonna hurt him?" he said.

I flipped him another half imperial. He nodded, went away, came back with the wine and two cups. Later, we had him bring us slices of a goose that was drenched in so much wine the poor thing probably drowned, but had been stuffed with enough garlic, lemon, and boulder mushrooms to make up for it. We ate a lot. The host pretended not to see me slipping scraps into my cloak for Loiosh, who informed me that, from now on, he would only eat goose, and I was to keep him supplied at all times. I reminded him who had the big office, and he bit me, but not hard.

We waited so long we were considering more goose, or maybe some of the kethna that was now on the spit, when the host caught my eye and nodded as Tuppi came in. By that time, the place had filled up a lot: Teckla, Jhereg, a couple of Chreotha.

"Let's wait a bit," I said.

"Sure."

Tuppi went upstairs with a tag who was kind of pretty in a Dragaeran sort of way but whose hair was in danger of escaping to freedom and going off to live its own life. We got the kethna, which was salty but not bad. They used the same boulder mushrooms they had with the goose. Maybe they'd gotten a big batch of them in, but I decided I'd have to try to cook with them at some point.

Tuppi came back down, took a table near the bar, and ordered a beer. By now we'd been there pretty much the whole day, and the place had gone from empty to full and was now clearing out a little. Tuppi finished his beer, stood up, and so did we. We followed him out, then Kragar tapped his shoulder. He turned around, and I got behind him, and tapped his shoulder. He turned again, saw me, and started to make some remark, probably about me being an Easterner. I saved him from being rude by saying, "What do you know about a Tsalmoth named Bereth?"

"Never heard of him."

"Did you hear about someone losing ten pounds of hishi?"

"Nope."

"*Anyone around, Loiosh?*"

"*You're good, Boss.*"

I put my palms together and brought them up against his jaw. He fell back against the wall and I moved in and pulled a knife.

"What we have," I told him, "is a problem of perception. See, because I'm holding this dagger to your throat, with the point pressed against your chin and kind of angling up, you perceive me as threatening you. This interferes with our relationship. We need a way to work past it. I'd suggest maybe you tell me what I want to know, which will show a willingness on your part to put our relationship on a friendlier basis. Then I'll remove the knife, and then maybe your perceptions will change. What do you think?"

He was in the same pose everyone in that situation takes: knees locked, head back, arms stiff at his sides, palms toward the ground, fingers spread.

"Ughla," he said.

"Okay, I can see your point of view," I said. "But to, you know, put our relationship on a sound footing, I think you need to say more than that. Or, if you want catharsis, I can arrange that." I pushed the dagger a little.

I was hoping he'd ask what catharsis was, on account of I could answer, but instead he sort of squeaked out, fast, like he wanted to get it all said in the few seconds left to him, "A guy asked me if I knew anyone who could process hishi."

I put the knife back into its sheath under my left armpit. "There, you see? Relationship restored. Why would he have asked you?"

"Before the Interregnum I did some sorcerous preservation of perfumes, so I knew a few people. I guess I still have a reputation."

"Did you give him a name?"

"Everyone I knew is dead."

"Tell me about the guy. What was his name?"

"He didn't tell me."

"What did he look like? In detail."

A guy like this, once you get him talking, he's just gonna keep going. He did. "It was a Jhereg, a little shorter than me, kind of a wide mouth and a flat nose, and thin as a, um, as something very thin."

"What did his hair look like?"

"Light brown, thin braid on one side. The left."

"Where was this?"

"Right in there," he said, gesturing toward the door we'd just come out of.

That's one thing about Hawklords: you can count on them to see and remember. Which thought reminded me, "Good man. I can find you whenever I want, do you get that?"

He nodded.

"Now, you're going to forget about this conversation, and you've never seen me, right?"

He nodded again.

I patted his cheek. I was doing that a lot. I guess it was my new tough-guy thing. "See you around," I said.

He didn't run, but he walked quickly, looking behind himself only once on his way down the street.

"Back in?" said Kragar.

"Why not? It's a nice place."

"The kethna was too salty."

"Look who's suddenly a food critic."

We went back in and ordered more wine and gave the host another half imperial. I had now spent twelve and a half imperials trying to get my eight hundred back. Still a good investment. I mean, if it worked.

The host pocketed the coin and waited.

I gave him a description, just as Tuppi had given it to me. "Know him?" I said. He looked like he was about to deny it, but I'd been watching his face, and he'd been watching me watch his face, so I guess he decided it was no good.

"Who is he?"

"We call him Fisher. He's my boss."

"Your boss," I said. "Great. And, let me guess, he works for Toronnan."

"Yeah."

"Perfect."

I looked at Kragar. He was looking at me. Neither of us said, "Now what?" but I was thinking it, and three flats to one round he was too.

"Thanks," I told the host. "I'll be in touch."

"Thanks for the warning," he said.

Everyone's a smartass.

3

THE PROPOSAL

So, let's talk about proposing marriage, because I've heard a lot of marriages start that way. Those Dragaeran Houses that have things arranged ahead of time don't have to bother with that, except for the Lyorn, who I guess have to go through some sort of formal proposal and acceptance even though they know what the answer is going to be, and they have all sorts of rules about who does the asking based on who is the older family or some garbage like that. It feels like cheating to know what the answer will be, but it also makes me wonder what would happen if someone said no.

I guess those other Houses that don't arrange things have all sorts of different traditions for how it's supposed to be done, but for my people—I mean Fenarians, or at least Fenarians living in the Empire—there's no real custom. Someone just says, "Let's get married," and if the other one says, "Sounds good," then you're on. After that, sure, there are all sorts of customs and traditions. But the proposal itself, well, it's like one day you're single, and the next you discover you're engaged.

Your life can change pretty fast sometimes.

❧

We didn't say much on the way back to the office.

I settled into my chair—I'll have to tell you about that chair sometime—and, after a moment, spotted Kragar sitting opposite me in the chair he always sits in. I pretended not to be irritated and said, "So, do I give up?"

"Yes."

"Let me rephrase that."

"Uh huh."

"Do you have any ideas other than me giving up?"

"I don't suppose you could ask Toronnan for the money?"

"If he were willing to do that, he'd have offered when it came up."

"Yeah. So, like I said before, you write off the eight hundred."

"Eight hundred and twelve."

He gave me a Look. I shrugged. "I'm not going to war with Toronnan over eight hundred," I said.

"Good decision," said Kragar. "He'd squash us like, ah, like something that gets squashed easy."

"Yeah. Now, if it was eight-fifty . . ."

"Uh huh. Okay, then. Look, the game on Garshos is getting popular. Osivra wants to rent a room in the flat next door and open up another couple of tables. Thing is, the flat next door is technically in Paquitin's area, so—"

"Handle it," I said.

He sighed. "So much for writing off the eight hundred," he said.

I hardly heard him; I was thinking.

"What I need," I said, "is a way to get my money without making an enemy of Toronnan."

Kragar kept still, which I'm going to guess required some effort on his part.

"But if I mess with Fisher, that's messing with his boss, and that's liable to be unpopular."

Kragar continued the silent act.

"Unless there's a way to mess with Fisher without messing with him."

Evidently, Kragar couldn't stand it anymore. "Seems reasonable," he said. "Then you can walk while sitting, and sing while you hold your breath, and kill someone while you sleep."

"That last one I can do," I said.

He didn't ask.

"Find out where Fisher lives, and where he hangs out."

"Right, and when he brushes his teeth, his favorite color, his—"

"Naw, skip all that for now."

"Vlad? You feeling all right?"

"I want this soon."

"I thought you wanted me to handle the game on Garshos."

"I'll do that. It'll keep me busy while you do the unpleasant stuff."

"Same old," he sighed, and headed out.

I got out paper and a graphite pencil and started scratching out some numbers for the new game on Garshos.

Kragar was back in less than an hour. I didn't notice him come in until a scrap of paper was slipped under my nose. It had an address in Little Deathgate.

"His home," said Kragar.

I knew the area, and could almost picture the house: most of them were tiny little bungalows, spaced close together; most of them had bars over the windows and heavy doors. And it was in an area where people minded their own business, which is helpful to those of us who think of laws as either inconveniences or opportunities.

"Good," I said. "And?"

"He owns or part-owns three inns, two brothels, and five long-standing games. He spends most days going from one to the other, or else playing s'yang-stones in the back room of a place on Blackbread, or at the Stolen Boat."

"Sounds like he's in about the same place I am."

"Pretty much."

"Okay. Good. That's all I need for now."

"Vlad, are you going to do something stupid?"

I considered. "Possible," I said. "I'm just thinking, maybe he's the one who stole the hishi. Or maybe whoever stole it ended up giving it to him. Either way, we know he's involved in it somehow, since he was trying to sell it."

"Okay, and?"

"Did he manage to sell it? If not, the hishi might be at his house. And what would happen if it suddenly went missing?"

"First of all, Vlad, that's a lot of *ifs*."

"*Ifs* are all we have so far."

"Also, well, what *would* happen?"

"I dunno. Maybe he'd get an anonymous offer to buy it back for eight hundred gold."

"Or eight hundred and twelve?"

"Yeah."

"Right. Good thinking, there. And of course, since no one knows that's the amount you're missing, no one would trace it back to you, and then, I don't know, kill you or something."

"Oh, is that that stuff you call sarcasm? Okay. Maybe I'll make it nine hundred."

"Yeah, that'll put them off the scent for sure."

"More sarcasm, right? Just want to be sure I'm catching this." I shrugged. "Okay, there might still be some details to work out."

The next morning—

Sethra, this is weird. I mean, you're a Dragonlord last I checked, and I'm about to talk about, well, you know, a crime. Are you sure—? Okay.

Heh. Yeah, well, if Aliera or Morrolan were here, I'd be talking about what wine to serve at my wedding, instead of my plan to break into this guy's house and steal the hishi.

If you're looking for where I made a decision that set everything in motion, I suppose that was it, but I still think it was a sound plan, and I had no way of knowing how it was all going to turn out.

But before then, I met with Cawti, and we spent a while in South Adrilankha, east of Twovine where the Easterner's ghetto starts, wandering around temples and talking to priests of Verra. We passed a small group of Easterners and Teckla marching and holding up signs I didn't bother reading. I was going to make a remark about them, but the way Cawti was looking at them made me change my mind.

There are a lot of temples to a lot of gods where they conduct services in a lot of the Eastern languages, and neither Cawti nor I generally went to any of them, so it was a long process, and neither of us enjoys being in the Easterner's ghetto. I mean, it stinks in a couple of different ways. But being with her made it pleasant, and I think she enjoyed it too.

Eventually we found a priest named Father Farkosh, who usually conducted his services in Fenarian, but spoke Northwestern too and was willing to do the service in that language. He did hesitate a little when he learned that most of our guests were "*elfek*," but he got past it. It got easier for him when we mentioned what we were willing to pay for using his temple.

Then she came home with me, which made things even better.

The next morning I was up early, which made things worse again. I don't like getting up early. I mean, I can't say that's why I chose the profession I did, but it's one of the bonuses, you know? But there it was: instead of lying there twirling Cawti's hair in my fingers, I had to get up and go out. And when I had to wait three hours outside of Fisher's door for him to leave, I was in a worse mood. It wasn't the waiting, it was that every hour there was another hour I could have slept or, you know, finger twirled. If I'd bothered to ask Kragar what time the guy left his house, I'd have gotten three more hours of something worthwhile.

Oh, and to be precise, I didn't see him leave his house, Loiosh did; I was sitting at an outdoor cafe just down the road listening to Loiosh's clever remarks about me not thinking of asking Kragar what time the guy left his house.

So, yeah, I was in a bad mood, and when I got up to his door, I wanted to just kick it open, but I didn't. Burglary, or at least the breaking-in part of burglary, comes in three varieties. So do assassinations, now that I think of it, but that's for another conversation. The three varieties of breaking in are: you don't want anyone to know there's been a break-in, you don't want to leave proof it was you, and you don't care. Kicking in the door in broad daylight would be the last of those. I was hoping for the first, so I went around to the back of the house, looking like I belonged there, and checked the back door. Loiosh told me no one had seen me. The back of the house had a thin garden with a path to the door, and behind it the equally thin garden of a two-story house facing the opposite way.

I made myself invisible—just about the first sorcery spell I ever learned, and one of the easiest—and got to work. I checked for sorcery, and found a pretty simple alarm which I sucked up, then I checked for mechanical alarms and didn't find any.

I studied the lock, and wished I'd thought to bring Kiera. Kiera is—never mind. She's someone none of my people knew that I knew, and I sort of wanted to keep it that way, though I couldn't tell you why. Maybe just to enjoy the looks on their faces when I showed up with her one day. But in any case, she wasn't here. It was me, Loiosh, this lock, and the set of tools I keep in a small pouch on my right hip behind the knife.

I opened up the pouch, knelt down, and got to work.

The guy was serious about his locks: he had what's called a "turnpin."

Picking a lock isn't hard. You just need the right tools, and about five minutes of instruction—not even that much for the ones you can just sort of scrape, which is a lot of them. Locks work by having little pins that need to be at the right height in order to permit the thing to rotate. You insert something that lets you adjust the pin heights, and something to turn the lock with once you've got it. Well, a couple of thousand years ago, some anti-social Vallista whose name I don't remember invented a lock where the pins not only have to be at the right height, but have to rotate to the right position, individually. If I could time travel, I'd find her and express my opinion of the horrible thing. Meanwhile, I use them in the office and my home.

Kiera could have gotten it open in a minute or two. It took me a solid hour, including three times when I had every pin but one positioned but then let them slip before I got the last one. I am not proud of this. But hey, it opened. I stepped in, closed the door, and started looking. Or, rather, listening. The first thing you do when entering an empty house is listen, because it might not be empty, and this is information that you want to have. I listened, and heard nothing. Also, Loiosh said there was no one there, which I gotta say is more reliable than me listening, so I wouldn't have had to listen at all, but I did anyway. I always do. Shut up.

Playing it safe, I figured I had the place to myself for six hours. It wasn't a big house, but Jhereg are good at hiding things.

Yeah, I could give you all the stuff about how you search a place when you don't want anyone to know you were there, but I already told you about breaking in, and about locks. There's only so much of that someone can take, right?

So I searched for the hishi. I found out that he was more careful folding his clothes than I was making *palaczinta;* I found out that, like most people with no real kitchen, he didn't have a lot to eat except hardbread and butter; I found his wine collection and was not impressed; where he kept a few pieces of jewelry and wondered on what sort of occasions he wore them. On the wall was a psiprint of a kid, a boy, who would have been about six if he were an Easterner; I figured a nephew or something. On the mantel above the fireplace he had a reproduction of a famous sculpture I don't remember the name of, but it's a woman holding a horse's bridle and staring off into the distance. I guess a lot of people like that one. I didn't find the hishi, but I kept looking.

For a minute, I got a little excited, because he had, concealed in a bedpost, a stack of newly minted gold coins that would have put a good dent in the eight hundred, but fortunately, I stopped and asked myself why he had them concealed but not banked, and took a closer look. They were gold all right, and "newly minted" in the sense that they had no signs of ever having been passed, but they were private coins, the head of someone I didn't recognize on them, and no imperial seal. The Empress had passed an edict forbidding private coins, which meant that I'd have had to melt them down and sell the raw gold, and by the time I paid someone to melt and cast them, plus the amount you lose no matter how careful you are, it just wasn't worth it. I left them there, though I admit with some regret.

And I still didn't find any hishi.

I did find something else, however.

As it was getting toward the time I was about to give up and go home, I found a concealed compartment in the floor under his bed.

I had to push the bed aside—carefully, so I could replace it without making it obvious I'd moved it. That's harder than it sounds, but I managed, then turned my attention to the compartment. It opened a lot easier than the door had.

In the compartment was a box that wasn't latched at all. I opened it.

"*What,*" said Loiosh, "*is that?*"

"That" was a polished black stone, rounded, about the size of my fist. It appeared to be sucking the light out of the room. And the rock started pulsating.

You don't find these things every day, you know. Although as I looked at it, I realized I'd seen something like it once before, I just couldn't recall where.

"*It's magical,*" I told Loiosh.

"*Brilliant.*"

"*I do believe I'm going to steal it.*"

"*Boss, that looks like one of those things that does all kinds of bad stuff if you touch it.*"

"*I know. Exciting, isn't it?*"

I picked up the stone and put it in my pouch. Nothing happened.

"*Fine,*" said Loiosh. "*But you still haven't found what we came here for.*"

"*So let's keep looking.*"

I continued the search a little longer, then gave up, made myself invisible again, spent half an hour re-locking the door, and got out of there.

I made it back to my office without incident, then pulled out my prize. The room, lit by a few lamps, darkened at once and the surface of the stone shimmered. It felt a little warmer in my hand than I'd have thought. I had seen something like it before, and it annoyed me that I couldn't remember where.

"*Loiosh, why does this look familiar?*"

"*It's like the stone Morrolan has on the pommel of his sword.*"

"*Oh. Yeah. I knew that.*"

"Kragar!" I yelled.

"Yeah?" he said from the chair opposite me, making me jump about halfway to the ceiling.

"You're a son-of-a-bitch."

"We already knew that. What can I do for you?"

"I need to see Morrolan. Set it up."

I would venture to guess that, in the entire, vast criminal organization to which I have the honor—or maybe dishonor—to belong, I'm the only one who is liable to utter those words, and my people are the only ones who are liable to nod and say, "Okay."

Kragar nodded. "Okay," he said.

An hour later he'd arranged a teleport for late the next morning. I took the rest of the day off. I'm the boss, I can do that.

I had a nice dinner with Cawti, then we went back to my place. I asked her what she'd been up to, and she said she'd been looking for a coming-of-age gift for some niece of Norathar. When Norathar was an assassin, she didn't have relatives, but now that she was a princess I guess she did. We talked about what "coming-of-age" meant to a Dragonlord, but neither of us knew, so we talked about what to get a Dragonlord for a gift, which led to a conversation about daggers versus fighting knives, and which kind were best for what. She asked what I'd been up to, and I told her my plans. She said, "Want company?"

I said, "Are you suggesting I bring the woman I love into the keep of a short-tempered, incredibly powerful Dragonlord who carries a Great Weapon and who hates Jhereg?"

"Yeah."

"Sounds good."

Then we argued about who was going to pay the additional cost of a second teleport. In the end, I surrendered and agreed to let her pay, but she had to use physical force to convince me. And I still say tickling is cheating.

Then I explained we were going to Castle Black to talk about the wedding.

"The wedding?" she said. "I thought it was about that stone."

"No, the wedding. If we were going to talk about the stone, I'd have to add the amount of the teleport to how much it's costing me to get the eight hundred back, and that would make me feel bad."

"Well, all right then," she said. "Can't have you feeling bad." Which settled it.

An hour before noon we were at my office with a sorceress from the Left Hand who was ready to do the teleport. We explained there was a second, and paid her for it. She was—ah, who cares what she looked like? Never saw her again.

She nodded, kind of twitched, and we were at Castle Black.

We were also sick. We knelt and took deep breaths, our heads down. We did it together, but it wasn't as romantic as you might think.

"Why is it?" said Cawti, "that teleporting to or from Castle Black is always worse than everywhere else?"

"I've noticed that too. Altitude change?"

"Maybe. Is it the same going to Dzur Mountain?"

"Tell you the truth, love, every time I've gone to Dzur Mountain I've had too much else on my mind to pay much attention to that."

Cawti stood up a little bit before I did, and waited. I stood up and nodded to her. The various guards on the various walls recognized me, and I exchanged slight bows with a couple of them. No doubt Morrolan was being informed of our arrival. And Lady Teldra, of course.

"How do you feel being back here?" I said.

"It's a little weird," she said. "I'm not sure."

"All right. Let's do this."

We walked up to the great double doors of Castle Black, which swung open as we approached. They do that. If I knew how to make my doors do that, well, I guess I probably wouldn't. But it's a nice effect, you know? And even nicer with Lady Teldra framed in the doorway, in her green and white and smile and all like that.

"My lord Vlad," she said. "My lady Cawti."

Okay, I gotta stop here and explain something so you'll understand Lady Teldra. If we were being formal—which she usually is—

she ought to have called me, "Lord Taltos," on account of that's my name, right? Vlad is just my friend-name, and you don't use that if you're being formal. But, you see, the thing is, Cawti has never told anyone her patronymic, and doesn't use it. There's a story there that I'm gonna find out one of these days. But the point is, if Lady Teldra had said, "My lord Taltos and my lady Cawti," that would have been placing Cawti below me on the social scale, and that would have been much more rude than addressing us both by our friend-names. See how she is? That puzzled me at first, but it kept kind of gnawing at me until I figured it out. See how I am?

She stepped aside for us as graceful as a, well, as an issola, and we entered. "I will inform the Lord Morrolan you are here," she said, as if he hadn't already been informed. Good manners means lying a lot.

She escorted us through the hall toward the sweeping marble stairway. Every time I was there, something different caught my eye; this time it was a sculpture off to the right below the top of the stairway that seemed to be two people joined together, one with arms raised, the other holding a two-handed sword, facing in opposite directions. I decided I'd try to remember to ask Morrolan about it. Of course, I forgot. Maybe next time I see him.

Huh, really, Sethra? Then how did Morrolan end up with it?

Oh, that's funny! Good story. You should be talking instead of me.

No, no. I don't mind the interruptions.

What was I . . . ? Right. Lady Teldra. She escorted us up the stairs to the library, past the huge chain-bound tomes. Morrolan was inside and rose to greet us: tall, skinny Morrolan. Today his hair was long and straight in back and short in front. It looked weird. I thought about telling him so, seeing as he wasn't carrying a weapon, but I didn't. I mean, he could have gone and gotten one.

"Cawti," he said. "Vlad."

"My lord Morrolan," I said.

Cawti dropped him a brief curtsy.

"Sit," he said.

We did that, and a moment later Lady Teldra appeared with

wine, poured, and left. The wine was white, chilled, and not too sweet, because Morrolan is a good person in spite of it all.

"How are things?" I asked him. "Killed anyone lately?"

"No," he said as if the question were reasonable. "You?"

I pretended to yawn. "I don't remember. The little stuff slips away, you know?"

He was polite enough to chuckle. "What brings you here?"

"You don't think it could just be your company?"

"No," he said, and smiled.

He was patient. I suppose if you can expect to live two or three thousand years it's easier to be patient, but I admired it anyway.

"I admire your patience," I told him.

"So you continually test it?"

"Uh."

"Perhaps," said Cawti. "You should get to your question, Vladimir."

"Perhaps you should," said Morrolan.

"Your sword," I told him. "Can I have it?"

"No," he said as if the question were reasonable.

"Can I see it?"

"Why?"

"I'm trying to learn to overcome my fear of things that anyone with the brains of a norska ought to be afraid of."

"Makes sense," he said. "What's the real reason?"

"I found this," I told him. He didn't ask about the "found," he just waited while I pulled it out of my pouch. "It reminds me of the pommel of Blackwand."

He didn't reach for it, just looked at it.

"Verra's tears," he said.

"Never heard that one," I said. "I've heard, 'Verra's tits and toenails,' and—"

"No, that's what that is called."

"What is it?"

"Obsidian that has been polished for thousands of years by Dark Water."

"Oh. Well, that explains everything then."

"It has certain properties."

I waited.

He hesitated, gave a sort of nod, and closed his eyes for a moment. When he opened them, I said, "Hmm?"

"I've asked the Necromancer to join us, and sent for Blackwand."

"Oh," I said. "I see."

I felt Cawti turn and look at me. I looked back and shrugged.

Morrolan's sword was delivered. He didn't draw it, which was a relief. He held the pommel next to the stone in my hand, and, yeah, they were the same, except that the one in Blackwand's pommel seemed to have a sort of glow from deep within it. It was subtle, like, I wasn't sure for a while if it was there or if I were imagining it, but, yeah, there was something.

I shrugged and sat back; Morrolan leaned his sword against his chair.

We drank some more wine, and in a few minutes the Necromancer came in. So skinny she made Dragaerans look fat, what stood out was the contrast between her pale, pale face and her black hair, which today was pushed back and held in place so tightly it seemed to stretch her forehead. If you meet her, don't look at her eyes. I mean, it's not like your soul will be sucked into a screaming void or anything, but, I dunno, they're just weird. Uncomfortable. Oh, skip it, you'll go ahead and look no matter what I say and then you'll know what I mean. And you're more likely to meet her in person than anyone else I'm talking about, including me; she gets around a lot. So don't say you weren't warned.

While I'm talking about her, I should tell you that I've heard four different stories about how she ended up living at Castle Black, and they all contradict each other, some of them from the same people, and for all I know they're all true. My favorite is that Morrolan summoned her to help in some ridiculously complicated necromancy spell, and by the time she'd finished and he released her, she was so fascinated by it that she wanted to stick around. I don't know, believe it if you want.

Morrolan moved a chair so we had a sort of circle, and the Necromancer moved into it like she was made of water. It was kind of creepy, the way she could move, though that wasn't the creepiest thing about her—not by a Serioli mile. (I don't know what the difference is between a Serioli mile and an Imperial mile, or even if the Serioli have miles. It's just an expression, okay? Do I really have to explain this kind of stuff, or can I skip it?)

The Necromancer gave me an inquiring look, and I held out the polished stone. "What can you tell me?" I said. She didn't look at it right away, just kept looking at me, which was weird. Maybe she was trying to figure out if I was alive or dead, and then finally decided I was living, so there was no point in bothering with me, and she looked down at my hand.

She tilted her head, frowned, squinted, and reached out toward it. She touched it. Then she glanced at Blackwand and looked an inquiry at Morrolan. He handed the sword over without hesitation, which I guess told me a lot about how much he trusted her.

The Necromancer set one hand on Blackwand's pommel, then touched the stone in my hand with the other. I glanced over at Cawti, who shrugged as if to say, "I don't know what she's doing either," and we both turned back.

"It has certainly been enchanted," said the Necromancer.

"What can you tell me about the enchantment?" asked Morrolan.

"Necromantic, of course. It doesn't feel like summoning, and there's no similarity to the enchantments on your weapon. Almost the opposite, in fact."

"Explain?"

"Instead of a narrow band of pulling, it is more like a broad field of pushing."

Morrolan nodded like he understood what she meant, and maybe he did. I hoped so, because I had a better chance of getting an explanation I could follow from him than from her.

"All right," said Morrolan. "Let's do a few tests. If that's all right, Vlad?"

I nodded.

"What did you have in mind?" said the Necromancer.

"I want to isolate—" He stopped, frowned, stood, and picked up Blackwand.

"We're under attack," he said.

Cawti and I stood too.

"What the—" I said.

"A spell," he said. "A powerful one."

He drew Blackwand, which did nothing at all to calm me down, since being anywhere within a mile of that bloody thing makes your guts sort of turn into water and your eyeballs want to crawl back into your skull.

"What kind of spell?" asked the Necromancer. "If I can help—"

"It's through," said Morrolan, and raised Blackwand and the world went away.

Let me tell you what happened. It was . . .

Okay, the short version is—

No, there is no short version.

I remember the stone suddenly getting very cold—like, icy cold— and I was thinking maybe I should drop it. Then I felt woozy. You know, the way you feel right after someone's cracked you a good one on your head, except without the pain and the sick feeling, just feeling, I don't know, seeing a single leaf, green and broad with edges like a saw blade floating away like it came out of my forehead, but wing flaps sounding like falling, falling into something or away from a single point that is all there is until hands reach for me but I slither past them, fear is so far back I must have left it with my body, *wait!* where—what is happening? am I—silky sheets of pure blinding white engulfing, darkening to pale blue, blue, up and down meaningless now, there is no *where* to find, and I'm no longer sure there is a *who*.

4

CHOOSING THE VENUES

Venues means places. And, no, I don't know why they don't just say places, but they don't. So, this part is about picking where you want stuff to happen, like, the wedding, and then the gathering after the wedding. You can't figure out a date for the wedding until you're sure you can find a place on that date, and you can't settle on a place unless they're available when you want to get married. So, if you want my deep thoughts, I dunno, something about where and when being all tied up with each other or something.

Anyway, it usually takes a lot of legwork, although some Houses, like the Tiassa, keep it simple by doing everything at someone's home. We couldn't do that, so we ended up doing a lot of walking around before we settled on a couple of places. I mean venues.

＊

I/He/I . . .

I? He.

He felt something cold against his throat, and looked up to see Cawti staring down at him.

"You will get him back," she said.

"You aren't helping," he said.

She hesitated, then took a step backward, the knife vanishing. "I'm sorry. I didn't mean to do that, it just—"

"It's all right," he said. "And, yes, we'll get him back."

She seemed embarrassed as she sat down again, and Morrolan wondered what it would be like to care about someone that much, then he pushed the thought aside.

He looked at Vlad, sitting, his face slack, his hand still holding the stone, but limp, Loiosh on his shoulder screaming. Morrolan hadn't been aware that jhereg could scream.

"What happened," said Cawti, and there was an intensity in her gaze that seemed almost palpable.

Morrolan raised Blackwand, holding her up in front of his face, and let himself flow into her. Whatever it was hadn't had any effect on her, at least.

"What happened?" said Cawti again.

Morrolan sheathed Blackwand and looked at the Necromancer.

"Something triggered the stone," said the Necromancer.

"It was like an arc," said Morrolan. "From the stone to Blackwand."

"And the sword?"

"Fine. No spells, no effect."

"Except on Vlad," said Cawti.

He nodded.

"I'm going to touch the stone," said the Necromancer almost too quietly to be heard over the jhereg's screams. "Maybe I can learn something."

Morrolan frowned, looked over at the jhereg, and said, "Shhhh. We're trying to fix this."

Loiosh, still on Vlad's shoulder, quit screaming and just glared.

The Necromancer got up, bent over a little, and covered the stone in Vlad's hand with her own. She seemed unaware of being the intense focus of everyone in the room, including the jhereg.

She straightened up and frowned. "Interesting," she said.

"What did you feel?"

"I felt the stone," she said unhelpfully.

Morrolan reached Tuvin and said, "*Ask Aliera if she'd be kind enough to join us in the library.*" He could, of course, have reached his cousin directly, but they had just had a furious argument about precedence among the families and he wanted to hold off the un-pleasantness as long as possible. The servant gave his usual terse acknowledgment, and Morrolan turned his attention back to Vlad, who still hadn't moved, then Loiosh, who was still glaring, then

Cawti, who seemed to be trying to avoid showing anything, then the Necromancer, who looked back at him with those eyes that he could never quite describe to himself: empty? haunted? bleak? It wasn't the eyes themselves, of course; it was the way they were set so deeply in her head, and the way she kept her eyelids, partly closed and never moving. But it *seemed* like it was her eyes.

"I've asked Aliera to join us," he said. "Shall I also see if Sethra is free?"

"Why?"

Morrolan blinked at her. "To help Vlad."

"Oh. Does he need help?"

At last he settled on, "Yes."

Around that time, his cousin Aliera came in, wearing her, *what have you bothered me about* this *time?* expression. Morrolan took Blackwand from where she rested against the table, buckled her on, and successfully resisted the temptation to use her on Aliera. It was never a very strong temptation, just a frequent one. Tuvin discreetly looked around, then made himself scarce; Morrolan didn't employ fools.

"What is it?" said Aliera.

Morrolan gestured at Vlad with his chin and waited.

Aliera looked at the Easterner and said, "What—" then stopped and looked closer. She approached him, touched his head, and Morrolan felt the tunneling flare of energy from the Orb coming to and from her. "He's gone," said Aliera. "What happened?"

Cawti, except for a sharp inhale at Aliera's words, was still motionless and silent, gripping the arms of her chair.

"Accidental astral projection," said the Necromancer, which, in Morrolan's opinion, she could have said before. Not that it explained anything.

"How can we get him back?" said Morrolan, shifting his gaze between Aliera and the Necromancer.

"What?" said Aliera. "You admit there might be something I know more about than you?"

Loiosh hissed at her before Morrolan had the chance to do the same. Cawti also glared. Aliera nodded to the jhereg. "All right," she said.

She knelt in front of Vlad to study the rock in his hand, and Morrolan suddenly wished for the skill and equipment to make a psiprint, just to show Vlad later.

If there was a later for him.

He frowned. There would be a later for him.

"It seems," said Aliera, "to be a perfectly normal sample of Verra's tears."

"Enchanted, however," said Morrolan.

"No enchantment," said Aliera at the same moment the Necromancer said, "Not anymore."

"Oh," said Morrolan. "So whatever was on it, it triggered."

The Necromancer nodded.

"Tell me," said Aliera, "what you felt when you touched it."

Morrolan found his hand had drifted to the hilt of Blackwand, and deliberately removed it; she was hungry these days, and he didn't need either the guilt or the distraction just now.

The Necromancer studied Aliera, as if she'd find the answer in her face. "What did I feel?" She said it the way Morrolan would repeat things when talking to someone in South Adrilankha who was speaking with too strong a Muskov accent.

Aliera could be patient in the face of frustration; something Morrolan hadn't known before. She said, "As you touched it, tell me of the thoughts, sensations, effects that you perceived."

"Oh." The Necromancer frowned, considering.

How does her mind work? Morrolan wondered for the ten thousandth time. *And is she even aware that Cawti is staring at her hard enough to bore holes in her skull? Or would she have a clue about why?*

"There was," said the Necromancer, her voice oddly even, almost monotone, "a sense of place becoming color, and time becoming sound. Of course, that is quite normal."

To you, maybe, thought Morrolan, but he didn't say anything.

"However," she continued, "the colors began to bend back on themselves, which as you know is unusual."

Morrolan, who knew nothing of the kind, nodded. Aliera was showing no trace of expression, but appeared to be listening intently.

"I don't understand what it means," concluded the Necromancer.

Morrolan took a chance on touching his cousin's mind. *"Do you know how much of that is metaphorical, and how much literal?"*

Aliera chose not to be sarcastic, which meant she was interested in the problem. *"No,"* she said. *"That's what I was just wondering."*

"Can you think of a way to find out?"

"Working on it."

A moment later, Aliera said, "Did the colors bend to or away from the stone?" which made no sense to Morrolan, but must have to the Necromancer because she seemed to be considering it.

"Away from both the stone and the sword," she said at last. "They formed a sort of arch."

"All right," said Aliera. "Do you think, if you were to lay your hands on both stones at once—the one Vlad is holding, and the hilt of Blackwand, and this time attempt to bend the colors back to the way they were, you might be able to reach Vlad?"

The Necromancer blinked. "It might work," she said.

Aliera nodded to Morrolan, who nodded back and extended the hilt toward the Necromancer. "I can't think of what harm it could do at this point."

He heard Cawti inhale sharply, but she remained where she was.

The Necromancer, ignoring them all, once more laid a hand on the stone that still rested in Vlad's open hand, and the other on Blackwand's pommel.

Nothing happened, and Morrolan exhaled. He saw Loiosh looking at him, and was suddenly sure he was being laughed at. He looked at the Necromancer, who was frowning. Again.

"Well?" he said, hearing the impatience in his voice and regretting it. No one else seemed to notice.

"That was useful," said the Necromancer. "I think I know what happened."

Things—by which I mean my head—stopped spinning, and left me with one of the oddest feelings I've ever had. You know how you, like, look in one direction? I was looking, or I guess seeing, everything around me, and that experience was even more unsettling than what I was seeing. And that was even before the voices started in.

Okay, okay. I know, I gotta slow down and give it to you. But it was all there at once, and giving it to you slow enough so you'll understand makes it seem like it was happening a piece at a time, so you won't understand. How the hell do storytellers do this stuff? I guess they don't tell stories about things this weird. Or they lie. Yeah, that's it, they probably lie.

There was an impossible mountain just a few miles behind me. It was impossible because it was too perfect for a real mountain, a perfect, smooth black stone coming to a point that, from where I stood, looked actually sharp. And if you're thinking of the stone on Blackwand's pommel, so was I.

To my right—and, remember, I wasn't turning around or anything, I was just seeing things—to my right was a landscape of pits and mounds in harsh grays that went on forever. I didn't have any idea what that might mean.

To my left was a troop, a battalion, an army of whirlwinds, all of them white against some sort of pale background; they remained in place, the closest so close it seemed I could touch it, but I didn't try, and I didn't feel anything like wind.

In front of me was a long trench leading away from me; on either side were black ocean waves, looking like they were held back by an invisible force, permanently, soundlessly crashing into nothing, and at the top of each of the waves on either side was massive yellow flame.

Okay, so, here I was.

I tried to reach Loiosh, failed. I'd never failed to reach him before. My heart pounded and I took some deep breaths.

Kragar might make jokes about how I don't think, and Loiosh makes even more. And, hey, they're funny. But I gotta tell you, the reason I'm still around to laugh at those jokes is because, when it matters, I do stop and think. Knowing when to stop and think will do more to keep you alive in this business than knowing when to duck and thrust.

Of course, you gotta have some skill at both.

But anyway, yeah, if there'd ever been a time to stop and think, this was it.

I could move, or I could stand still. Standing still meant waiting, and hoping something would change, or someone would rescue me. I had no idea what might change, but I wasn't hopeful about it being something good. Waiting to be rescued made some sense, I gotta admit, but I liked the idea of being rescued just about as much as you'd expect.

So the plan was to move, bringing up two more questions: could I, and which way?

I started to take a step forward, just to see if it would do anything, but stopped.

I mean, maybe everything would change with a step. How did I know? And—

It was then I realized that I didn't have my gear with me. No knife, no sword, no, well, anything. And, here's the strange part (yeah, I know, like everything else wasn't already strange?): I had no clothes on, but I didn't feel naked.

It took me a second to realize I didn't have a body, either. I mean, I could breathe, and I could even feel my heart racing, but I didn't have a body.

Now there's a sensation you don't get every day, right?

And I badly wanted to move, to see if I could move, to do something, to—okay, I'll admit it, to not panic.

The creepiest part was that I couldn't close my eyes. I kept seeing everything, all around me. I dunno. I've had sharp things pointed at me, and been sure I was about to "have my knowledge of the afterlife expanded," as one clever son-of-a-bitch put it, but just standing there, seeing all that, not able to stop seeing all that, was enough to scare me.

I started moving toward the black monolith.

Okay, I skipped a bunch of stuff.

There was a while there I don't remember. I guess I went off my head. There. I admitted it. Happy now?

The one good part of being in a scary situation where no one is trying to kill you is that you eventually come back and nothing bad has happened. The bad part is, you're still right where you were. So can we not spend a lot of time on all of that, which, like I said, I mostly don't remember anyway? I'm being honest here, so I'm letting you know it happened. If that isn't good enough, bugger off.

It also took me a while to figure out how to move. Trying to walk did nothing. I tried to summon a light wind, which should be easy enough, but at that point I discovered I had lost my connection to the Orb. That did nothing to make me feel better. I next tried, well, skip it. I tried a bunch of stuff, and what finally worked was to imagine myself moving. There was no sensation of motion, but things around me shifted, just like they do when you walk, and I felt like cheering.

I started moving toward the black monolith, or I guess massive cone would be more like what I saw. And, if you want weird, it was still behind me. What I mean is, I still had the same sense of "forward" and "backward," only now the cleft with the waves and the fire was getting further away from me.

The black cone got closer. My speed was constant, feeling like moving down the Adrilankha River from Jutrock to the Ferry on a skimboat. Okay, like that on a calm day; the River gets in moods when the wind's up. I wondered what was really happening, if "really" even meant anything, but then I tried thinking about stuff around me instead, because trying to guess what might be happening made me queasy, like moving down the Adrilankha River from the Ferry to White Dock in a rowboat on a windy day.

I got closer, and the big, black cone loomed over me. It was close enough to touch, so I did. I think I did. I guess I did. I tried to.

Then I couldn't see it anymore, and everything around me changed; I was now surrounded by black walls that emitted a faint glow. I tried to wrap my head around what that meant, failed, but

I kept thinking of Morrolan's sword, Blackwand, and the idea of being inside of it.

And then, I guess because things had been too normal, I started hearing voices.

No, check that. It wasn't hearing voices, it was, like, I was aware of someone's voice, but not exactly a voice. More like psychic communication, where the words form in your head and you mentally supply a voice to go with them, but without that last bit. This was words, and sometimes images, then more words, all disorganized. It was like when I'm not concentrating, when I'm just letting my mind wander, but it wasn't mine.

And that was it, of course. It had to be. I was now inside someone's thoughts, inside thinking, like echoing, disorganized, almost random awareness coming into my head that was like psychic communication only different, unfocused, unclear, and somehow familiar, like—

Morrolan.

Morrolan?

"Morrolan?"

I tried to reach him, but nothing. Whatever I was seeing/hearing/smelling/touching couldn't go back to him, it just came to me. I tried to concentrate, to force it to, what's the word? Coherence. Yeah, that's it. I tried to make it be coherence. Coherent, I mean.

Ever had the experience of feeling like your feet are on the ground, right where they should be, but also feeling like one was off the floor, that one leg was crossed over the other, that you were leaning back except you knew you weren't, and that your head was cocked, only it wasn't? Loiosh would have said I was losing my mind, and I don't think I would have disagreed with him.

⊰⊱

Morrolan crossed his legs, leaned back, cocked his head, and studied the Necromancer. "All right," he said. "I'm listening."

"He was holding the stone," she said, "when the spell hit, and it sort of jumped to Blackwand. I felt Vlad go in, and—"

"Wait, what?"

"I felt Vlad go in, and tried to—"

"What do you mean, felt Vlad go in?"

"To Blackwand," said the Necromancer. "I tried to follow, but—"

She was interrupted by a snapping sound, and now everyone was looking at Cawti, who was holding the arm of the chair in her hand. *I need better furniture,* thought Morrolan.

"Tell me," said Aliera into the sudden silence, "that Vlad's soul has not been absorbed by Blackwand."

"Not exactly," said the Necromancer.

They waited.

"His soul is still in place, it's only his consciousness that has been absorbed."

Morrolan turned to the Necromancer. "His consciousness is in Blackwand."

She nodded. "But his soul is perfectly fine."

"Oh," said Morrolan, letting fall the ironic tone he usually reserved for his cousin. "That's all right then."

There was another sharp inhale from Cawti, and Morrolan regretted the tone.

"How do we get him back?" said Cawti and Aliera, in chorus, as if they'd rehearsed it. Any other time it would have been funny, but neither of them appeared to notice.

Morrolan drew Blackwand again and slowly raised her. He looked at the length of the blade, the dull black that reflected no light, the elegant shape. So heavy when she hung in her sheath—so heavy, indeed, that every ten years or so he had to heal his back or side where the muscles objected to the unevenness of the burden. And yet, so light in his hand. He focused his thoughts. *"My friend, are you there?"* Blackwand was quiet. Asleep? He tightened his focus. No, not asleep. Busy.

There was no good reason for Blackwand to be busy.

The Necromancer was watching him, like she knew what he was doing, which she probably did. He shrugged. "I can't reach her," he said. "I suspect that means you're right."

"How do we get him back?" repeated Aliera, either because she thought no one had heard her the first time or because she was annoyed at not getting an answer.

"I don't know," said the Necromancer, and Morrolan felt a chill go through him, all the way through Blackwand. He lowered her carefully and licked his lips.

"Okay," he heard himself saying. "I'll try."

"I—" began Cawti.

"No," said Morrolan quickly. "My blade, I have the best chance of doing something."

He felt Aliera looking at him, and spared a quick glance. Her brows were slightly furrowed, her eyes bright green, and her mouth opened and then closed as if she had decided not to say something.

Cawti gave a terse nod.

The hilt in his hand—such a natural thing he was rarely aware of it—felt cool, and there was always a hum that he either felt or heard, he couldn't tell which. He focused his attention on that hum. He had spent hundreds of years studying sorcery, swordplay, and Eastern witchcraft, and perhaps the only thing they had in common was the importance of concentration; he felt like maybe he was starting to get good at it.

He had not, over the centuries, done this particular trick very often. But then, how often does an impulsive Easterner lose his consciousness within paired necromantic artifacts? And of those occasions, how many times would he care?

His grip on this world loosened; he concentrated on the other, and let go.

※

"Vlad?"

If there was anything I hadn't expected just then, it was Morrolan's voice, sounding exactly like a voice-voice. You know, I mean, not a mental echo, or some weird phenomenon from a dimension that didn't exist in reality, or even that peculiar almost-hearing you get with psychic communication, but, just a voice, like he was standing next to me.

He was standing next to me.

It never entered my mind to tell him I'd been inside his skull. That's a kind of invasion you don't do to friends, and I felt guilty about it even though it wasn't my fault.

"Where are we?" I asked him, because that's what was bothering me the most, I guess.

"Inside Blackwand," he said, which I'd known ever since the big black walls appeared around me, but which I'd kind of been hoping wasn't true.

"Oh," I said. "All right, then. How is Cawti holding up?"

"Badly."

"And Loiosh?"

"No better," he said. "Let's get you home."

I had no argument to make against this suggestion for our future. I wanted to know why I could see him, and he appeared the same as always (though not wearing his sword, which would have raised some questions that would have hurt my head), and I still seemed, to myself, like I didn't have a body.

This is a sensation, by the way, that I'm not recommending.

He did—something, I don't know what—and a stairway suddenly appeared in the middle of the monolith. It seemed tiny in that huge place, made of iron, and spiraling up a long way.

"How did you do that?" I said.

"Let's go," he said, informative as usual. "Follow me."

He started up. I put my foot on the first step and felt nothing except the floor—it was like my foot went right through it.

"Morrolan," I said.

He stopped and looked back at me.

I repeated the trick.

"Vlad," he said. "What have you done?"

"That," I told him, "is not what I want to hear."

"Vlad—"

"What did I do? I didn't do anything. I just appeared here."

He frowned.

"Morrolan, can you see me?"

"Yes, of course."

"I can't see myself. I don't seem to have a body. I'm just here."

He frowned.

"You look down, and you don't see your feet?"

"Right."

"Or anything else?"

"Right."

"What did you do?"

"Morrolan, do you see me?"

"Yes, of course."

"Do you see me glaring at you?"

"Yes, but there's nothing you can do about it."

I used my words. When I'd run down, he said, "So, I take it, as far as you know, you didn't do anything?"

"Yeah. You picked right up on that."

"Describe what happened, in as much detail as you can."

"Starting when?"

"When things got weird."

"You mean, when I first met you?"

"Be serious."

"All right."

I described what had happened as well as I could, pretty much as I've just told you.

He looked thoughtful, then said, "I'll be right back."

"Don't go," I said to the place he used to be.

⋰⋱

Morrolan opened his eyes, not aware of when he'd closed them, and saw the others looking at him. "Vlad," he said without preamble, "has gotten himself into a state where he is mentally present, but without, to himself, the appearance of a physical body."

"Do you see his body?" said the Necromancer.

Morrolan nodded.

"Then," she said, "he's half integrated with Blackwand."

"Why only half?" said Aliera. "What saved him?"

"Blackwand," said Morrolan and the Necromancer with one voice. Aliera looked back and forth at the two of them.

She said, "How—"

"No," said Morrolan. "There's no time for explanations."

Aliera's eyes turned icy blue, but just for a moment, then she nodded. "All right. What do we need to do?"

"We have to find him, and draw him out."

"Of Blackwand?"

He nodded, and out of the corner of his eye saw the Necromancer nodding with him, which was a relief. For a moment, the question popped into his head, *why do I care so much?* But he put it aside.

"Are you linked to him?" said the Necromancer.

Morrolan concentrated briefly, then said, "Almost. Blackwand is working on not destroying him, which puts her out of touch with me. I can feel Vlad is there, but there isn't anything solid enough to work with."

Aliera put her hand on the hilt of her sword. "Pathfinder?"

"Not if you plan to stab me with her," he said.

"I don't," she said. "At least, not as a first try. But can she find a way into Blackwand?"

Morrolan looked at the Necromancer, who was looking back at him. Loiosh and Cawti were staring at Aliera. The jhereg had his neck pulled back like a snake about to strike.

He outwaited the Necromancer. Eventually she said, "I don't know."

Cawti exhaled through her teeth, making a hissing sound not unlike Loiosh.

"But I can make a guess," the Necromancer continued. When she spoke, nothing else moved: no hand gestures, not even a bob of her head. Even after all of this time, Morrolan found it disconcerting. "It might be that he has not only partly integrated himself with Blackwand, but also with the stone, the Verra's tear. In that case, they're balancing each other, which is keeping him stable for now."

"Why can't he see his own body?"

Aliera answered. "He isn't trained to focus astrally, the way you are. It's automatic for you, but it does take training."

"It does?" said the Necromancer. They ignored her.

"Then the next question," said Morrolan, "is, does it matter? Is his inability to see himself a problem itself? Is it symptomatic of a problem that we'll have to resolve to get him back? Or can we ignore it?"

Everyone was looking at the Necromancer again. She hesitated. "I know about travel between worlds," she said. "But this is different." Morrolan tried to remember if he'd ever heard her sound hesitant before. "It's related," she went on. "Similar technique. But a world inside isn't exactly the same as—"

"There is," said Aliera, "as I said before, Pathfinder."

Morrolan started to object, but the Necromancer said, "You mean, as a guide?"

Aliera nodded.

"That might work," said the Necromancer.

Aliera drew her weapon and extended the hilt. The Necromancer shook her head. "Extend the blade."

"Um," said Aliera. "Are you certain that—"

"I'm certain."

Aliera pointed the sword at her; so much smaller than Blackwand, and with an entirely different sort of elegance: more businesslike, simpler. But the metal was the same: no light reflected from the blade.

The Necromancer laid a hand on it with an ease even Morrolan wouldn't have been able to manage. With her other hand she touched the stone Vlad was still holding.

She withdrew her hands after what seemed only a fraction of a second. "How very odd," she remarked.

Morrolan, and everyone else in the room, gathered breath for an outburst that the Necromancer preempted by saying, "I might be able to fix it. I hadn't thought it would be so similar to . . . let me try."

Morrolan felt himself flushing as he realized how relieved he was; he kept his face blank. Fortunately, everyone was looking at the Necromancer, who promptly dissolved into a shower of golden sparks, as per protocol.

⊰⊱

"Vlad?"

I'd have jumped out of my skin if I'd had any.

She—the Necromancer—appeared behind me, that is, what seemed to my odd all-seeing brain as behind me, at exactly the same instant she spoke.

"Hello," I said. "Fancy meeting you here."

"I'm going to try to get you out."

I started to nod, but I had nothing to nod with, so I said, "All right."

"Take my hand."

"With what?"

"Imagine you have an arm. Extend it, and take my hand."

She said it like I'd say, "Try some of the fish."

But I tried. I imagined an arm, and imagined extending it.

"Vlad?" she said.

"It isn't working."

"You're a witch," she stated, as if making an accusation.

"Uh, yeah."

"Isn't that just controlling the mind to direct your personal amorphia, just as sorcery directs the mind to control the amorphia through the Orb?"

I'd never heard it put that way before, and I wasn't sure she was exactly right, but, "What of it?" I said anyway.

"You still have your mind. Use witchcraft to create an imaginary arm."

"I don't know that spell."

"Make it up," she said.

Well, I had made up a spell before, and a pretty impressive one at that. In the Halls of Judgment I'd—No, let me concentrate on this.

Fix your mind on the effect you want, plant it like a seed in your head, then forget about it, because you'll need to focus on each step.

Taste the power, it's still there, even without a body, which brings up questions that are for sure and certain not for now.

Take it, feel it, taste it; it is movement with nothing to move, flowing unnoticed through the mind until you learn what you're reaching for. Like that song that's stuck in your head, and you can almost remember the words. Don't work at it, work around it. Tease it out, tease it out. An arm, you say? An appendage, an extension, the concept of *reach* made into something you can touch, and touch with. I would have been sweating if I'd had any sweat and shaking if there'd been anything to shake.

"I have it," she said, just as I felt something cold travel up the arm that didn't exist.

"Now what?"

"Hold on."

Hold on? To what? With what? What did that even mean?

I was about to ask for, you know, maybe a hint when—how to say it? Can you imagine a gust of wind literally picking you up and starting to blow you away, except that you're holding on to—something. Oh, and your hand doesn't actually exist.

I was smacked around and couldn't see anything for a while, which, surprisingly, was a relief. I guess I hadn't been aware of how much it was bothering me, that seeing-in-all-directions thing.

If it had gone on much longer, I'd have probably panicked, but then I could see again, in one direction, where I looked. I looked down and saw my feet.

That was the good news.

The bad news was that, except for my body, all I could see around me was darkness. Utter darkness. Blackness. Now, maybe you wonder how I could even see my body without there being any light. I wondered that too, but later, right then I didn't think of it, I just thought about how I couldn't see anything.

"All right, Vlad," said the Necromancer. "It isn't as bad as it looks."

I had mixed feelings about this bit of information.

"You aren't," she went on, "embedded in Blackwand. You're now only embedded in the other stone, the one you're holding."

I didn't try to figure out how I could be embedded in something I was holding; that was also only something I thought of later. Another thing that didn't occur to me until later was how weird it was that her voice sounded so normal, like she was just standing next to me, the way she appeared to be, only neither one of us was, like, really there.

Too much weird at once and you just gotta take what piece of it you can and deal with that, worry about the rest later.

I did, however, pick up on the "embedded" bit. I was embedded. That did not sound good. Also, "it isn't as bad as it looks" is not as comforting as you might think.

There was that sense of being pulled again, and then I saw sparks out of the corners of my eye. I figured the Necromancer was doing something, but I couldn't ask her what without distracting her, and, like, I'd understand the answer even if I did?

And then—

I don't even know how to say this.

A word formed in my head.

I didn't *see* it. I didn't *hear* it. It was just there.

The word was, no, wait a minute, what am I, stupid? I'm not going to tell you what it was. It was a collection of sounds, about as long as my name, but different, and it was from a language I'd never heard before. I knew how to pronounce it even though I hadn't heard it. It was in my head like, I dunno, blazing light or something; just there, and the not-sound sound of it went through me and filled me and was me, and while I was trying to figure out what it meant the Necromancer said some stuff that I'd swear was in the same language, and that word was right there, shining, in the middle of it, pronounced just like I knew it should be, and then everything went square and sideways and got thin and bright and I was staring into the Necromancer's eyes, and I felt Loiosh on my shoulder, and then Cawti was in my arms and I was holding her, shaking.

The air tasted awfully good.

5

EXCHANGE OF TOKENS

In Fenario, according to my grandfather, two people about to be married are supposed to give each other some sort of object to symbolize, I dunno, something. Love, maybe? Or an agreement to stay together? Whatever. Anyway, Noish-pa said it should be something you make yourself. I asked if triple onion beef would count, and he said no. I guess a lot of Dragaeran Houses do something like that. A guy named Daymar told me that in the House of the Hawk they have a ritual where they each share a secret into the other person's mind, which I guess counts as kind of the same thing? Maybe? I don't know.

In the end, I ignored the part about making it myself, and got her a silver-and-turquoise brooch in the form of a blue butterfly that had a little place inside big enough for, say, some poison or something. She gave me a frying pan with the curve you need to make your palaczinta come out perfect. She didn't make her token, either, so I guessed we were okay. I made her palaczintok, but she didn't poison me, and like they say, anytime you come out alive you gotta figure you're ahead of the game.

❧

"Would someone," I asked over Cawti's shoulder, "care to tell me what just happened?"

"I'm pretty sure we're all waiting for you to tell us," said Aliera.

I made some sort of sound and concentrated on holding Cawti. Loiosh squeezed my shoulder, which I guess was supposed to comfort me or reassure him that I was there. It was good to be there.

"I don't think I can describe it," I finally managed.

"Try," said Aliera. "If you try to describe it, it might help you under-stand it, and might even help us understand it."

"All right," I said. It took me a few minutes to get it straight enough in my head to even start, but then I gave it to them, a lot longer version than the one I gave you, with even more vagueness and "I don't know" and "kinda" and "it almost seemed" and stuff like that. Aliera was right, telling it the second time was easier, and it came closer to making sense. The fourth time—that is, this time, I'll tell you about the second and third later—it's almost coherent. You get the benefit of that. Rejoice.

And I guess that goes for you, Sethra. I mean, the thing about it being more coherent. So, like, maybe you can figure something out to—

Okay, okay. A guy can hope, right?

Where was I? Oh, right. As I was speaking, Cawti gave me a last squeeze, then pulled her chair closer to mine and put her hand on my arm. When I finished, Morrolan looked uncomfortable. I didn't know exactly what he was thinking, which I'm going to guess was a relief to him. I know it was a relief to me. I said, "Does anyone know what that sound might have been? Or, I guess it wasn't a sound. That word? The one I described—"

"Your name," said the Necromancer.

"Um," I said cleverly. "I know my name. Been pretty aware of it for a while now. That isn't it."

"What I want to know," said Aliera, "is how it happened."

"If that's to make sure it doesn't happen again," I said, "I agree."

"Where did you find the stone?" Aliera wanted to know.

"In a guy's house," I said.

She looked at me, and Morrolan coughed. "The important thing," he said, "is to try to understand what happened."

"The important thing," I muttered under my breath, "is my eight hundred gold."

"*Eight hundred and twelve,*" said Loiosh. "*And a half.*"

"What?" said Morrolan.

"Never mind."

"Whose house?" said Aliera. It took me a second to figure out what she was talking about.

"Oh, right. Just a guy."

Morrolan and Aliera were both staring at me. Cawti was studying the ceiling, and the Necromancer was looking off into space. I cleared my throat. "Do you want to know about Jhereg business? You know how you get." While they were thinking that over, I said, "Just what is that stone, anyway. Verra's tears?"

"Obsidian that has been polished—" said Morrolan.

"Yeah, for thousands of years by Dark Water. What is Dark Water?"

"Water that has never seen the light of day."

"Huh. And that's important?"

"It is useful for necromancy."

"Why?"

"Ask her," he said, gesturing with his chin.

"Hmm?" said the Necromancer helpfully. "What?"

I repeated the question, and she said some things I didn't pay much attention to about "all of life" and water and light and stuff.

"Is possession illegal?" I asked when she'd finished, leaving me knowing no more than I'd known when I asked.

"No," said Morrolan. "Though, technically, a lot of what you do with it is. Summoning demons, raising the dead, those sorts of things are against Imperial law."

"Technically?" I repeated.

"Depends on your House," he said. "No one near the top of the Cycle will be prosecuted, unless he does something especially terrible, in which case those charges will likely be added on."

"Huh," I said. "So, don't break the law if you're a Vallista or a Jhereg or an Iorich, but feel free if you were born an Athyra or a Dragon? Gotta love it."

"It's how things work," said Morrolan, which I guess I'd known already.

"Maybe," said Cawti, "we should just get back to what we were doing."

"What was that?" asked Aliera.

"Well, we came here to find out about the stone, what it was, what it could do—"

"How much it was worth?" said Morrolan with an ironic smirk.

"Of course not," I said. "But since you bring it up, how—"

"No idea," he said.

"None? I mean, think I could get eight hundred for it?"

"Maybe," said Aliera.

"Good, then," I said. "I win."

"This person whose house you were in," said Morrolan. "You said he was 'just a guy.' That isn't something 'just a guy' would have. They're rare, and only of use to necromancers."

"Can they be traced?" said Cawti.

I looked at her. I hadn't thought of that.

"Hmmm. Possibly," said Morrolan.

"Unlikely," said Aliera.

"I could trace it," said the Necromancer.

"You don't have to," I said. "It's right here."

She nodded as if I'd made an important point.

Meanwhile, I was regretting all the stuff I'd told Kragar not to bother learning about the guy. Fisher. What was he up to? Do I care? If I just sell this thing, will it turn around and bite me?

"What are you thinking, Vlad?" said Morrolan, who was staring kind of hard.

"I was wondering how much pasta to make, and how much time to allow for it. Cawti and I are going to cook—"

"Cut it out. Are you going to try to sell the Verra's tear?"

"I'm thinking about it. You want to buy it?"

"You should," Aliera told him. "Just to take it off his hands so he doesn't get killed when they find it."

"I'm touched that you care," I said.

She shrugged. "Usually I wouldn't. But we just went through a lot of work to save you."

"Yeah," I said. "And by the way, thanks for that."

"You will," said the Necromancer into an awkward silence, "have to let me know what sort of effects you notice."

"What sort of . . . What do you mean?"

"The after-effects of the transformation."

Cawti squeezed my arm.

"What sort of after-effects are we talking about?" I asked, using my I'm-so-unruffled-we-might-as-well-be-talking-about-card-games voice.

"Well," said the Necromancer, using her, if-you-want-to-talk-about-card-games-I'm-good-with-that voice, "Other than the obvious, there's no way to know."

I felt the others in the room staring at her, so, at least, it wasn't obvious to them. "What," I said, "are the obvious after-effects?"

"You know," she said, "the usual ones."

We all kept staring at her, and no one said anything.

"What?" she asked.

"What," I said, talking slow to make sure she understood, "are the usual ones."

"You know," she said.

We all waited.

"I mean, manifesting. In the normal way."

"Manifesting," I said. "What exactly do you mean, 'manifesting'?"

She looked like, I guess, I'd look if someone said, "How do you breathe?" She kept glancing around at us, and I'd have laughed if it wasn't about me and I didn't feel like maybe this was kind of important.

"You're manifesting now," she said.

"Is that what I'm doing?"

"We all are," she said.

"You mean, being somewhere."

"Yes."

"Oh. That's manifesting?"

She nodded.

Morrolan seemed satisfied with the answer, but Aliera was frowning, like she maybe wanted to keep digging at it. I was with her, so

I kept looking at her—I mean, Aliera—doing that thing where you look at someone, hoping the other people in the room will pick up on it. I guess it worked, because Aliera said, "There must be more to it than that, or why would you say manifesting, instead of just being here?"

See, that's Aliera. She's smart. That's why I let her hang around.

The Necromancer looked deep in thought. Maybe she was thinking about how smart Aliera was. I noticed that my hand was in Cawti's, and decided if Morrolan so much as raised an eyebrow I would throw something sharp at him.

"There is here," she said at last, "and then there's not-here."

"Ah, I get it," I said. "Kind of like there, only different."

She nodded.

I'd been being sarcastic.

"I meant manifest to mean being in both of those."

"At the same time," I said.

She nodded. "Well," she added, "time is sort of—"

"You mean like a god."

"Or a demon," put in Morrolan.

"So, I'm a god now?" I said.

"No, no. A demon," said the Necromancer.

I stared at her. I'd been joking. Cawti squeezed my hand.

"You don't mean it," I said. I looked at Morrolan. "She doesn't mean it." I looked at Aliera. "Does she mean it?"

They waited for the Necromancer to answer.

"It's nothing to be upset about," she said.

I had no idea how to respond to that, so I waited.

"It's a matter of precise definitions," she continued after a moment. "And you might fall into one category by strict definition, but in reality—"

"Reality," I muttered. "I'm thinking that doesn't have much to do with anything at this point."

"In reality," she tried again, "it won't make any difference. I mean, it won't change anything about you. Probably. It might, but that's what I meant about 'if you notice any—'"

"If I'm manifesting in two places," I said. "Why aren't I aware of it?"

"Most likely, you just haven't been summoned. Although," she continued, "it's possible that integrating the memories won't come naturally to you."

I shook my head. "You're telling me that I've changed, that I've been altered, that I'm a different Vlad than I was an hour ago, but it won't make any difference in my life? It just happened, but don't worry about it?"

"Yes," she said.

My heart was pounding like it does after a fight. I told it to settle down, but it never listens.

"I'm here, and somewhere else, and it doesn't matter?"

She nodded, then said, "Well, I mean, you might be somewhere else. Let me check."

I just looked at her.

"No, you're just here," she said.

"Well, that's good news," I muttered.

"Why?" she wanted to know.

"Okay," I said. "I'm here. I get that. I think it's time for me to be not here. I still have a collection to make, and this isn't helping. Morrolan, do you want to buy the stone, or not?"

"I don't," he said. "And I'd suggest you get rid of it quickly. It's possible, it seems, that it can be traced, and whoever owns it now is someone I think you will not want to engage."

"Okay, so—" I stopped. I'd been about to ask him for suggestions about a good place to unload it fast, but, on reflection, I'd know better than anyone else here. "So," I finished, "I'd best be going."

I stood up, and so did everyone else except Aliera, who said, "Are you just going to ignore it?"

"Ignore—"

"What the Necromancer just told you."

"She said it wouldn't matter."

"She's been known to be wrong."

I could have made a remark about talking about her as if she weren't here, but after all, maybe she was somewhere else. Who was I to say?

I said to Aliera, "It's fine."

My heart was telling me it wasn't fine at all, but that's kind of why I didn't want to be there—I wasn't sure what I was feeling, but I knew I didn't want to show it in front of Morrolan and Aliera. Also, I was thinking maybe some time to think about this by myself would help me figure out how to not think about it when I was by myself. Did you follow that? I hope not.

Meanwhile, Aliera said, "And what about the spell?"

I started to say *what spell* but then it came back to me, from what I'd overheard, and I said, "Yeah, good question. Who did this and why?"

Cawti still held my hand, the others all exchanged looks. At last Morrolan said, "I can't think of any easy way to find out."

"Not traceable?" said Aliera.

"If I'd done it right away, maybe. But we had other things on our mind."

"You said no *easy* way," I said. "Is there a hard way?"

"I hope so. I haven't had my defenses penetrated before, and I don't care for it, and I very much want words with whoever did it, so I intend to get to work on it."

"Would you like help?" said Aliera.

Morrolan nodded. "Thank you."

"You'll let me know?" I said. "I mean, being as I was kind of the target."

"Of course," said Morrolan. "It's likely to take a while."

I nodded. "I'm going to be doing some checking on my own," I said. "I'll let you know if I get anything that connects."

"Good," said Morrolan. "Would you care for a teleport?"

"Yeah, thanks. Have one of your people do it; I want to say good-bye to Teldra."

"Be careful, Vlad," said Morrolan, as if I hadn't planned to be. But I guess that's just one of those things you say.

We went down the long, curving stairway, with dragons and

Morrolan's ancestors watching us. Whether that felt creepy depended a lot on what I was doing there. Cawti said, "Hungry?"

"Yeah, but I want to unload this thing first. I didn't want Morrolan to know I'm nervous, but I'm nervous."

"Are you all right, Vladimir?"

"I don't . . . I'm not sure. My head keeps going back and forth between obsessing and not wanting to think about it. It's—I mean, am I an entirely different person than I was this morning, or is it just a weird thing that happened, or what?"

"You seem like the same person to me," she said after running a quick test.

"I don't think that's conclusive, but you're welcome to keep trying."

We took a moment to say farewell to Lady Teldra and to thank her for her courtesy. I know, that's kinda like thanking the Adrilankha River for flowing downhill, but a few words with her, like, puts you in a better mood. It was probably my imagination, but I thought for a second she looked worried. We said our farewells, she bowed deeply, and we left Castle Black.

One of Morrolan's guards, a lanky-armed guy with hair the same impossible blond as the Empress's, approached us in the courtyard and said, "I will perform the teleport, if you will. Where would you like to go?"

Cawti looked at me.

I said, "I'm heading to near the office, I guess, and to find someone to buy the, you know. Maybe I'll meet you—"

"I'll go with you," she said.

"Sounds good," I said, and nodded to the guard.

Teleports take way too long, if you ask me. Someone needs to invent a fast one. I mean, like, they take three, maybe four seconds, which is way too long when you're watching the walls in front of you start flowing like they're melting, and then you don't have anything under your feet, and then you aren't sure what you're seeing because none of it makes sense, and you feel like you're upside out and inside down and maybe you are because the blood rushes to your head hard enough and fast enough to almost hurt, except then you're standing on firm ground again with the door to your office in front of you.

Cawti had one knee and one hand on the ground, head down. I stood, bent over. After a minute or two, the sensation passed, and we each drew in a big breath at the same time and smiled at each other when we realized it.

"Where did you have in mind?" she asked.

"Three-Dice," I said.

"Because he's a Tsalmoth, or because he deals in that stuff?"

"Because he deals in that stuff. If I get my eight hundred, I'm not going to care about what was going on with the dead guy."

"Really?"

"Sure."

"You'll just drop it, and never know?"

"I'll drop it like a spitting slipsnake."

"Why would you ever hold a slipsnake?"

"If it had my eight hundred imperials . . ."

She chuckled, then said, "I still can't believe you're willing to never find out what Bereth was up to."

"Watch me."

"I always do," she said. I wasn't sure if that should please me or worry me, so I went with being pleased. "I'll meet you back in your office, then we'll head there together, all right?"

"I was thinking we'd go now."

She shook her head. "You have an errand to run first."

"I do?"

"You need to visit your grandfather."

"I do?"

"Yes."

"Why?"

"How are you feeling, Vladimir?"

"Fine, now that the after-effects of the tele—"

"No," she said. "How are you feeling?"

"You mean about . . ."

"Yes."

"I'll meet you back at the office," I said. "Also, I love you."

I wasn't going to kiss her on a public street, but I wanted to.

⇥

My grandfather lived in South Adrilankha. Supposedly, with Zerika on the throne, this was the reign of a reborn Phoenix, which, they tell me, means things are supposed to, you know, renew. You can't tell from walking around the Easterner's quarter, though. The ghetto where most Easterners live takes up most of the area of Adrilankha that's east of the bridges, although not the whole thing; there are a few hills to the north where various nobles keep their summer homes, and to the south there are the docks and the warehouses that continue all along the lower areas by the ocean-sea on both sides of the river, and then, further east, just above the docks, are the slaughterhouses. I've wondered if maybe they wouldn't have stunk so bad if they'd been built down closer to the shore, below the cliffs. I don't know.

The day was cool and dry. I mention that because when it was hot and muggy, I'd put my cloak in front of my nose when hitting the ghetto. Not just the slaughterhouses, but refuse was piled in the streets until it was burned. Burning it didn't make it smell any better.

Once I opened the flap on my grandfather's doorway, the smell vanished, replaced by a mild rose scent. Just so you know, there was magic at work there in addition to incense; the Eastern art of witchcraft may not be as flashy as sorcery, but it's awfully nice to be able to do. Trust me on that.

My grandfather was sitting at his table doing something with a few small bones in a pile in front of him. He looked up and broke into a gap-toothed grin. "Vladimir!" he said. It hit me that he and Cawti were the only ones who used the full form of my name. My father had, when he was alive, but only when I stopped mopping the floor to daydream about not having to mop floors.

I went over and kissed Noish-pa on the cheek. His familiar, a cat named Ambrus, jumped down from a chair, stretched, hissed at Loiosh as if discharging a duty, and curled up at Noish-pa's feet. I sat down in the chair.

He collected the bones and put them in a small, velvet-lined, silver-embossed wooden box that gave a satisfying *click* as he closed it. There's something pleasing about almost anything that's well-crafted, you know? Even a little box used to hold raven-bones.

"So," he said. "What is on your mind? Is it the wedding?"

"Well, no," I said. "Although, now that you mention it, I have a lot of questions about that, too."

"What is it, then?" He was suddenly serious. He picks up on things, does my grandfather.

"Something just happened."

He nodded, and waited while I searched around for the words.

"I think," I finally said, "that I may have been turned into a demon."

He sat back, his thick, white brows came together, and he said, "Tell me."

I described the experience as I remembered it, halting and stumbling and correcting myself, with a lot of, "no, that isn't exactly it," and, "something like that," and "maybe it was more like," and such.

When I'd finished, he looked very serious. "This . . . This is elf magic, Vladimir."

I nodded.

"I do not understand it, or what it means. When the elfs speak of gods and demons, they do not mean what we do."

"I know."

"How do you feel, Vladimir?"

"Physically? Fine."

"No, how do you *feel*?"

I thought about it. I mean, I gotta say, asking myself how I feel isn't something I spend a lot of time doing. But Noish-pa wouldn't ask on a whim.

"Angry," I finally said. "And, yeah, scared."

He nodded. "You must speak to the elfs. Learn what it means, and what can be done."

I nodded.

"You don't want to," he said.

I hesitated, then nodded again.

"You must anyway," he said.

"All right."

He fell silent, looking down, then raised his head and looked at me carefully. "You are still Taltos Vladimir," he said. "You must remember that."

I laughed a little. "I'm not sure if I know what that means anymore, but I think that's a good thing."

His eyebrows asked what I meant. "I mean Cawti," I told them. "It's different now."

His missing teeth showed again. "What do you wish to know about weddings?" he said.

⌈⌉

I collected Cawti at my office. She didn't ask how things had gone with my grandfather and I didn't feel like talking about it just then, so we just headed out.

Three-Dice's place was just a bit out of my area, on Garshos, past the point where it curves back and starts to go down Crackskull Hill. Crackskull Hill isn't its name, it's just what I started calling it after seeing one Vallista and three Teckla slipping and rolling down it during a rainstorm one day. The pawnshop, called Three-Dice's Pawnshop 'cause he had all kinds of imagination, was braced by poles on one side to make up for how steep the hill was. But the little porch—about three feet—was flat. The door was connected by leather straps that were only barely hanging on, and the front of the place was wood that needed a paint job and then to be replaced. Maybe with brick. I opened the door, which didn't fall apart.

When we walked in, he was reading a book, so his bald head was staring at us. I've known a couple of others who shaved their heads, and been curious about why. Three-Dice was the one I'd asked, a year or so before. He'd said, "I don't know. Felt like it."

He looked up as we came in. "Hey, whiskers. Whatayagot?" I can't tell you why, but he's one of very few people who can call me "whiskers" without making me want to hit him in the head with something heavy.

"Verra's tears," I said.

He sat back abruptly, and almost fell off his stool. "Do you, ah, have it on you?"

I nodded.

"Show me," he said.

I pulled it out, handed it over. He stared at it, turned it around in his hand, and showed no sign of suddenly having his personality vanish into it.

"Where—" he said, then stopped. "Is it traceable?" he finally said.

I shrugged, and his eyes narrowed; I guess he figured that meant yes.

"Lord Taltos—"

"Make me an offer," I said.

"I can't."

"Oh, come on."

"If it gets traced—"

"You can say you don't remember who sold it to you."

"And then whoever it is starts getting persuasive, and—"

"Yeah, I get it," I said. I did get it, and I didn't have a good answer.

"Can you recommend someone?" said Cawti.

I'd been about to ask that. No, really.

He scratched the top of his head.

"Let me think," he said.

I slid an imperial across the counter, to kind of help his brain work.

"Eight hundred and thirteen," said Loiosh. *"And a half."*

"Yeah, yeah."

"Sorivith," he said. "He works out of the upper floor of a rooming house on Seawatch Lane at the edge of Little Deathgate. Number eleven."

"Thanks," I said.

"Stay careful, whiskers."

"I always do," I lied.

We went back outside.

"Boss! Spell!"

And, if you want to make some sort of judgment, Loiosh noticed them first, Cawti second, me last.

There were two of them, and they were very fast, very good. I guessed they'd been sent to bring me in alive, or at least revivifiable, so their boss could ask me questions. If they'd wanted to kill me, I doubt I'd have come out of it. One of them was pointing at me. I swung Spellbreaker, and got at least some of it before it hit me.

Let me tell you about paralysis spells.

They're popular in the organization because all they need to do is work a bit. I mean, you get hit with one, your heart stops, your blood stops, your breathing stops, your life stops. End of problem. But if you're up against a sorcerer, or someone with sorcery protection, or, maybe a weird golden chain that interrupts sorcery, all you need is for a little bit of the spell to get through. Maybe you only get the muscles of his feet. Okay, now he can't run. Maybe his arms. Now he can't defend himself. The more gets through, the better chance you can finish the job and spend the money. Or stop worrying about the money you've already spent, whatever.

So, yeah, I swung Spellbreaker.

A tingling ran up my arm. I caught some of the spell, but not all of it. I'm guessing it was intended to stop short of killing me, but I don't exactly know. All I know is that I was suddenly frozen in place, like a statue, my left arm up with my gold chain in mid swing, and, I have no doubt, a stupid look on my face.

"Boss, I can't move."

"Yeah, that's two of us."

The good news is, there were three of us there, and whatever the spell was, it hadn't hit Cawti.

She didn't waste time seeing if I was okay, because if she had, she'd have been dead, and then I would for sure have been not okay.

I didn't see her throw, and I couldn't exactly follow the knives, but I saw three of them flying at the guy who'd cast the spell. They came fast, too, faster than—you promised no one in the world will ever hear this, right? Yeah. Faster than I could have thrown them, and on target. One caught the guy in his chest, maybe right below his sternum, and went in deep enough that it had to sting. He did something and the other two sort of flew off to the side where I couldn't see them—in case you missed it, I couldn't turn my head.

I'm pretty sure the knife wound wasn't fatal, but it wasn't any fun, either, and the sorcerer decided that this would be a good time to be somewhere else. I could still see the other guy, and, in a second, I could see Cawti, holding two knives and moving like a snake-dancer.

The other guy started circling to his right, holding a sword. Then he was also holding a dagger. My eyes started hurting and I realized I wasn't able to blink.

Cawti and the Jhereg circled each other. The one who'd been hit, the sorcerer, was out of my line of sight, but I knew he'd left the area, or Cawti wouldn't have been so totally focused on the other one.

Garshos is a pretty big street, so it was wide enough for them to stay out of range of each other even when both of their backs were to a building.

They kept circling, taking turns moving in front of me; the Jhereg gave me a perfect back shot, which I'd have taken if I could have, you know, moved.

Cawti made the first move, stepping into him. There are two ways to hold a knife in a knife fight: either point out, in thrusting position like a sword, or with the blade back in covering your forearm. That second position gives you better defense, and is good for slashing attacks, though you give up some range.

Cawti kept switching her left-hand knife between the two positions, the one in her right she kept covering her forearm, using it cross-body to deflect his sword and strike at his sword hand. Her left hand wove an ever-changing pattern, but mostly focused low to both keep his other dagger busy and interfere with his sword-work.

She never stopped moving, and she never moved predictably, but it was always in, toward him, interfering with his ability to get a good attack with the sword. Whenever their turning took her to a place where she had the advantage of height, she'd launch a series of attacks that made him defend himself, and when they turned so that he was higher, she'd slide in and out and never give him a chance to get a clear shot. And she was in complete control—he moved where she let him move; his thrusts were half-hearted and imprecise. She was dancing and flowing and deadly. It was, like, if I wanted to teach someone how to fight with knives, I'd just point at her and say "watch."

Gods of the Paths, she was beautiful.

Some blood started dripping from his hand. In a little while, he'd lose his grip on the sword, and that would be it, if it wasn't over sooner.

It was over sooner, but not how I expected: Cawti suddenly backed up several steps and sheathed her weapons. The Jhereg frowned, glanced over his shoulder, and hastily sheathed his. A moment later, when the pair of Phoenix Guards walked by, Cawti was standing in front of me like we were having a conversation, and the Jhereg was nowhere to be seen, at least by me. The birds didn't even slow down.

"Vlad? Are you all right?"

"Breathing okay, heart beating okay, and I just blinked, so I think I'm coming out of it. Except—"

"Except what?"

"Well, I'm suddenly terrified at the possibility of not spending the rest of my life with you. We are getting married, right? I mean, I didn't imagine that thing where you asked me—?"

"Glad you're doing better. And of course we are."

"Okay."

"Boss?"

"You all right, chum?"

"Yeah. Congratulations."

I was able to turn my head a little. Not surprising, because it seemed I'd turned Cawti's head. Little joke there, because in Fenarian, "turning someone's head" means you've, okay, just skip it. Can you go back and take that part out? Never mind, whatever you want.

She stood there as if we were just talking, and after a couple of minutes I felt her hand on my arm, and around that time Loiosh flew up onto my shoulder.

I wrapped Spellbreaker around my wrist again, still stiff, feeling like I was moving under water, but I could do it.

"We should," I told Cawti, "get on with wedding plans."

She took hold of my face with both hands and kissed me. "Yes," she said. "Let's do that."

"*I think I'm going to barf.*"

"*Shut up.*"

We started back to my office. I still wasn't walking right—kind of slow and lock-kneed—but most of the rest of me seemed to work. I'd once been hit by a paralysis spell (caught a piece meant for the guy I was guarding) that made my whole body numb, and I spent the next two days with all my extremities gradually waking up, and they were all in bad moods. I figured a little trouble walking was no problem.

We made it back to the office and up the stairs. Melestav took one look at me and was on his feet. "What—"

"It's fine," I said. "But tell everyone to stay alert. It seems I've annoyed someone."

"You? I don't believe it."

"You want to sit down?" said Kragar.

"Yeah, good idea."

I sat behind my desk and leaned the chair back—I really gotta tell you about that chair sometime, it's a work of mechanical art—and stretched my legs. They didn't crackle or anything.

Cawti went behind me and rubbed my shoulders, Loiosh flew over to his windowsill.

"Hungry?" said Cawti.

"Yes. I could eat the, I don't know, something inedible out of something disgusting."

"Right. But let's not do that."

"Should I grab something?" said Kragar, who, it seems, had followed us in.

I nodded and turned to Cawti. "Fish sound good?"

"Topo's?"

"Yeah."

"Yeah."

"I'll pick some up," said Kragar. I found an imperial in my desk and tossed it to him.

Then shook for a bit, and Cawti pretended not to notice. She pulled a chair around to my side of the desk, put a hand on my leg, and rested her head against my shoulder. We didn't say anything.

6

MEETING THE FAMILIES

There are, I'm told, all sorts of formal things that you say to each others' families to get approval for the match. Some of them the couple does together, some of them only the one who is asking to join the new family. With the Dzur, they meet by fighting a series of duels with each other, because they're Dzur. And kinda stupid if you ask me—people can get hurt doing that stuff. With Fenarians, it isn't that bad. There are questions you have to answer, some of them meaningless formalities, others things that family might actually want to know, like, "How do you earn your salt?" or whatever. The closest thing Cawti had to a family was her ex-partner, Norathar, who would have just looked blank. I had Noish-pa, who cut through all the other stuff by kissing Cawti on the cheek. That worked.

⚭

A bit later, the smell of vinegar entered the room, and there was Kragar, holding a small crate, which he set down and began emptying onto my desk.

I kinda know how to do this: you clean and gut a bluetail fish (I've done it, I hate it, I won't do it again), fillet it, dip it in some whipped raw hen's eggs, roll it in some white flour that's been ground down until it's nothing more than powder, then in the egg again, then in some breadcrumbs you've seasoned, then you stick it in some hot oil until it floats. What kind of oil you use is the big thing. Topo, who has a cart and "wheeled kitchen" just down the street, cuts slits in the fillets that he packs with lemon and garlic before frying them. When they're done, he drenches them, I mean, *drenches* them in some kind of magic vinegar that he distills himself and that he won't tell anyone about. Maybe one of these days I'll torture him for it. One of the many good things about Topo's fish is that they hold their heat for a long time, long enough that even after Kragar walked back with them and unloaded them, they were still too hot to hold.

I had Melestav bring us some wine, and offered him some fish because Kragar had, it seemed, spent the whole imperial on making sure we had enough. I ate fish and tried to decide if that imperial should be added to the 813. I finally decided not, because, hey, I'd have had to eat anyway, right?

The place was going to smell like vinegar for the rest of the day, but I didn't mind. Loiosh expressed approval of the whole thing, except for the part about other people eating his fish.

Cawti kept her hand on my leg for most of the meal. By the time we were done, I was back to my old self. Amazing what fish will do.

As I was taking the last swallow and showing off how cultured I was by licking vinegar off my fingers, Cawti said, "What now, Vladimir?"

I tried not to get all distracted by how much I loved the way she said "Vladimir."

"I don't know," I said. "I think it's safe to assume Fisher is after the stone."

"You can always kill him," said Kragar. I'd forgotten he was still there.

"You know who he works for?"

"Oh, right," said Kragar.

"Yeah, that would have, uh, what's the word?"

"Catharsis?" he said.

"Consequences."

He smirked.

One of my people came in sometime in there and distracted me with some business involving just who and how many were supposed to get paid off for one of my brothels. If the pay-off gets too big, I might as well get a license for the thing and stop paying the bribes

altogether, and then everyone loses. This is what they call "econom-
ics." Cawti taught me that word.

Once he was gone, I turned back to Kragar.

"I could always ask him," I said. "See if we can make a deal."

"Sure," said Kragar. "What if he tells you that he'll accept your
offer, which he will, and then tries to kill you, which he will?"

"I'll try to kill him right back," I said.

I glanced at Cawti, who was looking amused. I suppose I could
have been upset that she was amused by the idea of me getting all
killed and stuff, but I wasn't. I took the stone out and set it on my
desk. "I'll leave this here," I said. "Until I know if we can settle this.
I'm pretty sure they traced me using it."

Kragar said, "You have a plan, then?"

"We go back to that place where he hangs out, and I talk to him."

"Vlad—"

"Cawti will protect me."

"Yes," she said promptly. "I will."

"And so will Loiosh," I added, so his feelings wouldn't be hurt. He
flapped his wings. Kragar shrugged.

I wiped off my fingers on my jerkin, like a slob. Bad habit. I should
stop doing that.

We stood up. "Kragar, mind the till and—"

"Keep my hand out of the store. Yeah, yeah."

"I was going to say, find a couple of guys to keep a discreet eye
on me."

"How discreet?"

"Don't lose sight, but don't make it obvious, either."

"You want to play cat-string?"

"No, but I don't want to look like I'm worried."

"All right. I'll see to it. Keep your skin whole."

"That's the plan," I said. "That's always the plan."

I don't know who Kragar picked out to shadow me, but they had
nothing to do; we made it to the Stolen Boat with no trouble. Not
surprising; it was going to take Fisher some time to set something
up, now that his first try had failed. With luck, I could talk to him

and return the Verra's Tears, and he wouldn't kill me, and I could get back to trying to get my eight hundred imperials. Maybe he'd even be willing to pay me eight hundred to get his property back, though that wasn't very likely. But if you go right up to the guy who's after you, sometimes it'll throw him off. That's gotta help.

It was late afternoon when we got there, and the place was starting to fill up, mostly with Teckla, also a few Jhereg. Nice place, like a bar for wolves where norska like to show up. The host recognized me and nodded; if he knew of anything wrong he wasn't showing it.

"Get you something?" he said.

"I'm looking for Fisher."

"Not here."

"Will he be?"

"Probably."

"A bottle of wine and two cups, then. A Levier, maybe?" Cawti liked Levier.

He nodded, found a bottle, came back. He was deft with the feather, and kind of flashy. I've always liked that. I traded him a round silvery thing for the tall glass thing, and we took the bottle back to a table against the wall. I did a quick spell to chill it because Dragaerans know nothing about wine, and suddenly every Jhereg with sorcery detection—there were six of them—were on their feet, hands on weapons, staring at me.

"Sorry," I said into the sudden silence. "Just chilling the wine."

They gave me different sorts of glares, then sat down. I smiled an apology at the host and poured the wine. Cawti was smirking at me. "Did you know that was going to happen?"

"Mmmm, let's say I wasn't surprised."

"You mess with them just for fun, don't you?"

"Sometimes. Sometimes I just want my wine chilled."

We touched cups in the Eastern way and looked into each other's eyes in a way that would have made me want to slap someone else who did it, but there was no one around to slap me, so I drank some wine. It wasn't bad.

We talked about where we'd live. I wanted to find a new place

with her, she wanted to get out of the "hole in the wall" she'd occu-
pied since she and her partner had split up, and was happy to move
in with me for a while. We talked about moving stuff around. How
can a discussion of moving a table from one side of a room to the
other make you so happy? I don't know. It did.

Fisher came in. He had no bodyguards, which I respected. Unless,
maybe, some of the Jhereg in the bar worked for him. Probably. I
adjusted my respect down a notch.

Cawti and I stood, but she hung back so he wouldn't feel threatened. If he'd known how good she was at throwing knives, he'd
have felt more threatened, but that was all right. My plan wasn't to
threaten him. At least, not right away.

He looked at me, looked again, and his eyes narrowed. It's always
such a pleasure to be recognized, don't you think? To the left, at least
he didn't draw a weapon.

"Taltos," he said. He pronounced it "Tal-toss" instead of "Tal-tosh,"
so he'd seen it written, or whoever talked to him about me had. For
whatever that was worth. I didn't take the opportunity to correct
him.

"My lord," I said, giving him a token head-bob. "May I have the
honor of a few minutes of conversation?"

He looked at Loiosh, whose head was sticking out of my cloak,
and waited.

"Hang out with Cawti for a while?"

"Aw, Boss. All right."

He left my shoulder and flew to Cawti's. This caused a certain
amount of disturbance in the place—I guess they weren't used to flying things there. Then I got some looks that I ignored, while Cawti
scratched under Loiosh's chin and Fisher looked at her. "Who is
she?"

"My betrothed," I answered honestly.

He frowned. "Is she . . . ?"

"Yeah," I said. "But she'll wait out here too."

"All right. Follow me."

He led me upstairs. I felt eyes on me, but didn't hear any footsteps, and he had his back to me. Was he stupid, over-confident, or did he have something going on that I didn't know about? I assumed the latter. Besides, I hadn't planned to kill him anyway.

The room he led us to was tiny; there was hardly space for the two hard wooden chairs and small table to fit into it, and the instant I walked in I felt that little twinge in your head that tells you there is magic afoot.

Unlike those downstairs, I didn't instantly assume I was being attacked, I just said, "What was that?"

"A privacy spell. I don't like being listened to. Sit. What's on your mind?"

I sat. "I think you know."

He frowned. "Pretend I don't. I've heard of you, of course. But if one of my people has done something—"

"Really?" I said.

"Really what?" he said. "Spill it."

"You actually don't know."

"If you keep not telling me," he said, "I'm going to get irritated."

Okay, well, this hadn't been the way I'd expected the conversation to go, but, sure, let's run with it.

"I understand you're missing something."

His frown deepened. "Are all Easterners this cryptic? I am now irritated. Want more?"

This was *so* not how I expected the conversation to go.

"Your Verra's tear."

"My what?"

"Um. A stone? Black, obsidian, polished smooth by Dark Water?"

"What are you talking about?"

I opened my pouch, dug around in it, found a scrap of paper, pushed it over to him.

He glanced at it. "That's my address," he said.

"And there," I said, "in that house, is a hidden compartment under the bed, near the headboard on the right side as you face it."

His eyes narrowed and his teeth gritted. "And you know that, how?"

"Sources," I said. "And inside the compartment is a box, and inside of the box was a stone called—"

"There was nothing in that compartment," he said. "I haven't used it in twenty years. You've been misinformed, and I'd like to know just where this information came from, because I intend to have a talk with someone."

I sat back and stared at him. "Yeah," I said. "You probably should. Me too."

"What—?"

"You're not lying to me?" I asked, which is always a stupid question. I mean, who'd be lying and admit it?

"You had best—"

"Okay," I said. "Let me start at the beginning. There's a stone used in certain kinds of magic called Verra's tears. Some came into my hands, and I thought to sell it. I learned that it had been stolen from your home, so I came to you."

He was quiet for a bit, and completely still except for his nostrils flaring.

"What aren't you telling me?"

"I was kind of hoping for a reward for returning it."

"Uh huh. What else aren't you telling me?"

"All sorts of things."

"Who broke into my home?"

"A thief," I answered honestly.

"Was it you?"

"Of course not."

"Did you order it done?"

"No."

"Are you lying?"

"No."

See what a stupid question that is? He stared at me as if my answer had somehow not satisfied him.

"So," he said. "You claim that someone broke into my house and stole something I never had."

"Well," I said. "To be fair, some of that is your claim."

"Is it possible you were lied to about where it came from?"

"Hmmm. Yes, I guess it is," I lied. "But in case I wasn't lied to, who would break into your house and give you something like that?"

"No one," he said.

Was there a little hesitation before he said that? Just the least hitch, as if maybe a name had popped into his head? Maybe it was my imagination, but I was pretty sure I'd seen something.

"Um," I said. "Okay. Tell you what. I'll check my source again—"

"I think," he said, "that you're lying. I think you had my house broken into."

"I didn't," I said, which was technically true.

"How about you just tell me who that 'source' is."

"You mean, who broke into your house? Well, maybe you should report it to the Phoenix Guards, and they can conduct an investigation."

"Don't play games with me, Easterner."

"Why? I like games. They challenge the mind."

"You know, you're very irritating."

"If it helps," I said, "you're not the first person to—"

"You need to learn to control your mouth."

"I'll work on it. Got any, you know, advice?"

"You're on your own with this."

"I'll do my best, then."

"I think I'm going to kill you."

"All right. But next time, lead with that."

I slipped a hand into my cloak.

"Not right now though," he said.

"Then I appreciate the warning. I still want to know who it was who hid the thing in your house."

"None of your business, and you're going to be dead anyway."

"All right."

"Leave now," he said.

I stood up and headed out. It'd been a while since anyone had threatened to kill me. I'd been afraid I was slipping.

I went down the stairs, Loiosh flew over, and Cawti fell into step next to me as we headed out. A little ways down the street she said, "Well?"

"Did you bring the rest of the wine?"

"Of course."

"Good."

"What happened?"

"Either I've been effectively lied to for no reason I can think of, or there is something strange going on."

I filled her in on the conversation.

"If he really wants to put a shine on me," I said, "he'll have to clear it. We have the same boss."

"Think Toronnan will give him the go-ahead?"

"Hard to say."

"Then let's assume it's a real threat."

I nodded, and we kept walking.

As we got near my office, she said, "I've been thinking it over. If what he said is true, I very much want to know who would break into someone's house to conceal something valuable. And why."

"Well, yeah."

"So I think we can conclude that its value isn't the point. Either it's there because someone needed a place to hide it and Fisher's place was somehow convenient, or . . ."

She let her voice trail off.

"Or," I finished for her, "there is something necromantic going on and Fisher is the target."

"Right."

"If that's the case, and we can find out the details, we could probably use it."

"To get your eight hundred back."

"Yeah."

We reached the office and climbed up. I never did see whoever Kragar had sent to protect me. I went into the office, took the Verra's tear from my desk, slid it into my cloak.

"Vlad?"

"Yes, love?"

"You have a plan."

"Yeah."

"Can I hear it?" said Kragar.

I jumped, and Cawti almost drew a knife but caught herself. We glared at Kragar.

"Sorry," he said. "But that thing is worth a lot, so I thought I'd hang around here and keep an eye on it."

"Good thinking," I said.

"So," said Kragar. "The plan?"

"You don't even know what it's supposed to solve."

"Then fill me in."

I did, and he said, "Oh."

"Yeah."

"Okay, so, what's the plan?"

"We know someone took a shot at me."

"Yeah," said Kragar.

"Either it was Fisher and he's a very good liar, and he'll try again, or it's someone else, and he'll try again."

"With you so far."

"So we can assume I'm still a target."

Kragar nodded.

"From the looks of things, they don't want me dead, they just want me."

"Must be nice to be wanted," said Kragar.

I ignored him. "We need to find out who is after me, and why."

He nodded again.

"Before you asked if I was playing cat-string." I looked at Cawti. "Now I'm suggesting we do just that."

She looked back at me, thinking about it. Her eyes are such a perfect deep brown you could die.

"Vlad—" said Kragar, then stopped. We all knew the danger— you don't usually play cat-string when the cat knows you know it's there.

After a moment, Cawti nodded. "All right," she said. "When?"

"Let's give it a couple of hours, so they have time to get ready."

"That gives us time to finish the wine."

"See, I love how practical you are. When we're married, we have to remember that you're the practical one."

"What will you be?"

"The romantic, of course. Every marriage needs one of each."

She cocked an eyebrow. "Where did you hear that?"

"I just made it up."

"I'm not sure it holds up, love."

"It doesn't have to be true, it's romantic. And I'm the romantic one."

She was kind enough to laugh. Then she said, "I've heard of cat-string, of course, but never been involved. Best fill me in on what I'm supposed to do."

"Right. Okay, here's how it works."

A couple hours later, wine gone, I stood, and strapped on my rapier. I checked the stone, which was still in an inside pocket of my cloak. "Now is good," I said.

Cawti stood up, touched her daggers, and said, "I'm ready."

I nodded to Kragar. "Mind the store and all that."

"Don't die," he suggested.

We made it to the street, and Cawti said, "We ready?"

"Yep," I said. "Let's do this."

If you have someone after you, and you want to encourage that person to take a shot, and, you know, fail, there are a few ways to go about it, but they all come down to putting yourself into a situation where you look more helpless than you are. I'd been involved in cat-string three times. No, wait. Four. Never as the, uh, principal, though, just as part of the tail. It had worked on two of those occasions.

Typically, if you're dealing with an assassination attempt, it can take days or weeks, and, trust me, it feels like it goes on forever. And your feet get sore, and it seems like your eyeballs are itching from straining to see an attack before it happens. You work in shifts, because no one can stay alert all the time, and because that makes it less likely for the tail to be spotted, but it still drags. This time, I was working under the theory that whoever was after me was in fact after the Verra's tear, so killing me wasn't a priority, so it wouldn't take the careful planning that goes into an assassination, so it wouldn't take as long.

That was the theory.

And, I have to say, the theory was good, as far as it went.

Cawti dropped back about forty paces. It was afternoon on a Farmday, so there were a decent number of people, but not so many she couldn't keep an eye on me. Loiosh flew overhead. I slipped the end of Spellbreaker down to my left hand. Just the end, and I kept my palm in so it wouldn't show.

I went for a nice walk.

As I entered Malak Circle, the third floor of the Coppersmith's Guild building looked like it was bowing to me. When I was in a bad mood, it looked like it wanted to fall over on me. I'm convinced it's going to collapse one of these days. Someone should look into that. I continued around Malak Circle until it let out onto an unnamed alley that brought me to a curving, narrow little street named Nebbit that brought me outside of my area. Only houses there, not even a merchant's tent, and they're all three- or four-family places.

How you walk is important. Most of this I learned from Kiera, but Kragar also gave me a few pointers, in the early days. They taught me how to follow someone, how to blend into a crowd. Now, Kragar didn't need to know any of that, since he has kind of a natural talent for it, but he knew how to anyway, which I gotta say is to his credit.

Anyway, yeah. You gotta pay attention to how you walk. If you're in a crowd, like say in the market on Marketday, you walk so you'll blend in. No, seriously, next time you're in a group of strangers, if you look, you'll be surprised how many of them are all walking the same—arm movements, set to the shoulders, the way they're holding their heads. You walk like that too and they won't notice you, even if maybe you think you stand out. Try it. While you're there, pick someone's pocket or cut someone's purse. Let me know if you get anything good.

What was I talking about? Oh, right. Walking. If you want to be attacked, walk quickly, with your eyes straight ahead, like you have a destination in mind. That makes it seem like you're nervous about being attacked and you're acting like you aren't. If you want to not be attacked, saunter, looking around with a little smile on your face, like you're hoping someone, anyone, will try something, anything. If you want to be attacked, but want to look like you don't want to be attacked, you sort of go somewhere in the middle and hope for the best. Or the worst. I don't know.

Just before running into Imperial Avenue, Nebbit starts being called Lantern Way. I don't know why they called it that, never seen a lantern on it. Just past that point there's another tiny, winding street called Besindo that goes for about half a mile and ends in the Besindo Market. It was about a hundred yards before the market that Loiosh screamed into my mind. I ducked, turned, swung Spellbreaker, and took a dagger in my upper thigh that went deep enough to drop me to the ground.

It hurt like fire, and I had no idea what was going on around me. Loiosh was way up there, and Cawti was way behind me, and I was on the ground, bleeding.

So far, my plan was working perfectly.

I have to say, whoever threw the knife was very good, or very lucky; knives spin as you throw them, so the trouble isn't *hitting* a moving target as much as getting it to land point-first in a moving target. I can do it sometimes. Usually.

As I was lying there, I decided I'd assume he was good instead of lucky, because it'd be less embarrassing to be wrong. In any case, he was strong—that son of a bitch hit deep.

I pulled it out and someone made a gurgling noise. I think it was me.

"*Boss? You okay?*"

"*Remains to be seen. Who do you see?*"

I didn't know if I was bleeding bad enough that doing something about it was more important than standing up and drawing a weapon. Probably not. The Verra-be-damned knife had gone deep though. I was starting, as Kragar says, to regret my life choices.

"I see three of them, Boss."

So they wanted to capture me, still; because you don't send three people to kill someone. I'd tell you why, only I'm right in the middle of explaining about what these assholes were doing to me, and you'd probably get all pissed off if I stopped to explain stuff about how the Organization works.

So, yeah, where was I? Right. Lying in the street, bleeding like a boar.

I remember this stuff pretty good. I've been fighting for as long as I remember, but it seems like the older I get, the better I get at remembering how things played out in a fight. Little stuff, how the cobblestones of Bisendo hurt my elbow as I looked around, seeing Loiosh swooping down, realizing that Cawti had yelled my name even though I hadn't quite noticed at the time, and then suddenly spotting two of my attackers.

I was just bragging about how good I remember fights, but I can't for the life of me remember how I got to my feet, and what with how much my leg was hurting, you'd think that would be easy to remember. But there I was, standing, holding Spellbreaker in my left hand and my rapier in my right as they closed on me.

Spellbreaker, bless its non-existent heart, coiled up like a snake about to strike, which had to make them a little nervous. I mean, I didn't make it do that, I can't make it do anything, but sometimes it does things.

"Come and get it, you sons-of-bitches," I said.

This did not appear to frighten them as much as I'd have liked.

"Boss, the sorcerer is back, just around the cor—Never mind. He's down."

Cawti showed up from around the corner, and, speaking of details, I remember seeing a single drop of blood drip from her knife onto the ground. Not bad from, like, forty feet away.

Meanwhile, the other two Jhereg were much closer, and they were each armed with sword and dagger.

"We want you alive," said one of them.

"Now, there's a coincidence," I said. "I want me alive too."

"But we'll kill you if we have to, so you might want to make it easy on yourself."

I'd have said something clever right there, but they moved too fast for my wit to exercise itself. They timed it right: both of them striking at once, one high, one low, slashing, because a slash is less likely to kill someone than a thrust, and they wanted me alive. I parried the high cut and took a slash just above the knee on my uninjured leg—it didn't hurt, but I felt the impact. And then I was falling again, and I had the feeling that my plan could have gone better. I was getting woozy. I'd been getting woozy for a while, but now it was bad enough that I had to admit it.

The one who'd cut me suddenly stiffened. I know that look: it's what happens when you get a perfectly placed dagger in your kidney: you freeze, like all your muscles lock up. Then you go down.

The other one turned to face Cawti, but before they could engage, Loiosh landed on his shoulder and bit him in the neck. And held on.

He screamed and tried to twist away and swing at Loiosh, but do you know how hard it is to use a sword to get something off your shoulder? And the knife was on the wrong side. Poor bastard. Must have sucked for him, you know?

Jhereg venom affects everyone different. I mean, it kind of paralyzes you, and does bad things to your heart, but it might be slower hitting some, faster hitting others, only a little effect on some, a lot of effect on others. Like that. It won't kill most people.

But going right into your neck like that?

That just isn't healthy.

"We need one of them alive," I said.

"I know," said Cawti. "The sorcerer should make it."

"Sorry, Boss. This one—"

"No, no. Good job. He was going to do harmful things to me."

"This other one might make it," said Cawti. "But I'm more worried about you."

"I'm fine," I said.

"Then why are you on the ground?"

"Uh, well-earned relaxation after a successful venture?"

The plan had been for us to be attacked, win the fight, leave at least one attacker alive, and question him. The part where I was lying on the ground bleeding from both of my legs was an addition to the plan at the last minute, and maybe not such a good one, now that I thought of it.

The world was spinning, and also going up and down, but I was able to more or less keep track of what was happening around me. Cawti cut the sleeves off my jerkin and wrapped them around the wounds on my legs. "The sorcerer," I said. "Maybe we should—"

"He's unconscious," she said. "And Loiosh is watching him."

"All right. Can I be unconscious too?"

"Soon," she muttered. "Can you concentrate enough to reach Kragar? We need some help getting you and the sorcerer back to the office."

I started to say I wasn't sure, but Kragar said, "I'm already here. Sorry I was late."

I was still running down my list of bad names to decide which to call him when the world contracted into a pinpoint and went away.

7

INVITING THE GUESTS

The Fenarian tradition is that the couple each select a close friend, who then personally visits and invites each guest. Some Dragaeran Houses do that kind of thing. Lady Teldra explained that among the Issola it's a long, drawn-out thing where you have to ask certain family members to invite other people, and they have to respond in certain ways, depending on the exact relationships. She looked like she was being kind of naughty when she leaned over to us and whispered, "It's extraordinarily dull." We assured her we wouldn't tell anyone she said so.

The Fenarian thing is impractical in my situation. I mean, sure, Cawti could ask Norathar, but who do I ask? Kragar? Can you imagine him inviting Sethra to my wedding? Or, hey, maybe I could ask Sethra Lavode, the Dark Lady of Dzur Mountain. Or maybe not. Morrolan? Aliera? Any of these people would scare away most of the potential guests. I mentioned that to Cawti, who wondered why I thought that was a bad thing. Which led to a discussion of just how big a wedding we wanted. I said I wanted a big enough wedding to justify the amount of food I wanted there. She agreed, so it would have been small, except that we hadn't counted on the Jhereg. See, I was kind of a low-level boss. Well, it turns out that even if you're at the bottom, a boss is a boss, and so every organization expects to send people to show their respect. I don't want to go into how I learned that, because it's kind of embarrassing. The important thing is, I found out before making a mistake that could have had a bad effect on my career.

So we were going to have a big wedding, like it or not. That meant plenty of food, which I liked, and had the advantage that the Easterners we were going to invite wouldn't have had to find a way to make polite *talk with the Dragaerans, so it wasn't all bad. It wasn't what we wanted, but maybe sometimes you gotta sacrifice the wedding you want in order to get the life you want afterward.*

⊰⊱

Someone had found some blankets or something, and I was lying on them, staring up at the ceiling of my office. Loiosh, standing on the floor next to my right ear, said, *"Welcome back, Boss."*

"Thanks. How long—"

"About an hour."

My right leg hurt. My left leg hurt too, but my right leg hurt a lot. Loiosh picked up on that and said, *"Just a bandage and some stitches on the left, but the physicker did some sorcery on the right."*

"What kind of sorcery?"

"Well, he accelerated the healing, and, uh."

"Yeah?"

"He did something that smelled like cooking meat."

I figured that was enough information about that.

"He says you should be able to walk a little, but not too much. Probably a few weeks until you feel back to normal."

I knew Cawti was in the room by the scent of whatever she used on her hair. Something nice I didn't know the name of. I said, "I'm awake."

She knelt down next to me, and kissed me. "How are you feeling?"

"Pretty good. And nice work back there. You and Loiosh. Where is the sorcerer?"

"He left."

"What?"

"He did what he could, and—"

"No, not the one who healed me, the one we captured."

"Oh. In Kragar's office, with Kragar watching him. They did something I don't get, to keep him from doing sorcery."

"Okay. Then it's time to question him."

"I'll help you up."

She did. She's small, but strong. I put a hand on my desk, as much because of dizziness as because of weakness in my leg. Then I couldn't remember why I'd wanted to stand up, then I could.

Cawti said, "Vladimir, are you sure you should—?"

"The others are dead?" I asked her.

"The one I stabbed is. Probably the other one too."

"Too bad. I wanted to compliment the one who threw the knife."

"That was the sorcerer."

"What? Really?"

"Yeah, he just tossed it up and did a spell to send it at you."

"That's cheating."

"I know."

"All right, I'm going to talk to him about that, too."

"Need help walking?"

"I don't know, but I'd like my arm around you either way."

She smiled and I got that sensation again, the one it's worth getting both your legs cut for. You know the one. I hope you know the one. How does that even work? What is it that makes us weak in the knees and makes our stomachs fall out just because someone smiles? I don't get it.

It was only a few steps to Kragar's office, but they hurt a lot. The sorcerer was sitting in a chair, and a black stone was around his neck hanging off a gold chain; I figured it must be what was preventing him from doing annoying things with sorcery, because it didn't go with the rest of his outfit. I made a mental note to ask Kragar about it, but forgot.

Cawti helped me into a chair facing the sorcerer, and I noticed Kragar leaning against the far wall. He doesn't have a desk; his "office" is just a room with a chair and a bunch of hooks and shelves and cabinets where he keeps track of things. I'd get him a desk but there's no room for it.

"I'm Vlad," I said. "I guess you know that. Now, I'm going to talk to you while you glare at me, and then maybe we'll have a conversation, and then, depending on how it goes, I might or might not let you walk out of here."

He did his part by glaring. I like it when people around me do what they're supposed to, don't you?

I continued. "Now, I think you know what I'm going to ask you. I mean, the question is obvious. And I know you're considering whether to answer it. Here are a few things to take into consid—"

"Lady Shireth," he said.

I stopped.

"You were about to ask me who wanted you captured, weren't you? Lady Shireth."

"I don't—"

"Left Hand," he said.

I felt Cawti tense beside me.

Yeah, the Left Hand of the Jhereg. Sorceresses. They dealt in illegal magic, sold those little blue crystals used in pre-Empire sorcery, could help you locate Morganti weapons, and could be hired for just about everything else that involved magic and was against the law. They were, as a rule, very unpleasant people. I felt the weight of Spellbreaker around my left wrist.

"What did I do to *them?*" I said.

"I don't know. I was just paid to get you and the stone and bring you back."

"You tracked the stone?"

"My right boot. Shireth put an enchantment on it to search it out. We knew it was here, so we kept watch until you left. Uh, well played, by the way."

"On your boot. Nice." I wondered how irritating it would be to have your boot pull you around, but didn't ask. "Where were you supposed to bring me?"

"If I tell you, I walk?"

"Yeah. Well, after we've made sure you're telling the truth."

He grunted. "Second floor of a house on the south side of Turnbolt in the Highroad area. I don't know the number, but it's the only manor in the neighborhood; everything else is a small house. I was to let them know when I had you unconscious and somewhere private so they could teleport you in without anyone knowing."

The Left Hand.

The Left Hand was involved.

I should have figured it out, I suppose, as soon as I knew about the Verra's tears. But if you'd asked where this was on the list of things I wanted, it'd be pretty far down.

However, there they were, so that's where I was going, like it or not.

"I know the district," I said. It was a good neighborhood, just west of the Palace, not far from Pamlar. I didn't know it well enough to teleport, but I could find a sorcerer who did. I gripped the desk and stood up.

"Vlad," said Cawti.

"Hmm?"

"You're in no shape to fight."

"Fight? I thought they'd want to chat. They're friendly people, aren't they? I'm friendly."

"Vladimir."

"You don't think I'm friendly?"

"Vladimir."

"So, what would you suggest?"

"Let me go and take a look at the place, make sure it's there, and see if any sorceresses go in or out."

"How will you tell? Sorceresses. Teleport."

"I could go in and look around."

"Or not."

"So what do you suggest?"

Kragar cleared his throat, and we both looked at him.

"You're volunteering?"

"You're paying?"

"I'm paying."

"I'm volunteering."

He stood up and gave this ironic, smirking bow that was so him I thought maybe he was an impostor.

"Don't get killed," I told him.

"Mind the till," he said, "and keep your hand out of the store."

Then he left before I could organize my comeback. But I'd have come up with something good.

It was only after he was gone that I realized that left me watching the prisoner. I'd done some prisoner-watching before, when I was working for someone who was having a disagreement with someone else, and there were negotiations and interrogations and that sort of thing. The job involves sitting there, at least five feet away from whoever you're watching, and not falling asleep. It's not my favorite thing to do. Sometimes the person you're watching is talkative, but usually not, and this guy didn't seem the talkative type.

"Melestav!" I called.

His head appeared in the doorway. "Yeah?"

"Find someone to watch this guy. I don't want to watch this guy. I'm the boss. The boss doesn't have to watch guys. That's why we become the boss."

Cawti found that more amusing than I'd thought it was, but that's what love is, isn't it?

Then I set in to not falling asleep.

"You're actually going to let me go?" said the guy who'd tried to do bad things to me, although for a good reason. By which I mean money, of course.

I said, "If I weren't, would I tell you?"

He chuckled. "Just hoping for meaningless reassurance."

"You may have to settle for catharsis."

He looked puzzled, but didn't ask, so I didn't explain.

I hated watching the guy. I mean, even more than I usually hated just sitting doing nothing. I finally realized that it was because, with nothing to do, my head kept drifting from the pain in my legs to what had happened to me in Castle Black, and what it meant, and I didn't want to deal with thinking about either of those. I guess I wanted meaningless reassurance. I hoped I wouldn't have to settle for catharsis.

But that's where you come in, right, Sethra? I mean, you're going to help with—

Thanks for nothing.

No, no. It's fine. I'll just keep going.

Finally, after about half an hour, a guy named Shoen came in, we exchanged terse nods because as far as I can tell that's the only language he speaks. Then Cawti helped me back to my office, where I collapsed in the chair. See, I'm telling you about this stuff because it all took a lot of effort, okay? The physicker had fixed me up, and I could walk, but I was stiff and moving was hard. Also, there was, yeah, a lot of pain. I tried not to show how much pain I was in to Cawti because it would have just made her feel bad and not helped me, but I think she could kind of tell.

"I should run to your flat," said Cawti. She squeezed my shoulder and kissed my check. "I'll find you something to wear without holes in it."

"If I have anything."

"I'll look."

"But then you won't be here, and I'll be all sad."

"Naw, just do your tough-guy act and you'll be fine. Loiosh will keep you company."

Loiosh flapped his wings in agreement, which I guess settled the argument, because off she went. She cared how I looked more than I did, but that's what love is, isn't it?

A few minutes later I got that weird, *there's something I should be thinking about* feeling that I'd had ten thousand times before and still wasn't used to. Maybe it's because I'm an Easterner and that stuff isn't natural to us, I don't know. Or maybe it's weird for everyone but they don't talk about it.

I let it happen, and immediately got that happy, warm sense of Cawti's presence, sort of like how her voice made me feel, except there was no voice. I don't think I've mentioned her voice before, but I like the sound of it. Kind of low in the throat, and . . . sorry, where was I? Right.

She said, *"Vladimir? Can you make it down the stairs?"*

"Yeah. What's up?"

"Trust me."

"Okay," I said, because that's what love is.

It took me a while, but I made it down the stairs, past the card game, and out onto the street, and there was Cawti, holding a pair of leggings, with Aliera standing next to her.

"Aliera?" I said.

She scowled. "Come with me."

"Aliera?" I repeated.

"I am not going into a Jhereg lair, so come with me."

"What are you . . . why . . . ?"

She gave me a look like I was too stupid to be able to understand an explanation, then led us across the street and away from Malak Circle. She walked (technically, she floated, but never mind) slowly because I wasn't moving fast. Cawti supported me. Aliera had, in fact, been to my office before, but she didn't like it, and I didn't have any interest in talking about it. I didn't have a lot of interest in talking about anything, in fact—most of my effort involved not whimpering.

After a few steps, however, I said, "What—?"

"It isn't far."

"Why is Aliera here?"

"Why do you think?"

"I have no idea."

She kissed my cheek. "Because you're a dope. Now come on."

It wasn't far. There was a sketchy sort of tavern just a few steps away, sporting a sign that pictured a dog with big, floppy ears and was usually called "Shaggy's." I'd only been in there once before, because they have bad food, worse wine, and no one goes in there but Teckla. They often have a small, informal Shereba game in a back room that I could have demanded cut me in on the action, but I never bothered because it's small and only Teckla, so who cares?

The host was a Chreotha, whose eyes widened to see two Jhereg and a Dragonlord enter her place. She froze and stared at us. I think she recognized me, and I suppose what went through her head was that I was going to start demanding a cut on her game, or maybe even on the tavern itself.

"We need a room," snapped Aliera, tossing the host a coin.

"I—"

"On this floor. We aren't climbing stairs."

The host nodded, came out from behind the bar—such as it was—and led the way back, looking over her shoulder as she did and making noises in which "my lady" could be made out every now and then. That's when it hit me that she was more intimidated by Aliera's presence than mine, which kind of hurt my feelings. I didn't let it show, though. That's part of being a tough guy.

The room had an actual door instead of just a curtain, so I figured that was good. The bed was wooden, rickety, and just a frame with a couple of blankets to keep the splinters out of your back, and for amenities the room featured a washbasin and a white ceramic pitcher.

"Take your leggings off and lie down," said Aliera.

There have been things I've been more excited about doing, but I did so. There wasn't much left of the leggings anyway; the physicker had pretty much torn them to pieces while working on me, so my hairy legs were already on display.

Once I was lying down, Aliera looked at my hairy legs, sniffed disdainfully, and said, "Did you get bacon?"

"What?"

"When you went to the butcher who worked on those legs, I hope you picked up some bacon."

"Oh," I said.

"You don't cauterize a wound like that. You purge it, clean it, and suture if you don't have the sorcery to knit it properly."

"Um," I said brightly.

Then she put her hands on it, and I'd have cried out, but I couldn't do that in front of Aliera, so I just gritted my teeth. Cawti put her hand on my shoulder and rubbed it, and it was amazing how much that helped. There's some kind of magic there. Not *magic* magic, just magic.

"Hey, Boss. What was that thing we ate the other day? The one with the melted cheese and the hot pepper rings on top of it?"

"*I don't . . .*"

"*It was very good. We should have that again.*"

"*It was off someone's cart while we were in—I don't remember where we were. Trying to think.*"

A little later Aliera pressed on the wound, and even Loiosh's distractions and Cawti's magic couldn't help. I didn't scream, but I hissed kinda loud; I couldn't help it.

Aliera glanced at me. "Oh, go to sleep," she said, and the world quickly narrowed and went flat, then dark. She could have done that to start with. The last thing I remember thinking was, *I just want my Verra-be-damned eight hundred.*

When I woke up, Aliera was gone and my legs itched. I started to scratch them, but Cawti put her hands on mine. "Aliera said they'd itch," she said. "You aren't supposed to scratch them. The itching should be gone in an hour or so."

She gave me my new leggings. I sat up and looked at my legs; there was a pale scar on the right one, nothing at all on the left. Aliera does good work.

I got dressed, stood, and found I wasn't even shaky. All right, not very shaky. Okay, I did stumble a little for the first couple of steps, but that was all. Point being, if I was suddenly faced with the company of persons who wished me harm, I felt like I wouldn't be helpless. I was impressed. Aliera does very good work.

Sethra, do *not* tell Aliera I said that.

Good, then.

Once I had my cloak on and settled, I started to open the door. Cawti stopped me, took out a hairbrush, and made me presentable.

"You carry all sorts of concealed weapons, don't you?" I told her.

"I'd hug you," she said. "But I'm afraid I'll cut myself on your razor-sharp wit."

I grinned like a Verra-be-damned idiot and followed her out. I flipped the hostess an orb.

"*Eight hundred and thirteen and a half and a silver,*" said Loiosh.

"Oh, *shut up.*"

I walked back to my office like my old, jaunty self.

I'm jaunty. I can be jaunty. You should see me jaunt. I jaunted right up the stairs.

I poked my head into Kragar's office, and Shoen was still there. We exchanged terse nods. I can be terse, too.

I went back into my office and sat down behind my desk. "Much better," I said. "Aliera does good work. Now we just wait for Kragar."

That was usually the point when Kragar would cough to let us know he'd been there the whole time, but he didn't because he wasn't. However, he came back just a few minutes later. Better still, I noticed him come in, so if he'd planned to startle me, it failed.

"Well?" I asked him.

"Yeah, they're there."

"Okay. Want to tell me about it?"

"First, do I let the guy go, or kill him?"

"I said I'd let him go."

"Yeah. Do I let him go, or kill him?"

I considered, weighed the pros and cons, and finally said, "Let him go. But have Shoen stay with him until he's out of the building."

Kragar went off to do that. He was back a few minutes later.

"I see," I said, "that my office hasn't blown up."

"Can't get anything past you," he said.

"So, what did you learn?"

He slunk past Cawti, pulled a chair away from the wall with his foot, sat.

"They're on the upper floor," he said. "The lower floor belongs to some Jhegaala family, silk merchants. No connection as far as I can tell, except they own the house. I listened at the door for a while. No one noticed me, but I didn't pick up much. Mostly mundane stuff, like, where is the coffee, and who's going out to pick up lunch."

"You said, 'mostly.'"

"I heard 'Verra's tears' once."

"Well, well, well," I said.

"Also, they have a teleport block up, so they enter and leave just like us normal people."

I could have made some points about just how normal we were, but I let it go.

"So," said Cawti. "They're after Fisher?"

"In some sense of 'after,' yes. We don't know exactly what kind of 'after,' but it may still give me leverage with him, and that gives me a chance to get my eight hundred back."

"Vlad," said Kragar. "I think this has gone beyond the eight hundred by now, hasn't it?"

"Never," I said.

"And so," said Cawti, being the practical one, "what's the next step? Talk to Fisher again?"

"Get more information," said Kragar. "He always wants to get more information. I know, because I'm the one he tells to—"

"Get more information, Kragar," I said, because I thought it was funny. Kragar didn't, but Cawti did, because she loves me.

Kragar sighed. "What do you need to know?"

Come to that, I wasn't sure. Like I said, I just thought it was funny.

I chewed it over, then said, "Well, I'd admire to know what they were trying to do to Fisher so we could go to him with something specific. Especially now, when we know there is some connection to the Tsalmoth."

"How would you suggest finding all this out? And don't say, 'you'll think of something.'"

I *had* said things like that to him before, but this time I hadn't been going to. This time it was difficult. "Yeah," I said. "That's going to be tough. The Left Hand, from what I know, isn't keen on letting information slip. And, sure, I have a few sources, but none of them in the Left Hand. I don't even know how I'd go about setting something like that up."

"So?"

"So maybe I'll ask them."

"Ask who?"

"The sorceresses. Ask them what they're up to."

"Now there's an idea," said Kragar.

"What could go wrong?" I said. "Okay, sarcasm aside, a lot could go wrong. But I could also learn something useful."

"You aren't really considering this, are you, Vlad?"

"Boss?"

Cawti was giving me a look that said she was on their side.

"I'm open to other ideas," I said.

"Is it worth getting killed over eight hundred imperials?"

"I'll get back to you on that," I said.

"Vlad—"

"Kragar, aren't you even a little curious about what's going on? Why the Left Hand had the Verra's tears—is it tear or tears? Why the Left Hand had that rock planted on Fisher?"

"No," he said.

"I am."

"So am I," said Cawti. "But not enough to see you get killed for it."

"Well, I mean, I'm glad you don't want me killed. I'd be sad if you didn't care."

"Vladimir, we can come up with something."

"We meaning me?"

"Now you know how I feel," said Kragar.

I glared at him, but it was probably wasted.

"All right," I said. "I'll think about it."

Cawti was giving me that I'm-trying-not-to-smile-as-much-as-I-want-to look. Kragar looked at her, stood up, and said, "My time to leave."

Once he was gone, Cawti and I just sat there. Loiosh flew over to Cawti's hand and got some head scratching.

We were quiet for a bit, each with our own thoughts. I'm going to guess hers were more pleasant than mine. Then she suddenly looked up, and I realized I'd cursed under my breath.

"What?" she said.

I shook my head.

"Vladimir."

I sighed. "Sometimes my head goes places I don't want it to. That's why I like to keep busy."

"The demon thing?"

I nodded.

She got up, stood over me, and kissed the top of my head. That helped.

She sat down again. "Now that I've fixed that, let's figure out something constructive for getting your money back."

"Well, I have one idea."

"What's that?"

"You just heard it."

"Oh. Let's find something better." When I didn't answer, she said, "You're going to do it, aren't you? Just walk over there, clap at their door, and ask?"

"Well, I have two reasons. One good, one bad. The good reason is because it might work. The bad reason is it keeps me from wondering if I'm a demon, and, if I am, just what that means."

"The good reason isn't very good," she said.

"It's the best I got."

"Vlad—"

"It's direct," I said.

"You say that like it's a virtue."

"Sometimes it is."

"No, it's just something for when you don't have a better idea."

"True." I stood up. "And, as it happens, I don't have a better idea. See you in—"

"Right. As if I'd miss this." She stood up too, touching her daggers and checking a few other surprises about her person. I still wasn't sure I'd found them all, but the joy is in the search. I checked my various weapons, open and concealed, and nodded to her.

"This is pretty stupid," she said.

"It's direct," I said again.

"Yeah. Stupid."

I stuck the stone into a desk drawer, because bringing it with me would have been foolhardy even for me, and we headed out the door.

Loiosh wasn't saying anything, and he's usually right up there saying when I'm about to do something stupid. I guess he felt me thinking about that, because he said, *"You have a plan, don't you, Boss?"*

"Not exactly a plan. More like a reason to believe we'll be okay."

It's funny; sometimes he knows what I'm thinking, even when I don't direct the thought at him, sometimes he doesn't. I think it mostly has to do with how sharp and well-formed the idea is. Or, I don't know, maybe it's how much attention he's choosing to pay. Or something else. Or my imagination. I don't know. Sethra, do you have any—

Right. You aren't here. I keep forgetting because, you know, you're right here.

Cawti was relaxed as we headed toward the house. She always became, I was discovering, extra relaxed when things were about to get interesting. I try to do that too, but it doesn't come easy. At least I can fake it sometimes. As we walked, she said, "How do you see this working?"

"We go in, have a conversation, come out."

"It's that last part that concerns me. You remember the part about they wanted to capture you and bring you, where was it? Oh yes, here?"

"Yeah, but they wanted me by surprise, not walking in there on purpose. They could have invited me."

"Would you have come?"

"Hmm. Maybe. I'd probably have suggested we meet somewhere neutral."

We passed a baker on the way, a guy with one of those clever mobile ovens on an ox-cart. I wasn't hungry, but warm soda bread with butter swimming on it? You don't need to be hungry, you just need to be able to fit it in. I got us each one. They also sold beer, so Cawti got that, too. I'm not crazy about beer, but I like the metallic swoosh it makes when they pour it into the can—nothing else sounds quite like that. We ate as we walked. When we'd finished, and had each given Loiosh a few pieces, I said, "Thing is, I don't think they're going to want to kill us. It's messy, for one thing." I licked butter off my fingers. We tough guys do that. Shut up.

She waited.

"Would you commit murder where you lived or worked?"

"I'm not a sorcerer."

"There are still traces. The Phoenix Guard has sorcerers trained in looking for exactly that."

"You think that's enough to keep us alive?"

"They'll figure people are aware of our being there, and if I get the chance I'll kind of emphasize the point. They won't risk it."

She didn't say anything for a while as we walked, then she said, "This is it."

It was a big place, either a manor or an estate, depending on the House of whoever had first built it. White, with marble steps leading up to a reddish door with a clapper in the form of a snarling dzur. If a Dzur had it built, it was an estate. That's how that works. See, I know about all kinds of things.

All the nearby houses were much smaller. I wondered how the neighbors felt. Two clappers, one above the other. I pulled the upper clapper like there was no reason in the world not to. I tried to make it jaunty.

A youngish Dragaeran woman, tiny, frail-looking, in Jhereg colors, opened the door. She had a gray scarf around her neck and was wearing a loose-fitting black blouse with gray trim and trousers a lot like mine. She had remarkable deep blue eyes. By "tiny" I mean that she was only a little taller than me. But that didn't mean I wasn't intimidated just by her being there, because I was. I'm being honest here. I knew what these types could do. Spellbreaker itched on my left wrist, like it wanted to slither down into my hand. The sorceress looked at me, at Loiosh, at Cawti.

"Taltos," she said, pronouncing it correctly.

"A pleasure," I told her. "Oddly, that's my name, too."

She didn't twitch to the feint, as the Dzur say; she just looked at me. "I'm told," she said, "to invite you in."

I had seen no sign that she was in psychic communication. I mean, she didn't close her eyes, or even wrinkle her forehead.

I led the way in. Jaunty. Sort of.

The hallway was tiled, the walls were white. Two doors led off to the right, and at the end a straight stone stairway led up then turned right. We took that way, and our escort opened the door and led the way in. Instead of tiles, this story had hardwood floors and rugs, and the few furnishings I could see as we passed open doors looked elegant and expensive.

She brought us into a room that looked like a scaled-down version of one of Morrolan's sitting rooms, except the colors were darker and the lights were lower. There were a couple of bookshelves. I didn't look to see what the books were, but I'd guess most of them were in languages I couldn't read. I could feel Cawti looking around with that relaxed, alert tension that made me want to grab her and wrestle her onto the nearest flat surface.

That was a thought I had later, by the way. At the time, I was just trying my best to be the same as her, because, whatever I'd said about why they wouldn't kill us, the palms of my hands didn't believe me. Loiosh squeezed my shoulder, one foot, then the other. He was nervous, too.

"You nervous?" said the sorceress.

"No. Is there some reason I should be?"

She pointed us to some stuffed chairs. I thought about taking a different one just to be contrary, and safe, but I didn't. We sat, and a few others came in, all of them older than her, and one of them ancient. *Okay*, I told myself. *Here we go.*

8

OUTFITTING THE BRIDE AND GROOM

Fenarian tradition has the bride dressed in a long, colorful dress, usually a lot of blue and yellow, with flower designs and stuff. Noish-pa says that he's known bridal parties of six or more girls working with the bride for a Fenarian month (something like twice as long as a Dragaeran month, I don't know why) making the dress. The groom, by tradition, is less colorful, most often wearing a white doublet and black trousers, but he always wears a red-on-black felt vest, usually with some patterns and stuff on it. It's generally made by the groom's mother; I guess in Fenarian tradition men aren't thought to be skilled at sewing, so if they try they'll ruin everything! I don't know.

As usual, Dragaeran tradition is more complicated and not as much fun, except that those Houses that make a distinction between bride and groom—I don't remember which ones those are—always have the brides wearing those funny gold things on their shoulders, and I'd love to learn where that came from. Other than that, it varies by House, because, you know, what doesn't? And the Houses that don't have "bride" and "groom" distinction the way Easterners do usually have some sort of other distinction based on one of them being of a higher or lower nobility within the House, or military rank, or some other thing, that might have an effect on how they dress. The Tsalmoth have the couple prepare wedding dresses for each other, and how pleasing the outfit is to your betrothed indicates how much attention you've been paying. Or so I've heard. I don't know, I've never been married as a Dragaeran. Unless, you know, that reincarnation thing is real, and even then I don't remember, so ask someone else.

But I did find a Fenarian tailor and ordered the vest.

❧❧

Just to let you know, if we were Dragonlords, we'd have stood up when they entered; but to a Jhereg, that can sometimes be a threat, or at least a sign of mistrust, so we stayed seated. The old one sat, the others remained standing. I took it as a sign of mistrust but I didn't let it make me sad.

The old one spoke, of course. "What do you want?"

Was that polite? That wasn't polite. I looked at them all standing there and decided not to point out the rudeness.

"Lady Shireth?" I said.

She didn't even acknowledge the question, she just waited for me to speak. I suspected she was Shireth, but I could have been wrong.

"You wanted to see me, so I came."

"What do you want?" she repeated.

"See, that's just what I was going to ask you."

"Last time, Easterner. What do you want?"

All right, then. I said, "You planted Verra's tears on a guy named Fisher. What's your game with him?"

See, if you want to know something, just ask. That way, you might get an answer. As it happened, that time I didn't, but I could have, that's all I'm saying. What actually happened was that they looked at me. I felt Cawti to my left like a coiled spiralsnake, but I didn't look at her. The sorceress seemed not to be pleased with me, which made me sad, because I like to please people. After a couple of breaths, the old lady spoke.

"I want you out of here in the next ten seconds."

"That's fine," I said. "But there's something you need to give me first."

"I don't need to give you anything."

"I think you do."

"What?"

"A reason to care what you want."

"Ever felt your heart burst in your chest? Your blood boil in your veins? Your legs rot and fall off while you're standing on them?"

"Thank Verra I'm sitting down."

"You some kind of tough guy?"

"Every kind. I got it all covered. What do you need?"

"You think you're safe here?"

I shrugged. "People know where I am. Could make it uncomfortable for you if we were to vanish. Why let yourself get annoyed by the Empire when you could just be annoyed by me? And, hey, if you don't like the annoyance, answer my questions and I'll go away. Besides, we have you outnumbered."

There was a silence, and I'd have bet the eight hundred she was communicating with one of the others. Her expression didn't change, but she nodded a little.

"What," she said, "is your interest in the matter?"

"Fisher is a friend of mine."

"No, he isn't."

I smiled. "You got me."

"Well?"

"I just want a little harmless information, is all."

"You'll understand," she said, "if we tell you nothing."

"You've already told me something."

"Indeed?"

"Unless you want to make me believe you've been following me close enough to know who my friends are, and I kinda think you haven't, that means you've been following Fisher close enough to know who *his* friends are. That's something. I just want—"

"Maybe you should leave now."

Yeah, I was getting even more nervous, but I was on a roll. I said, "Is what you're working on going to pay enough to offset all the trouble I'm going to cause you?"

"Now why would you do that?"

"Sheer cussedness."

"I do not think you're much of a threat, Lord Taltos."

I smiled.

"You Easterners always underestimate what sorcery can do."

"And you Dragaerans always underestimate what witchcraft can do."

She sniffed. It was what they call disdainful. Cawti taught me that word. I like it. I want to be disdainful to someone, just to be able to say that.

"Why," she said, "do you want to put yourself through this?"

"Eight hundred gold. Or, well, more like eight hundred fifteen now."

"Who owes it to you?"

"It's complicated. Anyway, if you feel like giving it to me, I'll go away."

"I don't think so."

"You don't think I'll go away, or you don't think you'll give me the money?"

"Both."

I hadn't thought they'd give me the money. But there'd been a pause before she answered, like she'd had to think about it. Kind of like the one I'd gotten from Fisher when I'd asked him if he could think of anyone who'd want to plant that stone on him. I looked at the sorceress, and waited to see what else would happen. She seemed bloody old, but her eyes were sharp as, you know, something that's sharp. And kind of scary. Okay, very scary.

"Boss! Spell!"

There was hardly any motion or change of expression from the old woman who may or may not have been Shireth, but I'd been ready all along, and was in motion the instant Loiosh started his cry into my mind.

Anytime you're attacked, whether it's physical or sorcerous, or even verbal, you react before you decide how to. You duck out of the way, or maybe counter-attack, or sometimes you just freeze while your brain catches up and tells you what to do. That last is usually not the best reaction, but it does happen.

If you've been expecting the attack, waiting for it, that gives you an edge, both because you're aware of it that much sooner, and because you already have your reaction ready.

I let Spellbreaker fall into my hand, and swung it in front of me. I don't know exactly what she'd been trying to do, but I felt a disorientation that usually means someone is trying to mess with your thinking or your perceptions or maybe get into your head to find out what was on your mind.

Cawti was on her feet, Loiosh had his wings spread and I felt that tension that meant he was ready to fly.

I held up my right hand, and smiled. "Now now. Was that friendly?"

The one who may or may not have been Lady Shireth didn't answer.

In case you've never experienced someone tossing a spell at you, even if you don't know exactly what it is, you sometimes get an idea of, what should I call it, the degree of hostility? No, that isn't right. What I'm trying to say is, you can sometimes tell if someone is snapping off a spell that is probably going to harm you, or just sort of casually casting something on you to maybe get some information, or encourage you to relax, or do something to the area around you. It's hard to say how you know—something about the way your brain tingles, maybe? That's as close as I can come. This felt like the second of those. What I mean is, I didn't think they weren't trying to attack me.

I wrapped Spellbreaker around my wrist again. Loiosh relaxed, Cawti sat down.

"What," she said, "is that?"

Spellbreaker has that effect on sorcerers. I'm kind of proud of it, but I ignored the question anyway. "Here's my thinking," I said.

Her eyes stopped being so scary. She'd cast a spell and I'd stopped it, which I hadn't been at all sure I could do. I was pleased—and a little surprised—at how even my voice sounded in my own ears.

"I must worry you a little if you're trying to cast spells on me."

The old woman reacted just the way I would have, by which I mean, you know, not. I continued, "That's the sort of thing witch-craft works better for. Things like messing with someone's head. I could teach you if you want. Lesson is cheap, only eight hundred of the beautiful gold coins with the Orb on one side and the throne on the other, or maybe someone's face on the other, depending how old it is. I'm not fussy. In fact, if you have some that are worn down, I'm willing—"

"Get out of here."

"Sure. Just one thing. Is it Fisher you're after, or are you using him for something else?"

Nothing. Not a flicker or a hint. Damn. "Are you certain," she said slowly, "that you want to make an enemy of us?"

"In truth, I'd rather not. But there's this matter of my eight hundred gold."

Her eyes would probably have narrowed if they had any narrowing room left. "I suspect there's more to it than that."

"There really isn't," I said.

"You're lying, Taltos. Or you are the most ignorant Easterner I've ever met."

"How many Easterners have you met?" I said.

"All right," she said finally. "I'll give you two things, then you'll leave."

I nodded.

"First, yes, it was us who tried to get you here, because I wanted the Verra's tear back, and because there were things I wanted to find out from you."

I nodded again; it seemed to be working.

"Two, we won't attempt to have you brought to us again."

"All right," I said, and stood up. "I guess I'll be going now."

"*Boss?*"

"*We got as much as we're going to get.*"

"*You mean, nothing?*"

"*I mean something.*"

"*If you say so. We getting out of here alive, Boss?*"

"*Of course. Almost certainly. Probably.*"

"*I love this job.*"

Don't mean to hold you in suspense or anything: they let us leave.

I'd expected them to, but the walk down the stairs and out to the street seemed to take a long time.

"*Uh, Loiosh?*"

"*We're good, Boss. No spells.*"

The air smelled good.

"Vladimir?"

"Nothing, just want to stand here for a minute and enjoy being alive."

"Okay. But maybe if we stand a bit further away we can enjoy being alive longer."

"Fair point."

As we started back, Cawti said, "You learned something, didn't you?"

"*See, Loiosh? Some people have faith in me.*"

"Yeah," I said.

"Okay, what am I missing?"

"Well, like I said, they've been following him well enough to know who his friends are. Also, she wouldn't believe this was only about the money I'm owed."

"Okay, and?"

"Doesn't it seem obvious that we've stepped into something big here? I mean, she practically said, 'you wouldn't get involved in something this big just for eight hundred gold.'"

After a moment, she nodded. "But we don't know what."

"Right."

"Vladimir."

"Hmm?"

"That was a lot of danger we were in just to find out, 'it's big.'"

"Well, I could argue that it was obviously worth it, since we got out alive."

"You *could*. But?"

"There's more than that. Follow it through. Something big, my love, makes ripples. Leaves traces. Almost always involves more people, which means more opportunities for something to slip."

She was quiet for a bit while we made our way through the city, then she said, "It's still pretty tenuous."

I didn't want to ask what "tenuous" meant, so I said, "True. But we also found out one more thing."

"What's that?"

"If there's only one of them, it's a Verra's tear, not tears. I'd been wondering."

"Well, thank the Lords of Judgment *that's* settled."

"Yep."

"What's next?"

"You got any ideas?"

"It's always easier when you just have to kill someone."

"I love you."

She grinned and squeezed my arm.

Not long before, when I'd been worried about people out to kill me, Cawti wouldn't have been holding my arm. This was better. Of course, there was still Fisher, but it'd take him a while to set something up.

"So," she said, "we're now involved in figuring out what the Left Hand is preparing, and stopping it?"

"Or maybe helping it, or maybe ignoring it. But yeah, we have to know what they're up to with Fisher."

"For eight hundred gold?"

"For eight hundred gold."

"Actually, four hundred."

"How do you figure?"

"By Eastern tradition, after we're married, half of it is mine."

I couldn't keep from grinning.

After walking for a while, we got back to neighborhoods I knew, which always makes me feel more relaxed.

"Tenuous," she said, "means weak, or slight, or thin."

"I figured it was something like that," I said, "just from, uh—"

"Context?"

"Yeah."

"Want me to stop doing that, Vladimir?"

"Gods no!" I said, and we kept walking.

"Where are we going?" she asked after a while.

"To leave a message for a friend," I said mysteriously.

I made my way to a street called Vintner, walked down it, and found a woman who had a handcart for her bead work. She was a Chreotha of middle years, and I never got her name. She didn't seem to recognize me, but we'd only met once before. Like all merchants—okay, like some merchants—money mattered more than pride, so she gave us a sort of head-bob that would pass for a bow if you weren't particular. She said, "May I show you some—"

"No," I said, and handed over a few coppers. "But if you wouldn't mind, tell Kiera that the little guy is feeding the ducks."

The coins disappeared, and this time the head-bob was a tiny bit deeper—after all, if I was friends with Kiera, there must be more to me than whiskers, right?

"Kiera?" said Cawti as we walked away. "Kiera the Thief?"

I nodded. "Do you know her?"

"I know of her."

"She's been good to me."

"What was the thing about feeding ducks?"

"Zerika's Fountain on Ricebowl."

"Oh, of course. We're going to meet her there?"

"We—or at least I—am going to go there and wait, maybe for hours, and maybe she won't show up, in which case I'll go back tomorrow and wait some more."

"Good communication method," she said.

"She's Kiera the Thief," I said. "Can you suggest another?"

"Fair point," she said.

We got there, bought some bread, and fed the ducks for a few hours, then went home. We went back the next day and fed them some more, and a little after noon she showed up.

She kissed my cheek and nodded to Cawti.

"This is my betrothed, Cawti," I said. "This is Kiera."

Cawti smiled—a bit hesitant maybe, but not cold. Loiosh flew over to Kiera.

"It's a pleasure," said Kiera while scratching Loiosh's head. "Shall we get something to drink?"

Loiosh returned and climbed into my cloak. We found a place nearby that was mostly Teckla, so we got a table with a lot of distance between us and anyone else, and a hostess—also, surprisingly, a Teckla—who bowed and rushed to get us the best wine in the house, which wasn't very good. Most of her bowing was to Kiera, but what would you expect?

"So," said Kiera. "The Dagger of the Jhereg. Of course, I've heard of you. I'm impressed."

"Thank you," said Cawti. "I don't do that anymore."

"If it isn't a rude question, what do you do now?"

Cawti chuckled. "Still working that out. I might continue as an independent, might try a few other lines."

Kiera nodded. "Well, if you're interested in becoming a property redistribution specialist, look me up."

"I will, thank you."

"So," I said. "Coming to our wedding?"

"I'm sorry, Vlad. I don't attend weddings. A bad experience once, many years ago. I'll have to tell you the story sometime. But I'm certainly very happy for you."

"Thanks," I said. "I understand."

Kiera touched the wine to her lips, swallowed a little. "I'm guessing you didn't get hold of me just to deliver a wedding invitation."

"Yeah. I'm kind of tangled up with the Left Hand, and hoping you can give me some advice."

"Sure. Don't."

"Heh. Thanks. Anything else?"

"What's it about?"

"Eight hundred gold."

"A good sum," she agreed. "What do you have to do for it?"

"That's what I'm trying to work out."

"Vladimir," said Cawti, "you aren't giving her a lot of details."

"I was going to tell him that."

"Yeah, sorry." I took a deep breath. "A guy got shined while owing me eight hundred. I started checking into him to try to get it back, and it turns out he was involved in illegal perfume, and so I started checking that out, and it led me to the Left Hand."

She frowned. "I've never heard of the Left Hand having anything to do with something as mundane as gray market perfume."

"Nor had I. But here I am."

"Lucky you," she said. She seemed to think it was funny.

"So, anything useful you can tell me?"

I poured us some more wine, then signaled for another bottle. The hostess brought it even though I wasn't Kiera.

"Vlad, just how involved with them are you?"

"I don't exactly know yet. They're doing something that involves extracting hishi, and something that involves Verra's tears, and—"

"The stone?"

"Yeah."

"I came across one once. Isn't that mostly used for necromancy?"

"Yeah."

"That's dangerous stuff."

"Tell me about it."

"Oh?"

I shook my head, not wanting to get into that part of it. "But speaking of hishi, have you heard anything about a Tsalmoth getting lightened of a good supply of it?"

She sat back a little. "Yes, in fact. I heard about an Orca, strictly amateur and not very bright. He got hold of some and was looking to unload it. It was quite the score for him, compared to rolling drunks for a few coppers."

"Huh," I said. "Got a name?"

"No," she said. "But it probably wouldn't help you anyway."

"Oh, did he, uh, move on to the next world?"

She nodded. "At least, that's what I heard."

"Any idea who did it?"

"Rumor has it a mid-level boss named Fisher did it himself."

"Well," I said. "Now that's all kinds of news. But it tells us how Fisher ended up with the stuff."

"Glad to help."

"Any pointers about the Left Hand? Thing is, I'm over my head here. Whatever they're involved in is big, but I have no contacts inside their organization. Any ideas?"

She shook her head. "Sorry. I'll give it some thought, and maybe ask around a bit, but don't count on anything."

"Fair enough," I said. "You've already helped. Thanks."

"You're welcome. And be careful with the necromancy."

"Too late."

She frowned. "What do you mean?"

I shook my head. "Never mind. Good to see you again."

"And you. And a pleasure to have met you, Cawti." She started to say something else, but then didn't.

Cawti chuckled. "Don't worry," she said. "I'll watch over him."

Kiera smiled, and I had the feeling that I ought to be offended, but I couldn't quite manage.

We finished the wine, said our farewells. There was still most of the day left.

"Where to now?" Cawti wanted to know as Loiosh resumed his place on my shoulder and we started walking. Well, strolling.

"The office, I guess. I still need to figure something out."

"I think," she said after another half a mile, "I might have an idea of how to get more information."

"You have my attention," I said.

"I always have your attention."

"True. Except when someone is trying to kill me. And sometimes then, come to think of it. What's this idea?"

"Loiosh."

"What?"

"Uh, go on."

"Just that he can keep an eye on Fisher, and let you know if he does anything interesting."

Loiosh hissed at Cawti.

"He likes the idea," I said. And, "Ouch. Little beast."

"He'll be great at it," said Cawti.

"*Tell her that flattery—*"

"*Shut up.*"

"Loiosh is delighted at the opportunity to help," I told Cawti. "He's all about being helpful."

Loiosh hissed.

Cawti nodded. "I get that. You know those pepper sausages we had that time? We should get some of those to keep around, in case we run into any helpful jhereg who deserve a reward."

"*Bribes,*" said Loiosh. "*Bribes work.*"

My jhereg was corruptible. I wonder where he could have gotten that.

As agreed, we stopped at a local restaurant and had a cup of wine while they prepared the sausages and wrapped them up for us. Loiosh said incentives worked better than rewards. I incentivated him by letting him have a sniff, then sent him off to find Fisher.

When we got back to the office, Cawti said, "You need some books here."

"Why?"

"Well, you could read them. And they'd make you look smart and cultured. But I was thinking more so I could read them when you're busy."

My cold, murderous heart gave a flutter: she'd just said she wanted to hang around here, around me, even when we weren't busy together. I opened my desk and pulled out a whetstone and sharpened a dagger that didn't need it.

"I love you too," she said. I glanced up, and she was smiling.

"Shut up," I said.

I glanced up again, and she was smiling even more.

"*She thinks you're adorable, Boss.*"

"*I'm bigger than you, Loiosh.*"

"*I'm faster. And higher than you can reach. And five miles away.*"

"*Then get back to work.*"

He snickered into my head.

"Yeah, I'll get some books."

She laughed a little. "We'll go find some together."

I nodded.

"Then I'll make you read them."

"Hey, now. That wasn't part of the deal."

We discussed the deal for a while, and what all it involved, and who had agreed to do what, until Loiosh interrupted us.

"Boss! Got something!"

Cawti had been about to say something—probably something adorable—but I guess she saw on my face that I was distracted.

"Talk to me, Loiosh."

"Fisher went for a walk to Monument Square and is leaning against the statue of Undauntra."

"Good place to see all around, make sure you aren't being watched."

"Yeah, and he just got joined by someone."

"'Someone,'" I repeated. *"Could you be a little more vague?"*

"Someone interesting."

"Loiosh—"

"Remember the dead guy's brother?"

Well now. What to make of that? I'd asked the guy straight out if he knew anything about what his brother had been up to, and he'd said he didn't. Had the guy actually had the balls—and, you know, the skill—to lie to my face? I didn't think so. I mean, maybe I was kidding myself, because pride and all that, but where does some random Tsalmoth get the skill—and, you know, the balls—to do that?

No, if the brother was involved, something had changed. And not only that, but it proved I was on the right track, because there was now a link between Bereth—remember him, the guy who died owing me eight hundred imperials?—and Fisher. And Fisher and the brother hadn't known each other very long. How do I know that, you ask? Because they were meeting in person, which meant they didn't know each other well enough for psychic contact.

So there was something new; something had changed since I'd started looking into all of this.

I filled Cawti in on what was going on. She frowned. I like her frown, too. "Do we head over there?" she said.

"Not yet. I need to come up with a theory to explain this so I can go out and prove it wrong and be embarrassed."

"It's good to have a system," she agreed.

"I just can't figure out what led to this."

"Simplest explanation is that Bereth turned out to own something valuable and his brother didn't know it when he talked to you, and now is trying to get something for it."

"Will you be embarrassed if you're wrong?"

"No. I have a different system."

"You'll have to teach it to me."

"I think I'm going to be sick," said Kragar.

I jumped, Cawti jumped. She sat down again and said, "How are you still alive?" She turned to me. "How is he still alive?"

"It's a mystery," I said. "What do you want, Kragar?"

"Just learned something I thought you'd like to know. Unless you two would rather keep staring soulfully in each other's eyes."

"Ever had your skull used as a whetstone?" said Cawti.

"Not this week."

"Let's hear it," I said.

"Remember Matiess?"

"Uh, no."

"Bereth's brother?"

"Oh. Heh. I never bothered to get his name." For some reason, Kragar thought that was funny. "What about him?" I asked his smirk. "I hope you're not going to tell me he came across something, and is now negotiating with a Jhereg."

Kragar lost his smirk. "Vlad, have you been, uh, seeing other intelligence sources? I thought we had something special, something—"

"What did you get?"

"Seems you already got it. The brother meeting with someone from the Jhereg. Which means you got the other part of it, too, right?"

"The other part? No, I don't have the other part. Why don't you tell me the other part."

"I'm happy again. I've had a watch kept on that place with the sorceresses."

"Huh." At first, I had assumed there'd be nothing to see, that they'd all teleport. Then Kragar had told me there was a teleport block, but I didn't make the connection to there now being a reason to watch the place. Embarrassing.

"Oh," was what I said. "Right. Good work. So, you had the place watched. And? The brother, Materss, showed up there, too?"

"Matiess."

"Yeah."

"No. Someone else showed up."

I waited. Kragar needed to play these games sometimes, and I was willing to go along.

"It was a woman in red and silver, wearing a headband with a big ruby."

He waited.

I waited.

"What?" I said eventually.

"Headband, ruby?" he said. "Red and silver? Princess? Tsalmoth heir?"

"Oh," I said. "Well, now *there* is a nice piece of maize in my teeth."

"Bigger than you thought?" said Kragar after giving me a couple of seconds.

"Bigger than I thought when it turned out to be bigger than I thought," I agreed.

"What?"

"Never mind. This changes things. We need to find out how the Tsalmoth Heir is connected." I considered. "This is getting tricky."

"Complicated," agreed Kragar.

I nodded. "I don't like complicated."

"Right," he said. "You're a sim—"

"Yeah, yeah. And good job watching that house, I should have thought of it. Stay on it. Increase it if you have to."

"We'll have to hire to do that."

"Take twenty. That should cover us for a few days."

"So now we're at eight hundred and thirty-three?"

"Does that count as an expense for recovering the debt?"

"Why wouldn't it?"

"Yeah, I suppose it does. Eight thirty-three, then."

"Whatever you say."

"I love hearing that."

He snorted. "I'll take care of it," he said. "Anything else?"

"The game on Garshos. Anything?"

"He rented the place, has to spend a day setting it up, then he'll put the word out."

"Nothing from Paquitin?"

"Not so far."

"Good. That's it, then."

He nodded and took himself out of the room, leaving me alone with Cawti. I thought about kissing her, but didn't trust Kragar not to have forgotten something, and you know how I feel about love and murder.

"I need to find out how the Tsalmoth Heir figures into this," I said.

"How?"

"Yeah."

"I mean, how are you going to find out?"

"Erm," I explained.

She gave me some time to think it over, which is what I needed. "Okay," I said. "I might have something."

The guy's name was Fentor. Some time back, Morrolan had hired me to help out with security, and Fentor was in charge of security at Castle Black, so we'd worked together a little. I'd impressed him when we started because I'd gotten hold of him psychically, which I shouldn't have been able to do.

Most of you don't think about psychic contact all that much, you just do it, because the Orb—or whatever you have instead of it, I suppose, I don't know how things are wherever you're listening to this—provides most of what you need, and you don't spend a lot of time trying to touch the minds of people you don't know well.

But in my work, that does come up sometimes, and it's hard. First thing you think about is what the guy looks like. Fentor looked like a Tsalmoth, with those weird eyes that look too big for their faces and the nose that looks like someone shoved them into a wall, but, first of all, he wasn't a Tsalmoth, and, second, what the guy looks like doesn't help you all that much. What helps is if you can bring up the sound of the guy's voice, remember some of the expressions on his face, maybe how he stands, what pisses him off, that kind of thing. It's hard with someone you barely know.

Fentor was military through and through: House of the Dragon, and raised with strategy, tactics, siege engineering, logistics (whatever that means), and other stuff I'll never need to know. You wouldn't think that kind of background would make for a good head of security (you say "security," I say "spy"), but he'd done it, just by making himself learn, and being precise, and asking questions, and paying a lot of attention to little details. I'd concentrated on this, and reached him, and he was impressed. By now, of course, it was easy. I just brought his image into my head, and all of the emotional resonances came with them, and I reached out, casting, casting. . . .

"Who is this?"

"Vlad."

"What do you need?"

"Nothing urgent. How are things there?"

"What things?"

"Just, you know, Castle Black, security."

"Everything's fine. Except—"

"Yeah?"

"I got you talking in my head, and I'm going a little nuts trying to figure out why."

"I need to check into the Tsalmoth Heir."

"The . . . why?"

"Some things have come up."

"Does this have anything to do with Morrolan's security?"

"No, but it could be of benefit to him."

"Oh?"

"*The connection I'm trying to learn about is with the Left Hand of the Jhereg.*"

"*And?*"

"*Hello? Left Hand of the Jhereg? Illegal sorcery? Morganti weapons? Little blue stones?*"

"*They're purple.*"

"*Whatever.*"

"*Okay, I'll see if I can find a connection.*"

"*Just getting me some background on who she is would be helpful.*"

"*Okay, then. I'll get started. It'll take a while.*"

"*No hurry. Tomorrow will be fine.*"

It took me a moment after that to figure out that he was no longer there. Psychic communication is weird.

"Now we wait?" said Cawti.

"Now we wait."

"Wait at my place?"

"I like how you think." That sort of took care of things for the rest of the day. Oh, except for one very important point: Cawti admitted I was right, that the thicker pasta is better with clams. This was important, not because I was right, but because we could now face the future certain that, if we survived, our future clam sauces would have the right accompaniment.

9

THE FIRST FEAST

It's telling that some Dragaeran Houses, like the Vallista, have no marriage traditions involving food. I mean, I assume they eat, but there's no established ritualized eating. Laugh if you want, but ritualized eating is something I like. Fenarians have three different feasts, which doesn't count the food at the wedding itself, or the reception.

The first feast is seven days before the wedding, and given by the groom's mother for the bride, the groom, and one attendant each. I suspect, way back in the dusty reaches of time, it was a way to tell the bride, "this is the food my son has grown used to, and you'd better not disappoint him or I'll make your life miserable." Some Fenarian traditions are just weird, and what they came from is weirder still. The groom's attendant and the bride's attendant have special names, by the way, but neither Cawti nor I could remember them, and I was too embarrassed to ask Noish-pa. The parents of the bride and groom are also expected to be there.

Our feast was pretty small. Cawti brought Norathar, I brought Noish-pa and Kragar. (Oh yeah, all of the attendants for the groom are supposed to be men, and for the bride are supposed to be women, which probably makes more sense if you dig into religious traditions and folk beliefs of Fenario, but I'd rather dig into the food.) We rented the back dining room of a comfortable tavern called the Iron Kettle, and I hired the chef from a place called Menlo's to cater. I picked him because Menlo is a decent cook and had bought the place my father used to own. A little nod toward family, right?

He served us raw oysters with lemon and tomato juice and pepper sauce and vodka. Then we had a roasted goose covered in a sour cherry sauce along with soured cabbage in beet juice. Then came his specialty, "bandit's meat," which is skewers of barely cooked marinated beef with seared onion and bell pepper. It's all in the marinade, and I'd tell you what was in it if I knew, but there was wine and tarragon, anyway. He made poppy seed cake for the fruit course, and there was no shortage of wine.

Of all of those things, I think the goose was the one that stood out, because of how unexpected the sour cherry sauce was, and how it hit your mouth with a kind of, "How did that happen?" followed by, "of course that would happen, how did I not expect it?"

It's always interesting when something like that happens in your mouth, or your life.

⸙

The next morning, I had to deal with Loiosh's complaints that he was bored and hungry and wanted to come home. I was firm with him, and after he got home I only fed him a little of the sausage.

I wanted to walk by that manor where the Left Hand was operating, but Cawti pointed out that it was already being watched and no good could come of me being seen there. I mean, she was right, and I ended up not doing it, but it was hard. I wanted to be doing something. Sometimes the right thing to do is nothing. I hate those times.

The morning dragged.

You want to know something weird? It was only then—sitting around my flat doing nothing—that it hit me that the Left Hand had wanted to capture me, that they probably wanted information from me, that they would have interrogated me using sorcery. I'd never had a full-on sorcerous interrogation, or what you might call a brute-force mind-probe. I'd heard stories. And I'd heard stories about what was left after something like that.

I always get scared long after I should have, but I make up for it by being very scared. Being scared doesn't help anything, though. In fact, once you're scared, you might start making bad decisions. It can twist up your head, to where maybe you do something stupid just because you're afraid your reason for not doing it is because you're afraid. Did you follow that? The other thing is that when you're scared, one of the weird things that happens is that you're suddenly filled with the desire to *get it over with*. Not your best mindset when in danger, know what I mean?

Fortunately, I had a familiar around to make fun of me until I admitted that I'd been stupid enough yesterday to last a year at least, and that I should wait until I knew more before doing anything.

Having accomplished this, he went back to watching Fisher, not without some grumbling. Kragar was making sure we watched the house the Left Hand gathered in. Fentor was getting information about the Tsalmoth Heir. I was doing nothing. In a desperate effort to accomplish something, I went out and sat down next to Melestav's desk to see what needed doing, and we ended up arguing about the best courtball players we'd seen, which led to a discussion of how to hold the stick. It got heated, mostly on account of neither of us knowing much about the game except for how to make book on it. It passed the time, though.

My mind kept drifting back to what had happened at Castle Black. Was I a demon now? I didn't feel like a demon. But then, what does being a demon feel like? I suppose I could ask the Necromancer. Yeah, I should do that. "Hey, Necromancer," I could say. "What does it feel like to be a demon?" I was sure that would produce some useful results.

I'm being sarcastic there, in case you missed it.

I was still wandering around the office thinking when Cawti showed up and said, "Noish-pa says hello. Why are you grinning?"

"You called him Noish-pa. You didn't say, 'your grandfather,' you called him Noish-pa. Melestav, shut up."

"I didn't say—"

"You were thinking."

"Yeah, sorry, Vlad. I gotta not do that here."

We went back into my office. "What did you talk about?" I asked.

"Mostly how polite Norathar was."

"Yeah, I guess that'd surprise him, with his experience. And did he comment on Kragar?"

"It was like he didn't even notice Kragar was there. Also, Noish-pa says you need to learn to dance before the wedding."

I sighed. "Yeah, he mentioned that once before."

"What is it? You don't like dancing?"

"No, I don't like learning. It means doing things I don't know how to do right, and I hate that."

"Taltos Vladimir, you know how to do all sorts of things right, which means you must have spent a lot of time learning."

"Yeah, that's why I know I don't like it."

"You know I'll be there, right?"

"Okay, that helps. Did he give you the name of someone to teach it?"

"Yeah, I know where to go. South Adrilankha, of course. Don't worry, you'll be great. It's just like ducking out of the way of a cut, only you don't die if you do it wrong."

"I might."

"You won't."

"If I look like an idiot, you'll love me anyway?"

"I promise."

"All right, then."

I was quiet for a bit, until Cawti said, "You aren't thinking about dancing anymore, are you?"

"What would you think," I said, "about taking another shot at the brother, what's-his-name, and seeing if we can pry some information out of him?"

"Matiess. I like it."

"Good. One other errand first, then we pay him a visit."

"Sounds good."

"Cawti and I are going out," I told Melestav. "Don't kill anyone who doesn't need killing."

"I never do," he said. "Okay, I rarely do."

This time, when we walked, her hand wasn't on my arm, which I took to mean she was thinking we were in maybe a bit more danger than we had been. Probably true. We headed west, out of my area. "Where are we going?" she said.

"I want to pick up a treat for my faithful reptile companion."

"Aw, Boss."

"You're welcome."

"I'm in a mood for shellfish."

"Didn't you get enough clams?"

"No."

"You're spoiled."

"Something in a cream sauce, maybe?"

"I am not carrying shellfish in cream sauce around the Verra-be-damned city for you."

"Yeah, you're right. Skip the cream sauce."

"Spoiled."

We found a seafood vendor and picked up a bucket of rockfish (which are neither rocks nor fish, but are very good deep fried with a breading seasoned with mustard, bay leaves, ginger, pistiro, and, I don't know, whatever else Leevi puts in it).

Loiosh was perched on a house across the street from Fisher's, and I didn't want to show up there, so he met us a few hundred feet away. We gave him the shellfish, and he made that hissy-growly sound that passes for "thank you" when he can't be bothered to say it into my head.

I waited until he was done, because I'm polite that way, then said, "Anything? Any movement?"

"Went out to the market a couple of hours ago, then came back."

"All right."

"So I suppose I'm still stuck here?"

"Sorry."

"I—wait, there he is."

"I am the king of timing."

"No, he is. He waited until I was done eating. I hope we don't have to kill him."

"So do I."

I filled Cawti in on the conversation. She suggested we follow Loiosh following Fisher, and I had nothing better to do.

Kragar once asked me if I believe in fate, and I said it was my fate to fall asleep whenever he brought up stuff like that, and he laughed. I have thought about it, and sometimes things happen that have to be fate, or coincidence, or conspiracy, and I need a lot of convincing to believe in coincidence.

But when it comes down to it, what is fate except a conspiracy pulled off by magic?

Anyway, that's why I wondered if it was a conspiracy when Cawti and I happened to be following Fisher just when he was taken out.

I gotta say, one professional to another, it was a good job. You know, respect and all that.

Fisher was out paying personal visits to his businesses, which is something I do, and a lot of guys at our level do: it's a good way to spot problems early, and to remind the people running those places that the boss is keeping an eye on things, know what I mean? As Loiosh reported it, he stopped at a couple of public houses, and a tinsmith that I'm sure was every bit as legit as my herb shop, and then at another public house, then at a brothel. It was coming out of the brothel that he was hit.

You'd think, since I know this stuff, that I'd be able to give you details about how it went down—I mean the kind of details the Empire would want if they were to prosecute someone, right? But it's because I know about this stuff that I get why I can't. I'd never before seen a shine put on someone where I wasn't involved in the proceedings. It happens so fast, and out of nowhere.

Here's what I can tell you: Fisher walked out of the brothel, and there was some motion from beside the door, and he was on the ground and a guy was walking away. If the Empire had asked me what the assassin looked like, I wouldn't have been able to tell them (I mean, even if I were willing to), and I couldn't have been twenty feet away from him.

"*Follow him, Boss?*" said Loiosh, who always reacts faster than I do.

"*Just enough so you'll remember his face, though I doubt we'll need it.*"

"*I'm not so good with faces. You all look—*"

"*Good. A chance to practice.*"

I started to approach the body, thinking maybe I'd see just how dead Fisher was, but Cawti put her hand on my arm, and I stopped. Right. I probably didn't want to be so much hanging around a recent corpse. Just because I hadn't killed him was no reason to get sloppy.

Speaking of sloppy, it was only then I noticed the spreading pool that gave me a pretty good idea of how dead Fisher was.

I nodded to Cawti and we strolled off in the other direction.

"Got it, Boss."

"Good work. Not that I expect it'll do much. Oh, and, um, you don't have to follow Fisher anymore."

"Thanks for making that clear, Boss."

We started walking. I'd forgotten that I'd intended to look up Matiess, and just wandered. Cawti didn't say anything. If I had to guess, she knew that I was thinking and didn't want to interrupt; she has good instincts about that. Since we were close, I stopped and saw a guy named Harbrough, who handles money for me, and dropped off what I was carrying because it was more than I like to have on me. Hey, there are criminals around, you know? That put us in North Hill, near Fallow Street, and if it had been later in the day I'd have suggested we see a play; the ones on Fallow Street always have a few seats open. But I was just walking and thinking. The thinking went in circles, the walking brought me back to the house where the Left Hand had been operating. By now, they knew Fisher was dead. Did that mean their plan was working, or that someone else's plan had spilled sea-water in the middle of theirs?

I stopped across the street from the place and stared at it like I'd be able to read their minds. I couldn't.

"You can't read their minds," said Cawti.

"I was thinking I could burn a hole in the wall with the fire from my eyes."

"That'd be a nice spell. I'll bet someone knows how to do that."

"Yeah, wouldn't work against these people, though. They're probably the ones who can do it."

"Probably. Vlad, are we here for a reason?"

"Not really. Just walking and thinking and ended up here. We should go, I guess. Not going to get anything useful—"

At which point, because sometimes the Gods of Timing like to have their fun, the door opened and the youngish sorceress I'd seen before came out and started walking directly toward us.

We waited.

She crossed the street and stopped about three feet in front of me. "I'll give you this, Easterner. Whatever else, you've got nerve coming here, after what you did."

"Good," I said. "Thanks. That answers my question."

"Good," she said. "That answers mine."

She started to turn away.

"Wait," I said. "Does this mean we have common interests?"

"No," she said over her shoulder.

"Don't you think you maybe want to ask the boss?"

She stopped, turned, and glared. If I'd been a wall, the fire from her eyes might have burned a hole in me. Then she pressed her lips together and nodded.

We waited. I wasn't expecting her to be told to turn me into a slimy pool of gunk or something, but then, I couldn't be sure she wouldn't. I was, let's say, very aware of the weight of Spellbreaker around my left wrist.

The sorceress, looking like the words tasted bad, nodded to me and said, "Want to come in?"

"No," I said. "But you know where my office is. Send someone by if you want to have a conversation."

As I turned away, she said, "Wait. Perhaps somewhere neutral?"

I turned back and pretended to think about it, then nodded. "All right," I said. "Got somewhere in mind?"

"You suggest it," she said after a long hesitation.

"I know a lovely place, well outside my area, called the Stolen Boat."

Gotcha. Yeah, I saw it register, and then she scowled at me as she saw what I'd done. A pause while she communicated with "the

tower" as they call it, then she said, "Very well. That will do nicely."
She gave me a sweet smile that let me know she would prefer to
turn me into a slimy pool of gunk. I returned the smile and the kind
thought behind it.

"When?" I said.

"Now is fine."

"See you there."

"We'll have the back room reserved."

"And be waiting there, after making your preparations."

She smiled. "What about you?"

"Just me," I said. "And maybe Cawti, here."

"Uh huh."

"Kragar, I need four guys at the Stolen Boat."

"Covert?"

"Deniable."

"When?"

"Now."

"On it."

"May as well take our time," I told Cawti. "Uh, assuming you're in."

"I wouldn't miss it."

A little later I said, "I didn't sign on for this much walking."

I didn't turn my head, but I knew she was smiling. I wish I could
describe that particular smile. It's like, she was trying not to, but
she wasn't really hiding it. Whenever she got that smile I had to
remind myself what a tough guy I am so I didn't suddenly turn into
a grinning idiot.

When we got to the Stolen Boat, the guys Kragar had sent over
were already in place. None of them seemed to notice me coming
in, but I knew them all: Sticks, Ustora, Tanglebones, and Ritt. Good
people.

Just to be contrary, I ordered myself a cup of wine and took my
time drinking it. Cawti knew what I was doing, and that I didn't
have any reason except to maybe annoy them a bit. She didn't say
anything, but she had that same smile as before while she drank
hers.

The sorceress I'd been talking to came up and did a good job of acting as if us just sitting there was what they'd expected. "If you please," she said, all formal-like, "we are now ready to receive you."

"What's your name?"

Her eyes got kinda narrow. "Why? You think your Eastern witchcraft can conjure with it?"

Cawti laughed, and Loiosh made a hissing sound, but you had to know him to know that he was laughing too.

"No," I said. "We don't do that. But if you're who I'm going to keep talking to, I'd like to know what to call you."

"Let's try not to need to talk anymore. Kindly do not keep the ladies waiting."

Cawti and I stood up.

"Just you," said the sorceress-with-no-name-she-cared-to-reveal. She glanced at Cawti and Loiosh.

"Oh?" I said. "And just how many of you are waiting to talk to me?"

She hesitated, then said, "Very well." Pretty sure she asked someone; I didn't figure her for having much power in that group.

The Stolen Boat had a good-sized back room with a table that had been through some wars. The faces of the sorceresses were familiar. They were seated against the near, long wall, with the head and foot of the table empty. I went around and positioned myself in the middle of the other side. Cawti went over to a corner, leaned against the wall, and waited. They looked at her, looked at me. The old one that I'd dealt with before started to say something, then closed her mouth.

There's a look I've seen in people in the organization, a look that says, "I'm so good I don't gotta prove it. I can cut you into pieces whenever I want." You know what I'm talking about. You've seen it. Well, that old sorceress had that look, and I took it seriously.

"Lord Taltos," she said.

"Lady."

"We may have a common interest."

"I was thinking that. So, what's the deal with the Verra's tear?"

"You first. What is your interest in Fisher?"

"I told you. Eight hundred gold."

She pressed her lips together. "If we're to work together, I need the truth."

"That's what I just gave you."

"Will you let me into your head to prove it?"

"Would you?"

"If I were telling—"

I used a bad word. It didn't startle her as much as it would have some.

She said, "If you won't let me verify it, why should I believe you?"

"I got an honest face."

"You really don't."

"Now you've hurt my feelings. Look, some son-of-a-bitch died owing me money. I'm trying to collect it. That led me to Fisher, which led me to the Verra's tear, which led me to you. Why are you having so much trouble with this concept?"

She looked at the woman next to her, and I guess they had some sort of conversation that didn't include me. Then she turned back and said, "All right. For now, I'll accept it."

I started to make some remark to express how touched I was by this sign of trust, but I've learned that sometimes it's best to just shut up, and once in a while I do. I waited.

"We have interests," she continued, "in places that are not of this world."

I waited some more.

"You appear neither confused nor startled," she said.

I nodded.

"Then it's true, what we've heard about who your friends are."

"Probably."

"These are things an Easterner shouldn't know."

"Why? Too powerful for us?"

She pulled out a contemptuous look, which I ignored because that's what I do, but I heard a quick inhale from Cawti and hoped she didn't feel the need to start putting holes in our new allies.

"No," said the sorceress. "Because it cuts into our advantage."

"Okay, I can respect that."

She shrugged. "Let's get back to business. We were negotiating with some beings—"

"Demons."

"—in these other worlds, and received a request. Would it be a problem if they were demons?"

"No."

"Good. In fact, they are not; if they were, our business would be easier to manage, as they would be able to appear in our world."

"So, let me guess: that's where Fisher comes into this? And the Verra's tear?"

She hesitated. "What do you know about Fisher?"

"Not much. Worked for Toronnan, owned a few businesses."

She nodded. "Do you know how he's connected with a Tsalmoth named Bereth?"

"I know there is a connection; that's what I was looking into. I don't know exactly what the connection is."

"Why were you—" She stopped, frowned. "Bereth owed you money when he was killed." She didn't put it as a question.

I nodded.

"Eight hundred."

I nodded again.

"Do you know why he borrowed the money?"

"I suspect it was to go into the perfume business."

Her old eyes were gray, with bits of brown, and no, she couldn't see into my head—even Daymar would have trouble with that if I had my guard up—but she was sure looking like she wanted to.

"You're right," she said. "As far as it goes."

"I'm listening. I can't wait to find out how gray market perfume connects to other worlds."

"Other worlds have gold," she said.

"And they want perfume?"

"Not exactly. They want one of its byproducts."

"I hadn't known perfume had any byproduct."

"Extracting the hishi does."

"What sort of byproduct?"

"A greenish gel. I don't know what they use it for; I never asked. The point is, they'll pay for it."

"Right. And Fisher?"

"We picked him as the go-between because he had a connection to the hishi source, and we find Toronnan easier to work with than most of you."

Loiosh squeezed my shoulder. Sometimes he can tell when people are leaving out important things. He's not entirely reliable that way, but I made a sort of mental note about it.

"You picked Fisher as the go-between?" I said.

"Yes."

"Were you going to tell him?"

"Eventually."

Several observations came to mind; I didn't choose to express them. "And the Verra's tear?"

"To prepare him, to acclimate him, so he would be able to do what we wished when we sent him over."

"I'm sure if I knew more, that would make sense. So that leaves one question."

She nodded. "Who killed him?"

"Well, I was going for why, but sure, *who* works, too. We get one, we get the other."

"So you'll work with us?"

"I'll let you work with me," I said.

She laughed, which was among the better reactions she could have had. Then she said, "You look from your end, I'll look from mine. Was this done to interfere with our operation, or for a completely different reason? Either way, who?"

"Huh," I said. "I started out trying to figure out who wanted a Tsalmoth dead, now I'm trying to figure out who wanted a Jhereg dead. You know, sometimes I wonder if the people I deal with are all that nice."

"I wonder the same thing," said the murderous old woman.

"About me, or you?"

She smiled.

I said, "You will, of course, share anything you learn, because now that we're working together, we got no secrets, right?"

"Of course. Just as much as you will."

"Glad we understand each other," I said. "Any suggestions where I should start?"

"If I had, I wouldn't need you."

I wasn't sure that made sense, but I didn't tell her that. I just nodded and tapped my chest like I'd seen Dragonlords do sometimes instead of bowing. Then I stood up, and we marched out of there.

"Okay," I said as we left the inn. "I have a plan. I have all the details worked out. I know exactly what—"

"No clue, right, Boss?"

"So you're saying," said Cawti, "that you have no idea what our next step is."

"Loiosh beat you to it."

"He's known you longer."

"Okay, now I have an idea."

"Uh huh," said my betrothed.

I reached Fentor. *"Who?"*

"Vlad. Got anything for me?"

"Not much."

"I'll take anything at this point."

"Let me guess: people are staring at you waiting for you to tell them what to do next?"

"Something like that. What did you learn?"

"Princess Chervik, Duchess of Gillirand and Tsalmoth Heir."

"What about her?"

"She's on the verge of losing her duchy."

"To . . . ?"

"Debt."

"To . . . ?"

"Don't know yet. I was waiting until I learned that before I got hold of you. But since you're—"

"*Yeah. Good. I'll be in touch.*"

Sometime in there we'd stopped walking, which I guess I do sometimes when I'm concentrating. Now that I wasn't concentrating, I was able to walk again. Single-minded, that's what I am.

"Kragar or Fentor?" Cawti wanted to know.

"Now, how did you know—Fentor. You know me too well."

"Yeah, dangerous. You should marry me."

"Guess I might as well."

"*We jhereg are able to vomit at will.*"

"So," she repeated. "What did he say?"

I gave her a quick summary.

"So, House of the Tsalmoth?" she said. "Tsalmoth Wing of the Palace?"

"Or we could wait for Fentor to learn a bit more."

"Good idea," she said. "I know how much you enjoy waiting."

"As much as you do."

"Yeah, we picked the wrong line of work."

"I shoulda listened to my father and become a full-time witch."

She knew enough about my father that I got a chuckle from her.

"And so?" she said.

"I think it's time we meet Her Highness."

"All right. Walking into the house with the Left Hand didn't work out badly."

"Now there's a hex if I ever heard one."

"What's the difference between a hex and a curse?"

"Curses are real."

"Hmm. Could you put one on our enemy? I mean, once we know who that is."

"I guess. But it's a lot of work. Usually easier to just stick something sharp into him and then say mean things."

"We'll go with that then."

"*And then eat him?*"

"Probably not, Loiosh."

Then . . . "*Kragar? Find out where Princess Chervik lives.*"

"*The Tsalmoth Heir, Vlad? Why? Inviting her to your wedding?*"

"Something like that."

"I'll get back to you."

"Let's eat," said Cawti, before I could suggest it.

We walked—okay, strolled—until we found a guy selling hand-sized meat pies, and we burned our fingers and tongues and enjoyed it. We were still eating when Kragar reached me. The best thing about psychic communication is that you don't have to worry about swallowing your food before saying something, so I kept eating. Kragar let me know that Her Highness lived in the House of the Tsalmoth itself (as opposed to one of her estates, or the Tsalmoth Wing; this stuff gets confusing). I told Cawti, and we set in to discussing how we were going to convince her to give an audience to a couple of Jhereg Easterners. The Tsalmoth was pretty low on the Cycle, so it wouldn't be as hard as it would have been a few thousand years ago.

We made it to the House of the Tsalmoth, a long building that got wider further back, so it looked like an arrow pointing at the Tsalmoth Wing of the Palace. It had smaller doors than most of the Great Houses, by which I mean you'd have had to squeeze a bit to get my whole flat through them. The tsalmoth engraved above the door in silver against dark gray was pretty lifelike—a husky, snarling thing standing on its hind legs with its massive arms reaching out to rip you apart and its tusks looking like they were sharp as a dzur's fang. Or maybe it was reaching out to hug you, I don't know. I think the hug would be just as dangerous, but it's not likely to come up.

"Here we go," I said, and we walked in like we had no reason not to be there.

10

THE GATHERING

At some point, you got to get people together to plan things, right? Unless you're one of those Houses like the Athyra or the Hawk that do everything through psychic communication. I don't think they do the actual marriage ceremony that way, but I could be wrong. In House Jhereg, there's a tradition to meet over three days: to decide who will make the plans, to make the plans, and to change the plans. Of course, that's the House of the Jhereg, and has nothing to do with the organization in the middle of it—the people in the organization I've known who got married do it pretty much the way we Easterners do: We just pick a time when bride, groom, whoever is going to do the ceremony, and anyone else in the wedding party can get together, have a few drinks, maybe a meal, and figure out what's going to happen. We had our gathering in the library at Castle Black, and Morrolan and Aliera ended up arguing about when in the ceremony the newly married or about-to-be newly married couple (that's Cawti and me, if you've been paying attention) were supposed to clasp hands. The argument got heated, and personal observations were exchanged. Cawti and I enjoyed it.

⊰⊱

The doors were standing open, with a pair of guards in red and silver planted next to them. They didn't challenge us, or even appear to notice us, but they did somehow manage to convey contempt without moving or changing expression. It's a nice trick. I think they teach it in guard school.

The door opened up into a hall that had no reason to exist. I mean, seriously, a big room, a huge room, with a set of long, thin glass windows at the top, and other than that, nothing—not a chair, not a cushion, and only one other exit, directly opposite. Unless, I suppose, there were secret entrances. Oh, yeah, and there were a bunch of paintings, portraits, I suppose of important Tsalmoth. Morrolan had better taste in art.

"This whole hall is stupid," said Cawti.

See why I love her?

After going through the big, pointless, empty place, we were in a smaller room with more doors going off in different directions, because maybe they figured the smaller the room the more useful it should be, I dunno. Anyway, there was a guy there who looked official, standing next to the door, and we gave our names and asked if we could see Her Highness on a matter of business.

He seemed kinda young, but who knows how the Tsalmoth conduct things. He looked startled when we asked, started to say something, stopped, then said, "Just go on up," and gave us directions for finding her chambers. In case you missed it, that hesitation is probably when one of us should have gotten suspicious. I have no excuse. Oh, I suppose I could find that guy and have a talk with him, but, hey, he pulled one, and it worked. My own fault. We followed the directions, which involved a lot of stairs, I guess because the more important you are, the more irritating it has to be for someone to find you.

I gotta tell you what I had in mind, because it didn't go the way I planned. As Cawti and I had it figured, Her Highness was working through various agents, which had included Bereth, and now his brother, to work with the Left Hand to export hishi to some other world. Someone wanted to stop it, and resorted to unsocial acts. So, who'd want to stop it? Not the Empire, because, except for Easterners and Teckla, they usually prefer to arrest people before they murder them. So, most likely someone with some pull—say an Athyra or a Hawk—was trying to cut out the Left Hand and get the deal themselves. So the idea was to talk to the Heir and see if maybe she had some ideas of who the rival might be. Even if she didn't want to just tell me, a Tsalmoth isn't a Jhereg, so I could maybe pull some information out of her. That makes sense, right? I mean, we weren't being stupid or anything. I just want to make that clear.

As plans go, it wasn't bad, and even seemed pretty low risk.

Trouble was, we were making an assumption in there we hadn't even noticed, and that was, since the Left Hand was involved, and the Left Hand is good at keeping their business out of sight of the Empire, we figured there was no danger that we'd have an uninvited third party there. What I didn't think about was that maybe the Tsalmoth weren't so good at that. I mean, as mistakes go, it was an easy one to make. But—well, let me just tell it.

What happened was, we followed the guy's directions and walked into a good-sized antechamber with glass windows all along one wall and a lot of gold upholstered stuffed chairs and full of Phoenix Guards who looked at us in a way that wasn't friendly at all.

Loiosh ducked into my cloak, and I'd have followed if I could have managed the geometry.

There were five of them, not counting a brigadier. Having a brigadier there seemed like overkill for a troop of five, but what do I know? Maybe you need a high-ranking officer to deal with an Heir. Custom or something. I'm sure Lady Teldra would know.

I recognized the princess, who was standing near a wall looking not at all happy with life, and there were a couple of other Tsalmoth I'd never seen. No weapons were out, which pleased me, because I only like weapons when I'm holding one.

They were all looking at Cawti and me, and whatever conversation was going on had stopped.

"Well, hello there," I said. "Is this the rehearsal for the Ascension Day pageant, or did I go to the wrong—"

"Name," snapped the brigadier.

"Taltos, Vladimir, baronet, House of the Jhereg, at your service, and the service of the Empire. Happy to help. Anything I can—"

"Shut up. What are you doing here?"

"Visiting," I said. And, "I didn't get your name."

"My lord."

There were a few chuckles from around the room, which annoyed me, but it was fair. He turned to Cawti. "Name," he snapped.

I thought it would have been funny if she'd said, "my lady," but she remained mute. Without turning to look at her, I was pretty sure she was glaring. She doesn't like the Phoenix Guards as much as I do.

When she didn't answer, he turned to the princess. "Your Highness, may I ask your connection to these individuals?"

"None," she said. "I've never seen them before."

"I see," he said in the tone they use when they don't believe you, which is pretty much anytime you tell them anything that isn't confessing to a crime, and sometimes when it is.

He turned his head, but still kept his eyes on us. "Escort them to the barracks, we'll talk there after we've finished here."

Well now, this had taken a turn I didn't like. There are situations where you can't solve a Phoenix Guards problem by slipping them a few imperials, and having a brigadier give them an order was one of those. Situations like that, in my experience, ran from the very bad to the much worse.

"If you want to ask me questions, uh, my lord, why not here? I'm here with a few questions of my own. Think how efficient it will be."

"Disarm them," said the brigadier, which I didn't take as a friendly gesture at all. I shrugged and handed over my rapier and two of my daggers. Then, when he looked at me, a third.

"How many more do you have?" he asked.

"I'm an Easterner," I said. "I can't count that high."

One of his little troop laughed, which earned her a glare and me a sense of victory. "Get them to the barracks," he said, "then do a careful search. I know these types, they always have one more weapon than you think they do."

More like twenty, but who's counting.

I said, "My lord, truly, I just came to ask Her Highness some questions."

"I don't care why you're here."

I wanted to say, "then why did you ask?" but sometimes I can control my more suicidal urges.

Two of them approached us. I looked at Cawti, who shrugged. Nothing we could do; violence against the Phoenix Guards is a bad idea in so many ways, an Easterner can't count that high.

Our escort indicated the door. I turned around and started walking toward it when Cawti said, "One moment."

I turned back. The brigadier narrowed his eyes. "What?"

"Name the charge," she said, which I'd never said to a Phoenix Guard in my life.

"The what?"

"You cannot have us taken anywhere against our will without a charge."

"I'll think of one."

"That's probably a bad idea," said Cawti with a lot more confidence than I felt.

"And why is that?"

"My name is Cawti," she said. "And this is Vladimir Taltos."

"And those names are supposed to mean something to me?"

"They might. Perhaps you should ask Her Highness Princess Norathar."

Oh, right. I'd forgotten about that.

The brigadier sniffed. "That's quite a name to be throwing around."

"If what you're doing is legal, it shouldn't worry you. If it isn't, I suggest you ask her. Or, if you wish, I will. And when she shows up, I imagine she won't be pleased."

He started to say something, stopped, frowned. It was like I could see his memory working. *Wait. Wasn't there some scandal with Norathar becoming a Princess? Something about her having been working with . . .*

"What did you say your name is?"

"Cawti," said Cawti.

He hesitated a moment longer. His face had become quite red. "Very well," he said. "You may go."

"We'll wait," she said. "We still have the questions we came here to ask."

Now, you see, I wouldn't have pushed it. But, okay, here we were.

"This," he said, "is an official Imperial investigation." I guess he felt on more solid ground again, because his voice got stronger. "Unless you have orders from the Empress, I don't care who you know."

"Okay," I said. "Then maybe let us help."

That left him kinda stuck between the point and the edge. He didn't want to take me up on the offer, because unless he was an idiot he knew I had no interest in helping the Phoenix Guards, but if he said yes, he might be able to find out what I knew. I didn't gloat. I mean, not so he could see. I didn't want to find out how strong his self-control was.

"If you have questions," he said, scowling, "ask me and I'll decide if I want to ask Her Highness. You're not to speak to her."

"Sure," I said. "My lord."

I had the feeling Cawti was trying not to laugh. I plowed ahead in case she failed. "I just have one question for Her Highness," I said.

"Ask," he said. His teeth weren't clenched. Quite. As for Her Highness, she was outright scowling.

"Ask Her Highness," I said, "if it is her own personal property, or property belonging to her House, that has all of that Dark Water running under it."

Her eyes widened. "How did you—I'm not answering that."

"Thank you," I said, bowing. "That's all I wanted to know." I turned to the brigadier. "May we take our leave, my lord?" I can talk good when I want to.

He stared at me.

"My lord?" I said, since he'd said that was his name.

"What is Dark Water, and what has it to do with this?"

"My lord, you never told me what 'this' is, so how can I know if it is in any way connected to Dark Water?"

Yeah, I knew I was playing a dangerous game, but it seemed worth it. Besides, it was fun.

"You'll stay here," said the officer.

"My lord?" I wanted to see what sort of expression Cawti was wearing, but didn't want to look at her. I guessed she was enjoying this.

"Explain," he said.

I wondered just how far name-dropping Norathar would take us.

"My lord?" I said again. Maybe I could just keep saying that until the problem went away.

"I want to know what is behind that question you asked her, what it means, and what conclusions you've formed from it."

"My lord," I said. I bowed and tried to make it polite, instead of like I was mocking him. "It has to do with business dealings with some associates, and I'm not at liberty to say who they are or give any of the details."

He sputtered like my grandfather's tea kettle. "You're not at—"

He stopped, cocked his head, and stared at me like maybe I had his dignity on my forehead and he was considering how to ask for it back. You don't often get the chance to get one over on a Phoenix Guard, especially an officer, and especially with royalty looking on. I figured there'd be payback, but I was going to enjoy it in the meantime.

"Taltos, Vladimir," he repeated. He gave Cawti the hard stare. "I shall speak with Her Highness." He was referring to Norathar, not the Princess who was here; this stuff can get confusing, so I'm explaining.

"Do that," said my bride-to-be.

"*Boss?*"

"Hmm?"

"*Were you striking sparks with that question, or do you have something?*"

"*Some of each. Mostly, I'm trying to get us out of here.*"

"*I approve of your goal, Boss. But I wonder—*"

He broke off as the brigadier said, "Get out before I change my mind."

"*Don't even say it, Boss.*"

I bowed to Her Highness and the brigadier. We collected our weapons, then made our way out.

"Well done, Vlad," said Cawti as we reached the street.

"I was going to tell you that," I said. "Also, I can hardly believe we got out of that."

"Yeah."

"What if he'd actually gotten in touch with Norathar?"

"I wasn't bluffing, Vlad. She'd have helped us."

"I know, but you'd have hated it."

"Yeah. But not as much as the grief I'd have gotten from her if I let myself be arrested without using her name."

"Oh, right. Yeah."

"Now what?"

"I need to think."

"So, food?"

"You know me so well. Office first, though."

I made it a point to look very carefully to see if Kragar was already in my office before calling out to him. I sat behind the desk. Cawti gave me a look of curiosity.

"So, Vlad—"

"Give me a minute, love. I have to think, you know how much effort that is for me."

She chuckled politely and waited.

After some thought, I figured out the next move. I looked for Kragar before calling for him, and there he was. A victory for me, that time.

"Kragar," I said.

"What?"

I licked my lips. "Got a job for you."

"Uh huh."

"You're perfect for it."

"Okay."

"In fact, you're so perfect, no one else could come close to doing it as well as you."

"Uh."

"It's almost like you were made just for this—"

"How much am I going to hate it, Vlad?"

"A lot."

"How likely is it to get me killed?"

"Not very."

His brows went up. "Then—?"

"It is," I said, "kind of indecent."

He stared at me, and I could see him trying to figure out what I might think he might think was indecent. Before he could get too far, I said, "A guy named Fisher took a shine today. One of Toronnan's people."

"Okay."

"His friends will be getting together, probably this evening, maybe tomorrow, maybe the day after, and swapping stories about him."

"Yeah," said Kragar.

"Find out where, go there, get into a corner, and listen."

He looked uncomfortable. "Vlad—"

"I know."

He looked over at the wall to his right, then turned back to me. "All right. What am I listening for?"

"I don't even know. There may be nothing, and even if there is something, you may not hear it. But he got involved with something involving necromancy, the Tsalmoth Heir, the Left Hand, and Verra's tears. I want to know, why him? So, anything that might be a hint about that, I want."

"Okay." He didn't look happy.

Cawti, who hadn't said a word the entire time, caught my eye and mouthed, "food." I stood up and followed Kragar out.

We just strolled for a while, her hand on my arm. We went south out of my area for no special reason, and then my stomach rumbled loud enough for her to hear, and she agreed. We stopped at the first place we found that had nice smells coming out of it—I don't remember what it was called, probably the animals doing the thing—and had wine and a kethna and shallot stew that was edible. It was the kind of place with more aristocrats than Teckla—that is, no Teckla at all. They might have thrown us out for being Easterners, but Jhereg colors and openly wearing weapons are good for something. We did get a Look or two, which I ignored. I felt Cawti tense up next to me, but then she shrugged it off.

"So, my dear future husband."

"Hmm?"

"What was that all about?"

"What?"

"That question you asked Her Highness. No, don't give me the smug look. Oh, okay, give me the smug look. It's adorable. But answer the damned question."

"We've been tracking a business deal—the Left Hand working with some kind of mystical, magical, uh, thingie, and now we find out the Tsalmoth are involved. Why? Why bring the Tsalmoth into it? They're near the bottom of the Cycle. They aren't powerful. So either they're the ones who started it, or they have something the Left Hand wants. If they're dealing with Verra's tears, they're doing something necromantic."

"And you just guessed it was Dark Water running under someone's property?"

"I don't know a lot about necromancy, but I know of two things it involves."

"Dead bodies, and—"

"Three things it involves. Okay, no. Two things that are rare and valuable specifically to necromancers."

"Verra's tears and Dark Water."

"Right. And there's no way she could have a stock of Verra's tears. Or at least, no way that didn't also involve having access to Dark Water. So I took a shot."

"What if she'd given you a blank look?"

"That would have meant she was the one starting it, putting it together. It would have meant she was behind it, and was using the Left Hand, instead of the other way around."

She was quiet for a moment, then said, "Vlad, is it illegal?"

"What part?"

"Well, any of it."

"I don't think possession of Verra's tears or Dark Water are illegal."

"What about the rest of the operation?"

"You heard Morrolan. If they aren't raising the dead or inviting demons in, I think they're safe. Uh, well, check that: they're bringing gold in from another world. I'd think it would be a special case of smuggling, wouldn't it?"

"Huh. I suppose it would."

"What are you getting at?"

"Why the Phoenix Guards were there."

"Oh, right. That would mean they're sniffing around our friends from the Left Hand."

She nodded. "Or will be."

"That might affect how this plays out."

"Also, how did they get into it?"

"Oh good. More questions."

"And I have another one for you, love."

"What's that?"

"How much do you know of what's used for necromancy?"

"Not much," I said.

"So it would have been possible that the reason they went to the Tsalmoth had to do with something else entirely, not with Dark Water?"

"Well, yeah."

"So you got lucky."

"That's one way to look at it."

"What's another?"

"The stew is good, isn't it? I need to cook with shallots more."

She gave me that smile again and I'd have melted if I weren't such a tough guy. That had been happening a lot. Good thing I'm such a tough guy. See, I keep repeating that I'm a tough guy because otherwise you might forget.

"So," she said after a couple of bites and an elegant sip, "now that your brilliant example of deductive prowess has revealed that the

Tsalmoth Heir's property is being exploited by the Left Hand, and that the Empire is probably investigating, what's our next move?"

"I understood some of those words. I just want to say that."

"The part where I asked about our next move?"

"Yeah, that."

"Well?"

"Eventually we'll reach the point where we can kill someone."

"We usually do."

"Meanwhile, we work with the Left Hand to find out who had Bereth and Fisher shined, while we also figure out if it was them. Well, Bereth, anyway. I'm pretty sure I know who had Fisher shined."

"Who?"

"Toronnan."

"What makes you think so?"

"Think about it, love."

She did, then nodded. "Ah. Okay. But what if we're dealing with two factions within the Left Hand?"

That stopped me. "Damn," I said after a minute. "I hadn't thought of that."

"Neither had I until just now. But if this were the Jhereg, I mean, the Right Hand, our people, wouldn't we figure one outfit going against another?"

I nodded. "Just had to make things more complicated, didn't you!"

"I kind of did, yeah."

"And maybe one of them drops hints to the Empire to start an investigation into the other."

"Right."

"We wouldn't do that, but they might. I don't know."

She nodded.

"So no problem," I said. I frowned. "If that is the case, why didn't our dear new friends that we're now working with 'cause we trust each other completely not mention it?"

"Wow, Vlad. Think maybe they don't trust us after all?"

I chuckled.

"Or," she continued, "that isn't what's going on, or it is but they don't know it."

I sighed. "It's so complicated. I like things simple. Everyone says that about me."

"No one says that about you."

"They would if they knew me. If there *is* another faction of the Left Hand, how do we find them?"

"Not fair, Vladimir. I was going to ask that, so you would have had to answer it."

"Yeah, that's what I was afraid of."

We clinked glasses, which is an Eastern thing that's kinda hard to explain, and I winked and she smiled, and we went back to planning what crimes we needed to commit in order to secure my eight hundred illegal gold coins. Or I'd have been fine with a hundred and sixty five-weights. Or even scrip. I've been paid in scrip before. Some don't like it, but I don't mind, it exchanges one for one with gold. Anything would have been fine, I wasn't picky. "That Vlad, he isn't picky." That's what everyone says about me.

"*Boss, no one—*"

"*Shut up, Loiosh.*"

Cawti said, "If I remember how you like to operate in situations like this—"

"Wait. When have I ever been in a situation like this?"

She gave me the lifted eyebrow. "If I remember right," she started again, "you like to just go charging in and make everyone try to kill you until something breaks and you find out who your enemy is."

I opened my mouth, closed it, and drank some more wine.

She waited me out. I said, "All right. Other than charging headlong at the Left Hand, which would be kinda stupid, or charging headlong at the House of the Tsalmoth, which would be even more stupid, or charging headlong at the Empire, which overflows the stupid bucket, where do we charge?"

"I wasn't saying it was a good idea."

"Ah. Well, I forgot about it in all the excitement, but I was thinking of finding what's-his-name, Matiess, Bereth's brother. As far as squeezing information out of people, he seems the easiest to squeeze. Safest too."

Cawti nodded. "Which, since everyone else will know that too, there are probably some factions in this who'd like to shut him up."

"Good point. Let's get on it, then."

So, it was back to his shop, which was still closed, and clapping got no result. We shrugged and headed back toward the office and saw him just coming out of it. How's that for timing?

"My lord," he said. "I was looking for you."

"Then let's step inside," I said. "This is Cawti. Cawti, this is Matiess, brother of the late Bereth. Follow me."

I led the way up the stairs and past Melestav, who said, "A Tsalmoth was in here looking for you, Vlad."

Everyone who works for me is a wiseacre. I suppose that says something about me.

"Sit down," I told Matiess once we were in my office. "What's on your mind?"

Cawti pulled the other chair away so she could face him and sat down. I love how she sits down—there's this unconscious grace to how she just flows into the new position, all in one motion, like she's dancing. Yeah, I'm getting distracted, but I got distracted then, too.

Matiess said, "You said to come see you if something happened."

I nodded. "What was it?"

"I got a letter from an advocate, saying I'd inherited some property, and then I got a message to meet with someone, who turned out to be a Jhereg."

I wasn't used to someone just showing up and giving me the information I'd been working on a way of finding out, but I didn't mind. Since it was going so well, I just nodded and let him continue telling it.

"His name was Fisher," he said. "And he asked if I wanted to sell my property."

"That is, the property you'd just inherited?"

He nodded. "I hadn't even looked it over yet, so I said I didn't know. He, I'm not sure, he might have threatened me."

"You're not sure?"

"He said I should think it over carefully, and there was something about the way he said 'carefully' that—"

"Yeah, he threatened you."

He nodded. "That's when I decided to come to you."

"Good thinking."

"Can you protect me?"

"Absolutely," I said. I mean, since Fisher was now dead, I was pretty sure I could protect the guy from him. I don't know if I've mentioned this before, but one of my specialties is protecting people from non-existent threats.

In any case, he seemed relieved.

"Tell me about this property," I said. "Where is it, and what is it?"

"I don't know what it is, but here's the address."

He dug around inside his jerkin and produced a scroll, unrolled it, and showed it to me. It was one of those legal documents hated by everyone except Lyorn and Iorich—and the Iorich only like them because they get paid to draft them. But the address was clear enough, right at the beginning of the third section. I memorized it, then handed the parchment back.

"Let's go," I said, and stood up.

"Where are we going?" he asked after a while.

"To look over this property of yours."

"Oh," he said.

"Don't worry," I told him. "We'll keep you safe."

As we walked, evening came, went, and lights came on. Some parts of the city are full of lights, as people hang lanterns out; others stay mostly dark; still others—by which I mean the Imperial district— have big sorcerous lights they keep on all the time. I don't know why they don't do that everywhere; how much work is a light spell? The area we went to, the Hook, was somewhere in between; our shadows danced and grew and changed as we moved out of the range of one lantern and into another.

I'll bet there's a great story about how The Hook got its name, maybe somebody with a hook-hand once lived there, or someone thought some part of it looked like a hook, or there was a house called The Hook there once. I dunno. The streets got narrower and the buildings—most of them flat houses—taller. As we kept going, there was less old stone and more new wood, so, like some sections of my own area, you started feeling like the houses were looming over you. Matiess gave us directions. If it weren't for Loiosh, I'd have worried about getting lost, because this was a part of the City I didn't know, and there were enough little curving hills to mess me up pretty good.

But his directions were good, and eventually we got there. It didn't look like much to me: a wooden storefront like a thousand others, oiled-paper windows, no sign, a few rooms above it.

"All right," I said as we approached the door. "Let's see what's—"

I stopped, because Matiess had stopped. He had also gone pale and was shaking.

"What is it?"

He shook his head, staring wide-eyed at the door. "I don't know," he managed.

"Spell!" I said.

"I guess so."

"Fear spell. Huh. I'm not feeling it."

"I don't think I can—"

"Take a step or two back," I said.

He did, appearing to think it was a fine idea.

"Better?"

He nodded. "Some," he said.

"So someone doesn't want you going in. Or maybe anyone going in, but it doesn't work on Easterners."

Cawti said, "Vladimir, isn't this the kind of thing witchcraft is better for?"

"Huh. Yeah. You think they might have a witch working with them? That'd be a first."

"*Loiosh?*"

"*Okay. You might want to warn him.*"

"*Yeah.*"

Aloud I said, "All right, you aren't going to like this, but just go with it."

"What—"

Loiosh flew over and landed on his shoulder. He jumped back, started to wave his hands, almost went over backward, then froze. I gave him what I hoped would be a reassuring nod. A minute later Loiosh flew back to me.

"I didn't get anything, Boss."

"No," I told Cawti. "It isn't witchcraft."

"At least we don't have to redefine everything we've ever believed."

"Uh, yeah. So that's good."

"How would you do something like this with sorcery?"

"I wouldn't. Doing things to someone's head is, I don't know . . . Hard."

"This is the Left Hand. We have to figure they're good. And remember that spell they threw at you when we visited them? Didn't you say that was some kind of mental thing?"

"Well, I figured it was an attempt at a mind-probe, but yeah, there are similarities, I guess. Okay, so, a sorcerous fear spell, either aimed at Matiess here, or at anyone who isn't an Easterner."

Matiess here, by the way, was listening to us and looking nervous. Maybe he was still close enough to feel its effect. Or maybe it was what we were saying. Or maybe he was picking up on the fact that when it came to sorcery, I was pretty badly outmatched by whoever it was who'd done this, and maybe he knew that trying to counter a spell from someone better than you is a good way to end up with your brain dripping out of your ears.

I shrugged. "Okay, well, I want to go in there and look around, so I guess I'd better break that there spell."

11

THE SUPPLICATION TO THE GODS

Maybe the biggest difference between Dragaeran marriage rituals and human marriage rituals is that human traditions—not just Fenarian, but all of the ones I've come across—involve, in one way or another, asking the blessing or favor or at least approval of the gods on the union, which no Dragaeran wedding does. Well, I guess the Iorich, as part of their vows, make a reference to the fires of Ordwynac, but they just refer to him, like, maybe their love burns like that; they don't ask him for anything. I mentioned this to Morrolan, who knows more about humans than most Dragaerans, and he said, "Well, you know, the gods probably have more important things to do, don't you think?" He had a point. Cawti and I talked about removing the bit from our service about asking the Demon Goddess for her blessing, but in the end decided to keep it. For one thing, the priest would have objected. And for another, well, you never know what will piss her off, so why take chances?

⊰⊱

"Thing is," I told Cawti, "he's in no shape to go in there, and we need him."

"Why?"

"To trigger the traps that would otherwise get us."

"Vlad."

"Seriously, because it's his place, and there could be other spells keyed to him, and it'll prevent legal complications if the owner is with us."

"All right."

"I think I can do this," I said.

"We could get help."

"*Yeah, might come to that. But I want to try first. If it's something that was done to him, this won't work, but if it's a continuous thing, I mean, something coming at him, then maybe.*"

She nodded, and, right there, on the street, I turned toward the Tsalmoth. "Okay," I said. "I'm going to try something."

"I don't know if—"

"Stand still."

Yeah. So, let's talk about sorcery, the magic of the Empire. The great mystical art. The secret of the power of the ancients. The supreme gift of the Gods. Blah blah blah.

All the way back when the Empire started, too long ago for me to even think about it, they put together the Orb, a device to make it possible for regular folk like you and me to take all the wonderful energy that is sitting in the Great Sea of Amorphia and use it to do miraculous things like cooling down a bottle of wine fast and lighting up a street so you don't trip over the winos. I'm sure wherever you are, you have something like it.

That sort of thing isn't hard—in fact, those are some of the first spells you learn—heat, cool, light, dark, fire. From there, if you want, you can get into sophisticated things that will twist your brain inside out trying to keep track of a million details while the power runs around inside, and if you screw up your brain will dissolve into mush, or maybe you will, but really, no problem.

If you're good at sorcery, you can do things like teleport to anywhere you have a good mental fix on, without the risk of, you know, bad things happening. If you're better at it, you can even do complicated stuff like putting a block around an area so no one can teleport into it or out of it. If you're great at it, you can make things up on the fly, spells no one's ever come up with, and have a fair chance of avoiding disaster.

I'm not great at it, but I can do some stuff.

But this was going to be, well, interesting.

"*Boss, don't kill yourself.*"

"*Isn't this kind of last minute for a change of plans?*"

"*Funny.*"

Matiess was looking at me, and I felt the breeze, kind of cool, on my cheek, and through my hair. The Orb was there, like a water pipe flowing into my head, and I opened it a crack, another crack, out on the street where anyone could walk by—no, don't think about that—the water swirls into me, but it isn't water, because I can direct it, change it, as effortlessly as moving a finger, enveloping me like a cloud, then moving from me to him; I can feel the beating of his heart, his breath, muffled by the layers of clouds that feel more solid than they are—and was something beating down on them?—no, which means this can't be working or I'd have found—

"I feel better," said Matiess, and he was looking puzzled now.

Vlad Taltos: sorcerer.

"What was it?" he asked.

"I don't know," I said. "I'm no sorcerer."

He looked skeptical, but before he could think about it too much, I said, "Let's go in and look around."

He nodded, looking much better, and when we approached the door, he seemed fine. I started to reach for my lockpicks, but caught myself. "You have the key?"

He produced it, dropped it, picked it up, handed it to me. I unlocked it and motioned him inside.

"What is this?" were his first words.

"Alchemy," I said. "In particular, a setup for making perfume."

"And that?" he said, pointing to the other side of the room.

"If I had to guess, it's set up for summoning, or something like that. Something sorcerous, certainly, but I can't say exactly what. Let's see what we can find."

"Is it safe?"

"Of course not. Come on."

I inspected the various basins, tubes, and barrels. I am far from an expert in this, but I know a little bit just from having been around it before.

"Never been used," I said. "It's set up and ready, but they've never done anything."

"It's all pretty clean," said Cawti.

"Yeah, and the barrels are empty. He hasn't gotten whatever it is he needs to process the hishi."

"Probably because he got robbed," said Cawti.

"He did?" said Matiess.

I nodded. "Some street punk took the stuff off him. Stupid move, since your brother was protected. If you get a much bigger score than you expected, there's a good chance you've stepped in something. Good thing to keep in mind if you ever decide to switch professions."

"Vladimir," said Cawti, who'd been continuing to wander around. "Take a look."

"What is it?"

"Hidden door."

"Oh, and a hidden room behind it. Nice."

"What's back there?" Matiess wanted to know.

"A cot, some dried food, a hole for wastes. Pretty deep, too. I'm impressed."

"Why would he have a place like this?"

"He was hiding from me until he could get his business going."

"Oh. What happened? Why was he killed?"

"I'm starting to get an idea," I said.

"Oh?" said Matiess.

"Sorry to tell you, but your brother wasn't all that bright. He had this nice hidey-hole, but whenever he went out—probably to get food or whatever—he kept the hishi on him, instead—"

"The what?"

"Something valuable. He kept it with him instead of leaving it here. I get it, I understand it; you got something that your fortune depends on, you don't like to leave it alone, but it was a mistake."

"How did that get him killed?" his brother wanted to know.

I didn't answer because I was busy trying to work it through, and the implications, and how to test it, and how to use it to get my Verra-be-damned eight hundred gold.

We spent some more time looking in corners and under things to see if we'd missed anything. I mean, aside from not knowing exactly what the big silver circle and various marks on the floor meant.

We finally decided we'd gotten what we could and headed out. Or, rather, we were about to head out. I had just opened the door, when Cawti said, "Wait a minute."

Loiosh and Matiess were already outside, and I was in the doorway. I looked back, and Cawti was staring at something. I looked where she was looking, and didn't see anything except floor.

"What is it?"

In answer, she walked over to the far corner and pointed toward the wooden flooring. "Look there."

The flooring consisted of the usual long slats you see in places like that, only one spot wasn't even.

"How did you even spot that?" I asked her.

"A flicker of light from the lamp across the street hit it when you opened the door."

"Good eyes."

We knelt down. It didn't take long to find the latch. I pulled the door up. It was either going to be a ladder down to a tunnel, or a hidey-hole. It was a hidey hole, and it wasn't empty.

"Well," said Cawti. "Will you look at that."

"A Verra's tear, a vial of something—Dark Water, if I had to guess—and a plain glass—or is it crystal? Yeah, a crystal rod that I'm sure has nothing whatever magical about it and isn't at all dangerous, trust me, and one of those little purple stones Aliera loves to play with."

"Yeah," she said. "Like, everything you could want to, I dunno, summon a demon? Cross to another world?"

I bent over and reached for the glass tube in the hidey hole.

"*Boss—*"

"*If I die, you can eat the Tsalmoth.*"

I picked it up.

I didn't die.

"What is it, Vlad?" asked Cawti.

"I don't want to say."

"What—"

"If I tell you what I'm seeing, and it isn't there, then I'm out of my head."

I handed her the rod. "Hold this and tell me what you see."

She did. "Oh," she said. "Silvery lines, running from the corners of the room to the circle on the floor, and—"

"And?"

"Another diagram, also silver, painted onto the floor as part of the first one."

"Good. Then I'm not crazy."

"Let's not jump to—"

"Shut up."

"What's going on?" said Matiess.

"We know why they wanted to keep you out, anyway. This is where they do the exchanges. Or are planning to do the exchanges. Or used to do the exchanges." I considered. "Planning to, I think, since they haven't done the hishi extraction."

"What exchanges?" he wanted to know.

"Uh, they're doing trades with demons. I'm sorry, I guess they aren't actually demons."

"If this is the place," he said, "Then why aren't they guarding it?"

"They are. Remember the spell that made you want to run?"

"Oh, right. I was trying to forget that."

"Don't blame you."

"So," said Cawti. "This is where they plan to do it. Right in the middle of the city."

I nodded. "I know. You'd think they'd find some nice castle tower for that sort of thing."

"Not enough castles nearby, I guess."

"After we're married, should we get a castle?"

"What would we do with it?"

"Necromantic rituals in a tower?"

Matiess was looking back and forth between us like we were mad, which I suppose we kind of were.

"So, what's the play?" said Cawti. "Wait here and see if something happens?"

"I was thinking I'd walk out the door and see if we're attacked, or followed. Or," I said, and glanced at Matiess. He had his nervous look back. I thought about warning him that if he kept it, it would settle on him permanently, but decided that wouldn't be helpful.

"Hmmm?" said Cawti.

"We know he's had a spell put on him. If I understand what I did—which I admit is only about fifty-fifty, then if I release it, it will take effect again."

Matiess said, "Can't you just fix it?"

"I don't have the skill. I can block it, but I can't fix it."

"What should I do?" he asked. "If I own this building, I'll need to be able to go in, at least to sell it. And if anyone else wants to see it—"

"Yeah, I get it."

"So what are you going to do?"

"We're going to figure out who's doing it, and why, and thwart them."

"Thwart them?" said Cawti.

I nodded.

"So," she said, "is it time to have another talk with our confederates?"

"Our which?"

"You know what 'thwart' means but not 'confederates'?"

"The guy said 'thwart' in *The Empty Room*, remember?"

"Oh, right. Confederates: the people we're working with. Maybe talk with them and see how much they know?"

"Yeah, them," I said.

"Who are you working with?" Matiess wanted to know.

"People," I said.

"Confederates," added Cawti.

"In any case," I said. "We have some ideas about who's doing this."

"We do?"

I nodded. "To do something like this with sorcery means we're dealing with someone who's very, very good. And we already know the Left Hand is involved, somewhere, with some of it. I'm tired of this. It's time to get some answers."

I'd expected an argument from Loiosh and Cawti, but Loiosh didn't say anything, and Cawti just said, "All right."

Matiess continued looking worried.

We stood up again, and headed for the door. We didn't make it out that time, either; this time it was because someone was thinking about me in the particularly demanding way that's kind of like a headache with no pain, if you can make sense of that.

I held up my hand, and they waited while I had a conversation inside my head, which I like to say because it makes it sound weird, and it's magic, right, so why not sound weird?

"Hey Vlad."

"Kragar. What's up? I know you didn't get my answer already."

"Yeah, how do you know that?"

"Kragar, what's—"

"Because I did, and I think you're gonna like it."

"How'd you get it so fast?"

"I'm very good, Vlad. Also, lucky. They gathered at a place called The Sleepy Eye, started telling stories, and, well, like the second story was it."

"Nice. Okay, let's hear it."

"This is going to take some explanation. Uh, where are you?"

"Half an hour east of you."

"Why do Easterners always answer distance questions with time?"

"We're practical people. Except for me, I'm romantic."

"Right. I'll meet you at The Flame."

"No, I'll come to the office. I'll have someone with me. A Tsalmoth. The brother. I'm protecting him."

"From what?"

"His imagination."

"See you in a while, Vlad."

I gave Cawti the short version as we walked. Matiess didn't seem to especially listen, or maybe he was afraid if he heard something he wasn't supposed to, I'd have him "shined like a new copper," as someone once said. These guys, I tell you, between the stories, and the theater, and, well, reality I suppose, they're so scared of us most of the time we don't have to do anything.

Okay, not fair—the guy's brother was dead, after all, and he'd had a spell cast on him. I guess he had more reasons to be nervous than most.

I nodded to Melestav and said, "This is Matiess. He's going to hang around for a bit while I talk to Kragar."

Melestav nodded, Kragar said, "I'm here," and Matiess jumped and I managed not to chuckle, but it was nice seeing someone else get the Kragar Effect once in a while. The Kragar Effect. I like that. I gotta remember that.

I pointed Matiess to a chair and went into my office with Kragar and Cawti, who shut the door behind her.

"Okay," I said. "Let's have it."

"Fisher," said Kragar. "From what I can pick up, people mostly liked him. Did his job, stayed out of things that didn't concern him, earned for his bosses, played fair with his partners."

I waited, listened.

"He had a pet cat, since adopted by one of his partners. He—"

"I didn't see a cat there."

"I smelled it, Boss. It was hiding."

"Sorry," I told Kragar. "You were saying?"

"He also collected sea shells. He—"

"Kragar."

"Hey, how do you know none of this is relevant?"

"The look on your face. Get to it."

He smirked. "Guy used to be a Tsalmoth."

"He didn't look like it."

"True though."

"Kicked out?"

"Don't know. From the story I heard, he said he just got bored, but he could have been lying."

"What? People lie?"

He rolled his eyes.

"Yeah," I went on. "Anyway, that gives us the connection, all right. Any relation to Bereth or Matiess?"

"I'm checking on that."

I nodded. "Nice work."

I found a few imperials and slid them across the desk before he could slyly figure out a way to ask for a bonus. I did it just to annoy him. He took them and headed out, crushed and defeated. Okay, I made up that last part.

"Now what?" said Cawti.

I started to consider my options, when I caught the look in her eye. It was starting to get kinda late, and we'd put in a long, long day. "Your place?" I said.

On the way out, I nodded to Melestav. "Find someone to escort this guy back to his house."

To Matiess, I said, "You should be okay now. Stay in your house until tomorrow. By then, we'll have this settled."

"Are you sure?"

"Count on it," I said.

"Thanks."

"*Eight hundred and forty-two and a half,*" said Loiosh.

The next morning Adrilankha was chilly, with a breeze coming off the sea. I don't usually notice the weather unless it has some obvious effect on things, like, making the ground slippery so I have to be careful if I'm planning to, uh, walk somewhere. And that day, it didn't have any effect at all, but I remember it, so I'm telling you. I guess it was the way Cawti's cloak sort of whipped back from the wind, and the way she drew it back around her because of the chill. There was something about the way she did that that put a lump in my throat, so I coughed and asked where she wanted to go for breakfast.

She knew a place, she said. We took ourselves across the Stone Bridge to South Adrilankha—by which time we were starving—and found a place that did an Eastern-style breakfast. We had palaczintok with various things rolled up in them, like orange marmalade or cinnamon, and some truly outstanding klava. It was an odd place, run by a tiny sect of Easterners who dressed in strange flowered blouses and skirts outfitted with ribbons and weird things decorating them. Cawti explained that a group of these people had left Fenario over a thousand years ago, and dressed and lived the way they had then, and wouldn't go near sorcery even when they could afford it, and only permitted certain kinds of witchcraft. I made a note in my head to ask my grandfather if he knew anything about them. I dunno. They cooked good.

After, we took our time going back over the bridge, talking about stuff. Like how odd it was that we both preferred the City itself to South Adrilankha, but we both felt a little more at ease on the eastern side.

Once we were in the City again, it was back to work. We hadn't talked about it at breakfast, but now she said, "So, what's our next move?" just as I'd been wondering that.

"It isn't," I said, "that we don't know what everyone's up to, as much as it is we don't even know how many players there are."

"So, how do we find out?"

"Stir things up and see who comes at us?"

"Sure. Old and reliable."

"Then let's start stirring," I said. "First stop, our good and trusty friends of the Left Hand."

"And when we get there?"

"We start asking questions."

"And if we don't get answers?"

"We start telling lies."

"Works for me."

It was afternoon before we made it there; in case you've never been there, the City is big, and the walk from the Stone Bridge to the Highroad District takes a while.

We approached the house, and were halfway up the walk when the younger sorceress, who'd never told me her name, came walking out the door to meet us and said, "What is it?"

I said. "I have some information for you."

"You could have left a note."

I just waited, and eventually she said, "All right. Lady Shireth will see you."

Ah *ha!* I knew it was Lady Shireth. I felt unreasonably smug.

She guided us in, showed us to the same room we'd been in before, with the same group, and we sat in the same chairs, and I felt the same nervousness.

Nice to have some things that don't change, right?

I said, "Thank you for seeing us," all polite like that.

She nodded in response and said, "You've learned something?"

I nodded.

"Let's hear it, then."

"You know, I really come here for the charming small talk."

She waited.

Hey, I wasn't *just* cracking wise. One of the things to remember if you're going to lie is not to seem too eager to get it out, so you start with other stuff. Also, asking questions is good, because it makes you seem less eager with the lies, and because, hey, you might even get answers. "All right," I said. "When is the last time you spoke with Toronnan?"

"Who?"

"Don't even," I said. "I don't have time for that. I've eight hundred in this, and I want it back, and that may be nothing compared to what you and Toronnan have going with the House of the Tsalmoth, but it's a lot to me. Now when is the last time you spoke with him?"

She hesitated, looked at me, and shrugged. "Three days ago."

"And did the name Fisher come up in the conversation?"

"Why?"

"Because I'm pretty sure I know who killed him and why, and it will give me great pleasure if I can tell you it's all your fault."

"No, his name never came up."

"Ah. Too bad."

"Sorry to disappoint."

"Well, in any case, I think I know who had Fisher killed and why."

"Toronnan?"

I nodded.

"All right," she said. "Why?"

"Why do I think so, or why did he have him killed?"

"Let's go with both," she said.

"How about this: I give you both answers, and in return you take the spell off that building so the guy who owns it now can go in there without getting the sweats."

That seemed to have startled her a little. "How do you know about that place?"

"The guy who owns it now brought us there. The spells worked on him, but not on us. Witchcraft would have worked better. So we went in, looked around, found the setup and the summoning area. So, you take that spell down, and I'll answer your questions."

She hesitated, then nodded. "Agreed. Now, how do you know Toronnan had Fisher killed?"

"Because you had no reason to, after all the work you'd done to prepare him for your big necromantic deal. And no one else in the Jhereg would have. Because that's how the Jhereg—that is to say, the Right Hand, works. You don't put the steel to someone who works for a boss without the boss's permission. People who do that get, uh, talked about. So either Toronnan had him done, or he at least gave permission. I mean, it could have come from someone higher up, but I haven't seen anything to indicate Fisher had any connections or was working with anyone in the Jhereg higher than Toronnan, so I doubt it."

"Fair enough," she said. "So, why did Toronnan have Fisher killed?"

"Fisher got greedy."

You know, now that I think about it, ninety-nine times out of a hundred, the answer to, "why did so-and-so get shined?" is, "he got greedy." But I just had that thought. At the time, I explained more. I said, "The best I can put it together, Bereth got robbed of his hishi by some street punk, probably an Orca. He complained to Toronnan, who put Fisher on the job of finding it. Fisher found it, but decided to keep it for himself—or rather, for certain other parties. Pretty sure he put the shine on Bereth so Toronnan wouldn't find out, but it didn't work."

"Certain other parties," she repeated. "Who?"

That gave the opening to launch into the lie, and, not to brag, but I think I was pretty smooth about it. "I know people," I said.

"Yes, we know."

"Some of these people have, let's say, fingers, inside of your organization, as I have no doubt you know people with fingers inside of mine."

"Well?"

"My people found signs that you have a rival."

"A rival?"

"Your organization? The Jhereg? What we call the Left Hand? You know, you? There's another group of you out there somewhere, and Fisher was working with them."

She still wasn't showing anything, but she studied me. "Interesting," she said after a while, which I thought was interesting.

I nodded. "You may want to look into that."

She nodded.

"Or," I said, "I could look into it for you."

"Seems you already have."

I shrugged. "Sometimes you get information you weren't looking for, and it's worth more than what you thought you were trying to find. You ever have that happen?"

"Sometimes."

I nodded, and the two of us settled in to outwait each other. It's kind of a power game, I guess.

I won.

"So, if that's all—"

"Are you going to look into it, or do you want me to?"

"I will."

"Good enough," I said.

We made it back to the street without being dissolved into mush or whatever, which still felt like an accomplishment.

"Nice work," said Cawti.

"You caught that?"

She did that thing where she tilted her head down and looked up at me.

"Right," I said. "Sorry."

She nodded. "If there weren't another group, or if they didn't know who it was, they'd have at least wanted more information on our source."

"Yeah."

"So we know they exist," she said. "And we can be pretty confident Fisher was working with them."

"Fisher was in between. Whoever this other group was, they had Fisher on their side, but Shireth and her group were the ones who planted the Verra's tear in his house, so he was either playing one side against the other, or, more likely, he was being used by Shireth."

"Why more likely?"

"I guess because I believed Fisher when he denied knowing anything about the Verra's tear, and because of some of his hesitations, where it looked like he was just figuring things out."

"I can accept that," she said.

"So we can be pretty sure there is some other mysterious group of Left Hand sorceresses, and they were working with Fisher, and they might or might not have something to do with the Tsalmoth Heir."

She nodded. "I propose we find them."

"I love how you talk."

"And what I say?"

"Yeah, that too."

She looped her arm through mine. "You should read more."

"Uh."

"After we're married, I'll read to you."

"Okay, that sounds good. Speaking of marriage, what are we going to do about the invocation?"

"Invoke?"

"What if she shows up?"

"We'll offer her cake."

"And if she doesn't like cake?"

"She can fuck off."

"Sounds reasonable."

We strolled, arms linked, and chatted about our upcoming wedding and how to figure out who to kill and stuff like that. Then we switched sides. You gotta take turns with whose weapon arm is free. But I guess everyone does that.

"I don't know how to find them," I said. "But I know how to start looking."

"Toronnan?"

I nodded.

"Tricky," she said. "He's kind of your boss. We'll have to be sneaky about it."

"Sneaky? I can be sneaky. Once, in the Halls of Judgment, I was devious."

"Sneaky it is, then."

"For starters, let's stealthily sneak to a stinky stable."

"Is it really sneaky if we just walk up to him?"

"If we're sneaky enough," I said.

"And," said Cawti, being the practical one, "what do we do when we get there?"

"Yeah, that."

"Do you have something in mind?"

"Sort of," I said. "I want to give him two choices he hates in the hopes he takes a third."

"But you don't know how you're going to pull that off."

"We can figure that out on the way."

"Walk into a potentially lethal situation without a plan? When have we ever done that?"

"See, like, you said 'potentially lethal.' I love that."

I felt her smile more than saw it.

"*Sometimes we jhereg throw up on our food to make sure no one else wants it. So if I suddenly vomit, that doesn't mean—*"

"*Shut up,*" I said.

12

THE PARADE

Who doesn't love a parade?

I don't, for one. Walking isn't my favorite thing, and watching other people walk isn't a lot better. It's one part of the Fenarian wedding tradition we didn't even have to think about. Besides, we were going to do a sort of parade anyway between the wedding and the reception, which was enough of that. But if you're curious, the idea is that three days before the wedding, the bride and groom and attendants and whoever else wants to all march through the street wearing all sorts of finery and making as much noise as possible. Noish-pa says that the tradition comes from making sure everyone knows these two are going to get married, so anyone who has an objection can say so early. That part—giving anyone who wants a chance to object—happens in a lot of marriage ceremonies, mostly different. The Chreotha, I'm told, have a thing where they go around the room and each person has to say yes or no to the wedding. You'd think it'd take forever, but that's what I've heard. I don't believe everything I hear.

⤜⤛

This time, the tough guys just nodded and let me past to see Toronnan without comment. I figured they were being polite to Cawti.

Toronnan looked up as we entered. It came to mind how easy it'd be to kill him right then and there. Also, how stupid it would be, since we'd have no chance of getting out alive.

"What," he said. He's good with conversation.

Every boss is different. Some of them need to keep reminding you how scary they are, or how important. Some of them just expect you to be loyal because of how much you're earning, or maybe because they treat you well. Some of them will give you the cold stare if you say something that might even hint at being disrespectful, some of them have a sense of humor. Toronnan, I guess, was somewhere in the middle of those, except about the sense of humor. I think he had it surgically removed. I dunno. Can physickers do that? Wouldn't surprise me.

The point is, your boss is pretty important to you. Like, how much you earn, how easy or hard you have to work, and once in a while, maybe, how likely you are to stay alive. And since sometimes you gotta get him to agree to things, or maybe even you need some information from him, you have to know what he likes, doesn't like, and how to approach him. He doesn't need to know any of that about you. That's what being a boss is, right?

I mean, I'm a boss too, I guess, at a low level, and I do try to keep aware of what people don't like, and all that, but that's because you can get more out of them that way. But that's off the subject. Sorry, get me talking and sometimes I don't know where to stop. What was it I was talking about?

Oh, right. Toronnan. So, kind of small, kept everything around him neat and organized, and a bit of an asshole. But who isn't?

"Here's the thing," I said. "I'm trying to work out this eight hundred gold I'm owed, and I was looking into Fisher, and then somebody put a shine on him, and I'm wondering if that was my fault, so I thought I'd come to you."

Just so you're clear, no, I knew it wasn't my fault. I was doing that thing where you say something you know isn't true. We call it lying. It's a useful skill because if you do it right, it can get you out of more jams than it gets you into. Barely.

Toronnan squinted at me, like he might have suspected I was playing him, though I don't know where he could have gotten an idea like that. He drummed his fingers on his desk. He was trying to decide which lie to tell me, how much information to give me, or if he should make me "gleam in the candlelight" as one wag put it.

Then he turned to Cawti and said, "You're the Dagger, right?"

She nodded.

"I'd heard you'd connected up with this guy."

She nodded again.

"I also heard you were out of the business."

"No, I still take a few jobs now and then."

"If you're interested, I could make it worth your while."

"I'm not going to send Vlad to the River. It would put too big a strain on our marriage."

"Okay, that's out, then."

"Sorry."

"You guys are funny," I said, meaning they weren't. Although I gotta admit, they kinda were. And here I was just saying he had no sense of humor.

Toronnan shifted his eyes back to me.

"What do you want to know?" he asked me.

I coughed. "I was just worried that—"

"Stop. Don't. What do you want to know?"

A few answers came to mind, like, *how to get my fucking eight hundred imperials, you asshole,* but I kept those sorts of answers to myself because it seemed like the smart choice.

"Who in the Left Hand are you working with to do the hishi deal?"

That got me the Hard Stare. Hey, I knew I was taking a chance, but since the bastard was seeing through my game like a Verra-be-damned Athyra, I figured playing straight was the least risky choice I had. And since I knew the answer already, or at least I was pretty sure I did, that'd give me a way to see just how straight he was going to play it with me.

When he felt the stare had gone on long enough to make his point, he said, "If I give you the eight hundred, will you drop this?"

"Yeah," I said.

"What if I give you six hundred?"

"I'll drop three quarters of it."

His face twitched a little, like it was almost worth a smile but not quite.

"What if I just tell you to drop it."

"Then I'll drop it."

"I could have told you that once before."

"Maybe you did and I forgot. I have a very bad memory."

"I'm thinking of ways to improve it."

"Eight hundred imperials would work."

He went back to the Hard Stare, I guess because he couldn't think of what to say. I'm not blaming him; I do that, too. Eventually he said, "Just what are you expecting me to do, anyway? Short of just giving you eight hundred imperials."

Well, I mean, that's what I'd been hoping for. He could afford it better than I could. But he'd made it my turn to draw cards, so now I had to think. The best I could come up with was to just stand there not saying anything and see if I could make it his turn again with committing to anything.

You have to understand, I knew he didn't want to just shine me out of hand. For one thing, I was a good earner for him, and for another, that sort of thing gets you a bad reputation that makes it harder to find good people, especially as by now word was probably getting around about Fisher, and for yet a third, it was liable to cost him more than the eight hundred. If I pushed him far enough, yeah, he might shut my door, but—

Shut my door? Uh, you know, send me to the River? Deliver me a rock garden? Have me worked on? Ask me to kiss the street? Thrill my heir? Cool me down a little? Tell me the last secret? Make me a statue?

Kill me, okay?

So he wanted to find a way to make me stop doing what I was going to do unless he paid me or killed me without paying me or killing me. You follow that? I waited while he thought it over, and my plan worked because he finally spoke.

"Okay," he said. "I'm going to bring you inside, because everything else I can do is worse, but I'm not happy about it."

That was a good time to not let my wit out to play, so I just nodded.

He called out for a chair, and one was brought in. There'd been one already, in addition to the one he was sitting in.

"Sit down," he said. "Both of you."

I tried to remember if he ever had me sit before. I didn't think so. We sat.

"I got an offer from a sorceress, Left Hand, named Shireth, to get in on a good thing early."

"Let me guess," I said. "Selling hishi to demons."

He didn't seem surprised that I knew. "You make it sound so vile," he said. "Like selling flashstones to East—" He broke off and coughed. "Anyway, yeah."

And no, before you ask, I've never had anyone try to sell me a flashstone. Never even seen one. As far as I know, they haven't been used since the Interregnum.

"So," I said, "how'd Fisher get involved in the whole thing?"

"He's the one who brought it to me, the sonofabitch."

"Wait, what?"

"He was hanging around here when this Bereth showed and said he'd been robbed in my area, and Fisher said he'd take care of it."

I laughed. I couldn't help it. My boss glared at me. "All right, what's the joke?"

"It's on Fisher," I said. "Poor, dumb asshole."

He looked like he was getting annoyed. "Maybe you'd better explain."

"Okay, there's some third party we don't know about yet."

"How—" He cut himself off again and just listened.

"This third party—call him or her Slick—Slick wants in on this demon deal, and there's some connection somewhere between Slick and Fisher. So Slick has Fisher get hold of the hishi, since it sort of fell into his hands. Which is the funny part—hishi isn't all that hard to come by, and if he'd played straight with you instead of wanting to save a few hundred imperials, this never would have happened."

"I'm lost."

"My fault, I got diverted. So, the thing is, Fisher gets pulled into this by Slick, gets you to have him recover the hishi, and since he's now right there in the middle between you and Shireth, she figures he's the obvious go-between with the demons, or the beings, I guess they aren't really demons, and so she—I mean Shireth—has someone plant a Verra's tear in his house, to sort of prepare him for necromantic travel. With me so far?"

"Kind of," he said. "Shireth said something about needing someone 'it would work on,' so I guess that makes sense. She didn't tell me she was using Fisher."

I nodded. I guess I was someone it worked on. Whoopee.

"So," I continued, "Fisher was worried that Bereth, since he'd come to you in the first place, might come to you again, and you might find out that he—I mean Fisher—had taken the hishi for himself. So he drops Bereth, and that's what brings me into it. But of course, you find out anyway, right? And you arrange for Fisher to have, you know, an accident."

"Accident? Fuck that. I had the sonofabitch killed."

"Um, yeah. I meant—Right."

"This Slick," he said. "I had the feeling there was someone else playing with this. That's why I brought you in. I want to know who it is, and what this individual is up to, and from what I've heard, you're good at finding things out."

"I might have some ideas on where to start looking," I said.

He nodded. If he had a suspicion that I knew more than just where to look, he kept it to himself. He just said, "Unless you got questions, that's it."

Questions? Yeah, I had questions. Just not many that I wanted to ask him outright. I did have one or two, though. "How long was Fisher working for you?"

"Uh. Around a hundred and fifty years, I guess. Ever since he joined. I sold him the title, and he started working for me right then."

"Yeah," I said. "He used to be Tsalmoth, right?"

My boss nodded.

"So, did you ever hear why he left?"

"I never asked," said Toronnan.

"Well," I said. "Okay. I don't have any more questions, then."

Cawti had one, though. "Tell me something, lord," she said, and I wondered if he knew just how far she was going to be polite.

"What's that?"

"If this is so valuable, and you were so worried about us messing around that you've finally explained it, why didn't you give Vlad the eight hundred the first time he asked?"

He tilted his head and his mouth twitched.

"Because I was thinking," said Cawti, "that the first time he came to see you, you came up with the idea of having him look into it, without paying him anything, just by telling him a few little lies. Could that be it, lord?"

My face might have gotten a little red, but only a little.

Toronnan studied her for a minute, then said, "If that's all, I got things to get back to."

I stood and bowed, because that's what you do when you leave your boss; Cawti bowed, I think, out of respect for a good stroke.

"I can't believe that worked," she said once we were out on the street.

I'd been about to say that, so instead I said, "I never doubted."

"You lie like an Orca."

"Is that an expression?"

"It is now."

"I like it."

A little later she said, "So, how do we find Slick?"

So I told her my idea, and it was a good idea but it didn't work, and I am *not* going to tell you about the next two Verra-be-damned days of running around and gathering crap and bringing it to people because if I do I'll just get annoyed all over again.

My idea was to summon Fisher's spirit, and ask him. It should have worked, especially because we had help from the Necromancer, and because Fisher had been living with the Verra's tear, so it should have made it easier, but the Necromancer just said, "Sometimes they won't show up, and there's nothing you can do."

But it was a good idea.

And it didn't work.

And that's all I'm going to say about it.

We were in my flat, doing dishes after eating up a reasonable portion of a cow that nobly gave his life for us. We had mushrooms and onion and garlic sauteed in butter with the cow.

"All right, Vladimir," she said. "We have eaten, we are cleaning, how do we figure out who Slick is?"

"I should have come up with a better name."

"We're stuck with it now."

"I guess so."

"So how do we find this Slick person?"

I thought about it, then I said, "We're seeing shadows of Slick, right? I mean, we're seeing the results of what Slick has done. So let's figure out what it would take to cast that kind of shadow."

"All right, that sounds good. What do we know?"

I almost dropped a plate, caught it elegantly, held it up triumphantly, and Cawti stopped long enough to applaud. I bowed.

"Slick," she said, "has a connection with Fisher that goes way back, before Fisher became a Jhereg."

"Which means," I added, "that Slick might be a Tsalmoth."

"A Tsalmoth who left the House around a century and a half ago?"

"Possible," I said. "Either jumped or was pushed."

"Maybe friends? Lovers? Family? One of them jumped or was pushed, the other went along? We're getting into some deep speculation here, Vladimir."

"I know. I just want to give Kragar something to work with when I send him out after this stuff."

"Poor Kragar," she said.

"Yeah."

"So, back to your office?"

"Afraid so."

"Poor Kragar."

We got back to the office, and "poor Kragar" moaned and whined and scowled and complained and got to work. Then I had a bunch of little crap come up: one of my brothels was changing management because the old manager wanted to strike out on his own, a guy wanted an extension on a loan, details on the new game on Garshos, and a few other things that I had to deal with when I wanted to just run off and spend time with Cawti while we waited to see what Kragar would find.

But I did it 'cause I'm a responsible guy. "That Vlad," they always say . . .

Yeah, okay.

Cawti went off to visit the farmer's market in South Adrilankha. This is, by the way, one of her special skills. She can find the most amazing things: rare and delicious peppers, odd varieties of bean, someone's overgrown tomato. I loved when she went to the farmer's market. We got together in the evening for the mushroom ginger kethna at the Blue Flame because neither of us was in a mood to experiment. Loiosh approved.

I don't talk about it much, I guess because I don't think about it much, but a lot of the time when we go into a place Loiosh slips from my shoulder to inside my cloak so as not to offend any delicate sensibilities. He doesn't mind; he says he likes it there. I think he enjoys the sneakiness of me slipping bits of food to him without anyone knowing. But one thing about the Flame is that we don't have to do that. They know me.

We went back to the office to see if Kragar was ready to report, but he hadn't returned, so we went back to her place.

Kragar was, to be brief, missing the whole next day. And then the day after that. If you know Kragar, you'd know that was a good sign. On the third day, he was in the office when I showed up. Cawti was with me, because we'd just had breakfast. Kragar was looking smug.

"Okay," I said. "Tell me you solved all my problems."

"Nope," he said. "But I got you a whole bunch of new ones."

"Yeah, that seems about right. Let's hear it."

"Tavissa," he said. "Or, as she was once called, Princess Tavissa. Just under two thousand years old, joined the Left Hand about a hundred and fifty years ago, following a dispute within her House about sixty years earlier."

"Tsalmoth, I assume."

He nodded.

"You know," I said. "I know nothing about how Tsalmoth do things. I mean, the internal politics of the House. Why would someone have left? I need to know—" I broke off because Kragar, looking more smug than ever, was pulling a couple pieces of paper out of his jerkin.

I guess if you're good at something, you get to be smug about it once in a while. I get smug about killing people and cooking and stuff like that.

"Succession within the House is hereditary," he said.

I nodded.

"But a scandal within the ruling family takes the entire family out of the running for Heir for at least a full Cycle. And by 'family' that extends to first cousins once removed, but no further." A Cycle, by the way, is a long time, like, maybe a hundred times longer than we poor Easterners can expect to live.

"Scandal," I repeated. "Is this where we get to the good part?"

"Not *that* good. I mean, as scandals go. It isn't the business with the black gloves. Or that thing before the Interregnum with the goblets. Or—"

"Kragar."

"Right."

"And stop enjoying this so much."

"No."

"All right."

"How much do you know about enclosures?"

"Something something land pasture something something," I said.

"Common areas in or around the villages," said Cawti. "Used for grazing, or sometimes for growing small amounts of vegetables for the villagers to share. Sometimes the landlord will give the peasants a one-time payment for it, enclose it in a fence, and make it his own. It never works out well for the peasants."

"Sometimes for the landlord, though," said Kragar.

"Doesn't sound all that scandalous," I said.

"The Empress has the final decision on enclosures."

"That's gotta keep her busy."

"They don't come up that often, and in practice, she just does whatever the Heir wants."

"Okay."

"So—" He stopped and looked at the paper, then looked up. "Lady Chervik—"

"Wait, who?"

"I'm just telling you. Countess Chervik, House of the Tsalmoth, owns property west of the Charis. Like, about a hundred miles west of the West Charis."

He waited, like that was supposed to mean something to me.

"Well?" I said.

He cleared his throat. "Just northeast of Adron's Disaster."

"Oh."

"It's been losing value since the Interregnum."

"Well, yeah."

"Mortgages on the mortgages."

"Okay."

"She wanted to enclose some of her commons, but the Tsalmoth Heir said no."

"All right."

"The Tsalmoth Heir was Princess Tavissa."

"Ah ha!"

He smiled. "See, Vlad? We got there."

"Good. Keep going."

"Chervik dreamed up a plot worthy of a Yendi. Want the details?"

"Always."

"She found the guy who checks out the enclosures, and offered him a bribe."

"Uh, wait."

"Stay with me. She bribed him to refuse the enclosure, and didn't offer him enough."

"Okay . . ."

"I see where this is going," said Cawti.

"Quit being smarter than me," I said.

"You'd hate that."

"Fair enough. One of you explain it to me."

Cawti said, "The guy—what was his name, Kragar?"

"I don't know."

"All right. Slim. Slim wasn't offered enough, and maybe he was honest anyway, so he at once runs to Princess Tavissa."

Kragar nodded.

"She, being a responsible Heir, at once orders an investigation into the bribe."

"Okay," I said.

"Meanwhile, Chervik is running to the scandal sheets and making a big stink about how she's being persecuted by the Heir."

"Can't have been that big a stink," I said. "I never heard about it."

"First," said Kragar, "it was, like, over two hundred years ago."

"Okay, point."

"Second, being surprised that you didn't hear about scandals within the Great Houses would be like a peasant in Guinchen not knowing what the daily special is at Valabar's."

"Valabar's doesn't have daily specials."

"How many peasants in Guinchen know that?"

"How many peasants in Guinchen have you met?"

"You were saying," said Cawti, trying to keep the smile out of her voice, "she made a big stink about being persecuted by the Heir."

Kragar nodded. "And it was obviously not true, because everyone knew that Chervik *wanted* the enclosures, so, 'everyone knew' the Heir was making up false charges, and next thing you know, Tavissa is no longer Heir."

"Nothing was established?" I asked.

"Didn't have to be," said Kragar. "An accusation is as good as a conviction in some circles."

"What would the Iorich say?"

"And after she was removed as Heir," said Cawti, "she resigned from the House and joined the Jhereg?"

Kragar nodded.

"Elegant," I said.

"There's more," said Kragar.

"All right."

"After she joined the Jhereg, Tavissa started looking into how it all happened."

"Oh, excellent. And she found out, of course."

"Uh huh. She put it all together with the guy—what were we calling him? Slim. He left the House too, changed his name, and joined the Jhereg."

"Oh," said Cawti, who's faster than I am.

I looked at her.

"Fisher," she said.

Kragar nodded.

"Well, damn," I suggested.

"Complications," said Kragar. "But I know you like those."

"Shut up."

He looked smug.

I like to reach into my desk, find a purse, or a few coins, and toss them over like it's no big deal, but this time I opened up the strongbox in the bottom drawer, pulled out some coins, and very carefully counted out twenty imperials in front of Kragar, one at a time, slowly.

"Good work," I told him.

"Thanks, boss," he said.

"*Eight hundred and sixty-two and a half,*" said Loiosh.

"*Where did you learn to count, anyway?*"

"*Taking my cut from your meals. Counting each grain of rice.*"

There are questions I should know better than to ask.

"That explains a lot about what happened when we visited Her Highness," said Cawti.

I nodded. "Especially if Tavissa is working to implicate Chervik."

"Which would mean it's working," said Cawti.

"Do we care?" said Kragar. "I mean, if this Tavissa gets Chervik in trouble with the Empire, so what?"

"We don't care," I said, "except that the more we know, the better my chances of getting my eight hundred back."

"Can we guess what her plan is?" said Cawti.

"I don't know. She's had a long time to plan it and put it into operation. Gonna be tough to figure it all out."

"There are," I said, "too many things we don't know. How did Shireth first get onto this deal? How did Tavissa? What is the connection? And of course, where is Tavissa? Is she someone we already know? One of those sorceresses of Shireth's hiding in plain sight? I mean, I doubt it, but it's possible."

"One thing we know," said Cawti, "is that there are two Left Hand factions working against each other."

"So," said Kragar. "Who do you help?"

"Whoever will pay me eight hundred gold."

"Maybe neither will."

"Or maybe both will, and they'll have a bidding war."

No one thought that was as funny as I did. After a moment, I said, "Okay, let's lay the whole thing out."

"Will there be diagrams?" was what Kragar wanted to know.

I made a suggestion as to where the diagram would be drawn and with what.

"So here it is, as far as I can tell," I said. "We have two intersecting chains of events. The first one is Chervik trying to hold onto her land and avoid surrender of debts, the second is the Left Hand trying to—and I'm still having a little trouble with this—the Left Hand trying to set up a trade with, what do we call them? I'm told they aren't demons. Uh, people from another world? So, yeah, Chervik and her debts, Shireth and the trade deal, is what is going on."

"It sounds a lot simpler when you put it that way," said Cawti.

"Oversimplifying and peppered kethna dumplings are my specialties."

"I can think of others," said Cawti.

"To get into the details," I said, "we have Chervik doing the dirt on Tavissa, she's removed as Heir, quits the House, joins the Left Hand. Then—"

"Wait," said Cawti. She was frowning.

"What?"

"Do we have any reason to believe Tavissa is a skilled sorceress?"

"There's that sixty years," said Kragar, "between when she left the Tsalmoth and when she joined the Jhereg. You could learn a lot of sorcery in sixty years if you devoted yourself to it."

"Yeah, that's possible," I said.

"Necromancy?" said Kragar. "Like, could she have been the impetus behind all of this from the beginning?"

I looked at him, at Cawti. "Okay, add that to the list of things we need to find out," I said. "How is her skill in sorcery in general and necromancy in particular."

"We don't even know where she lives," said Kragar.

"You didn't find her?"

"I found out *about* her. But she's done a good job of vanishing. No one has seen her in forty years."

"Where was she forty years ago?"

"Zerika's Point."

"So, she could still be there."

"Unlikely. She had a manor there that was destroyed during the Blackrock Rebellion, and it looks like she left the area."

I nodded as if I knew all about the Blackrock Rebellion.

"And no sight of her since then," I said, mostly to myself. Forty years of staying out of sight. Why? Plotting? Preparing? If I barged back into the House of the Tsalmoth and confronted Chervik, would I be able to get any information out of her? I doubted it and didn't feel at all inclined to try.

"Okay," I said finally. "Let's set that aside for now. I want to focus on this deal with a demonic world."

"You should be better equipped for that now," said Cawti.

"What?" said Kragar.

"Uh, never mind. But you're right. Maybe."

"Now I'm *really* curious," said Kragar.

"How much do you know about necromancy?" I asked him.

"Nothing."

"Demonology?"

"Less."

"Then never mind."

"Huh. Thanks."

But it did bring up the question of timing. If Cawti was right, it was a little much to put on coincidence that I'd stumbled onto the skill I needed just when I needed it. Someone more paranoid than me might suspect the hand of a certain goddess in this. Ever had one of those things where you kinda think something is going on, but you're not sure, and you flip back and forth about whether you're imagining it? It was like that. *Could* this all be my Demon Goddess setting me up for reasons of her own? I suppose, but why? Also, well, I went and stole a powerful necromantic artifact, and it did powerful necromantic things; doesn't take a conspiracy to make sense of that.

Does it?

No, it doesn't.

"What are you thinking about?" Cawti wanted to know.

"Divine conspiracies and whether I believe in them," I said.

"Any conclusions yet?"

"Not so far."

"So," she said, "we might as well get back to work on getting my four hundred gold back."

"What?" said Kragar.

I didn't explain. Instead I held up a finger, closed my eyes, and concentrated on Morrolan.

"*Vlad?*"

"*Yeah, just got a question.*"

"*Can it wait? I'm in the middle of something.*"

"*Sure.*"

Huh.

"What was that?" said Cawti.

"Nothing useful," I said. "So back to work."

The three of us kicked around ideas for a while, until I felt Morrolan's presence in my head. "Hang on a sec," I told them, and relaxed into the contact.

"What is it, Vlad?"

"Just want to know if there's any progress in finding out what happened to me, or how, or who did it."

"We've learned some things, but no real answer."

"What have you got?"

"Pathfinder attempted to locate the source of the spell, and failed."

"Huh. Surprising. I can't imagine Aliera is pleased."

"Not in the least. She got a location just west of Adrilankha, but it was empty. Nothing there, no sign of any spell having been cast. Anything that can fool Pathfinder is, well, I don't know who we're dealing with, but it's someone strong and very, very good."

"Huh. Okay. Anything else?"

"Yes, but I don't understand it yet. We're still working on it. Blackwand, it seems, interfered with the spell. It had its effect on you, but it was intended to do something different, which Blackwand prevented."

"What was it intended to do?"

"That's what we're trying to figure out."

"You know, Morrolan, this is not reassuring."

"Right," he said. *"I keep forgetting that truth is determined by how something makes you feel. You have to keep reminding me of that."*

I used some expressive terms and broke the connection. Cawti looked at my face and said, "Not good?"

"No, it's wonderful," I said. "I've had a lesson in truth."

"And here we thought the day was a failure," she said.

13

WRITING THE VOWS

Then you get to the part where you decide what you're going to promise each other. You'd think it would mention important things, like, who cooks, who cleans up, whose job it is to hide the bodies, stuff like that. Uh, that last was a joke; I've never had to hide a body. Point is, you usually only make promises about remaining faithful, and maybe swearing that you'll stay in love forever, and stuff like that. Noish-pa says that older, traditional vows have things about someone obeying someone. That makes me think no one ever took those vows seriously in the first place.

I wonder, do Yendi make promises to each other when they get married, and if so, does anyone ever expect them to keep any of them? Maybe they just sort of hint at things and it's up to the other to figure out just what the person actually means to do.

Anyway, Cawti and I sat down with Father Farkosh and a bottle of peach brandy and figured some stuff out. We decided that we'd promise to keep loving each other and to work out our problems and all that. That's when Father Farkosh told us that, traditionally, the vows had to rhyme. We looked at each other, and another tradition fell dead on the floor.

Don't know about the vows, but the brandy was good.

❧❧

Kragar stepped out to take care of some things, by which I mean, to do what I pay him to do. I filled Cawti in on the conversation with Morrolan, which I hadn't wanted to do with Kragar there, because I wasn't excited about him knowing what had happened to me.

"So, more waiting," said Cawti. "I mean, on that side. So we need to go at it from another."

"Right," I said. "And I can't help thinking that there's this mysterious spell and we don't know where it came from, and there's this mysterious Tsalmoth, who might or might not be a sorceress, and we don't know where she is."

Cawti nodded. "I see what you're getting at. So we need to find her."

Then she said, "Vlad?" with a kind of urgency that seemed odd. I tried to ask her what was wrong, but I couldn't talk, and then I realized I was staring at a wall that seemed familiar, but wasn't where it should have been; it certainly wasn't in my office.

"Vladimir, are you okay? Can you hear me?"

Right. The wall was the ceiling in the bed-room of my flat. I was in bed—my own bed. How had I gotten here? I tried speaking again, and managed, "What?" but my voice sounded weak and kind of crackly in my ears. Had someone just tried to kill me and almost managed? I checked for pain, and didn't notice any.

I was able to look around. Only Cawti was there, which was a relief. "What happened?" I tried again.

"We were talking, then your eyes rolled up and you passed out."

"How undignified," I managed. "How long?"

"A couple of hours ago. What do you remember?"

"I was telling you about my conversation with Morrolan. No, wait. After that. We were talking about finding Tavissa, and that maybe she'd done the spell."

"What about after that? We were talking about trying to get a spy into Shireth's operation, and see how much she knows about Tavissa."

"Uh. I don't remember that. Good idea, though."

"Thank you."

"Did we figure out how to do it?"

"Vlad, what happened?"

It took me a bit to manage, "I don't know," because I didn't want to say it.

"We need to find out," she said with a kind of finality I couldn't argue with.

"No need to worry," I said, and was happy that my voice sounded stronger. "I'm sure it was just some sort of mystical necromantic event."

Then I wasn't happy, because I suddenly realized that was probably just exactly what it was.

Bugger.

I think Cawti realized it at the same time I did. "We should talk to one of your friends," she said.

"I suppose. Tell me more about this idea of getting a spy into Shireth's operation. Did we discuss any specifics of how to go about it?" I sat up, put my feet on the floor. So far, so good.

"Vlad."

"What." I didn't make it a question.

"Ignoring it won't make it go away."

"You sure? We can try."

"What if it happens again, only this time it happens when someone is trying to do you harm?" When I didn't say anything, she added. "I'm not ready to lose you yet. I'll let you know when I am."

Yeah, she probably would, too.

I tried standing up, and it seemed fine.

"So," I said, "I'm supposed to drop everything and—"

"*Shut up and do what she says, Boss.*"

"*You too?*"

"*Yeah.*"

I think Cawti figured out what Loiosh was telling me, because she just waited.

"Fine," I said. "I'll just—"

At which point, because everything happens at once, I felt Kragar in my mind, and I felt some urgency there, so I held up a finger, and said, "*What?*"

"*Are you okay?*"

"*Still figuring that out.*"

"Damn."

"Wait, what kind of okay? You mean, okay with just having had another fucking thing turn my fucking life inside-fucking-out, or okay like there's something I need to be doing and you want to know if I'm able to do it?"

"That."

"Yeah, I'm okay."

"Then you might want to get back here. We have visitors."

"Who?"

"Some charming ladies wearing black and gray and who say they know you."

"You made up the 'charming' part, right?"

"Yeah."

"On my way," I said. "Entertain them appropriately."

"I don't have enough muscle here."

"Then be nice."

I told Cawti, "That thing I don't want to do has to wait."

"Tell," was all she said.

"The Left Hand just showed up at my office."

She stood. "Then let's go."

We didn't talk during the short walk from my flat to the office, but I could tell she was worried. I wasn't used to people being worried about me. It was weird.

When we got there, there were three of them: the young one I'd first spoken to, and two others I'd seen who hadn't said anything. Shireth wasn't there, but it was still more sorcerous ability than had ever been in that place at one time, and I didn't care for it. Spellbreaker felt heavy around my left wrist.

"Sorry to keep you waiting, ladies," I said. "I was—"

"Where can we talk?" snapped one of them who'd never spoken before. Her voice was too high-pitched for the expression on her face, almost squeaky, but I managed not to laugh. She had a long neck and a complexion as dark as a Hawklord's. I think her squinty eyes were something she did on purpose, but I could be wrong. Like all of them, she seemed to have taken a vow to never have any expression on her face. I don't mind that, except it's hard not to see it as a challenge, know what I mean?

"We could go into my office," I told her. "But the walls are pretty thin here. I do trust my people—I pay them well." I shrugged. "Up to you."

They glanced at each other, and probably had a conversation amongst themselves. I wondered if I'd ever get good enough to be able to hold two different voices in my head at the same time.

"Your office," she squeaked eventually. Then she glanced at Cawti. "Just us," she added.

"Three of you and one of me? I don't think so."

She started to object, then said, "Very well."

I led the way. There were only three chairs, other than mine, and there were five of us, so none of us sat—an awkward little bunch hovering around my desk. The young one closed the door. I was ready for one of them to try throwing a spell at me, but no one did.

"All right," I said. "What is it?"

"What do you know about our activities?"

I wished I'd been sitting, because that would have been a good time to stretch my legs and lock my fingers behind my head while giving them a Kragar-like smirk. Since that wasn't an option, I said, "Well, I've heard rumors that you're interested in money. But that couldn't be true, could it?"

"Lord Taltos," she said, with just enough emphasis on "lord" that I'd almost think she was being, what do you call it, ironic.

I shrugged. "How about we start with you telling me all the stuff you aren't telling me. Okay, some of the stuff."

"Listen, whiskers," she said. "If there's—"

"Whiskers," I repeated. "You people always call us that, but you never think about what it means."

She made her eyebrows go up. Pretty good job of it, too. "It means you have hair growing out of your face?"

"It means a lot of us, like me, do this thing called shaving. Once, maybe twice a week, we take a very sharp piece of steel and slide it over our faces, taking off those whiskers and not cutting ourselves up in the process. Some of us do it ourselves, but there are also professionals who do that for us sometimes. It's a whole cultural thing with us."

"What's your point?"

"We've gotten really, really good at putting very sharp edges on steel, and we know what to do with them when we have them."

"You think you can—"

"'No matter how subtle the wizard . . .'" I said.

"Yeah, I've heard that one. I won't turn my back on you. I came here to get—"

"You came here, to my place of business, and started laying down demands for the sort of information you have no intention of giving me, and were rude about it. What would the Issola say? Either you're a complete idiot, or you're here for something that isn't what you say you're here for."

"You know what bothers me?" she said.

"What?"

"Easterners who think they're both smarter and tougher than they are."

I nodded. "Yeah, that'd be annoying. You know what bothers me?"

"What?"

"Crumbly cheese. I wouldn't care if it didn't taste so good, but it does, and I try to slice it to put it on some bread, and—"

"I should have added," she said, "and think they're funnier than they are."

"*Vladimir?*" said Cawti into my head.

"*Hmm?*"

"*I love you.*"

"*Don't make me cry while I'm trying to be tough.*"

The sorceresses were looking at each other, and having a conversation, I suppose. Probably also with Shireth.

"Fine," she squeaked. "Information for information, then?"

"Sure," I said. "And if you tell me the truth, I'll even do the same, probably."

She must have practiced that glare.

Hey, look, I know I was being a jerk, but I was annoyed with her. And I also knew she was acting under orders, and I doubted the orders were worded like, "Get this information unless he pisses you off."

When she felt like she'd glared enough, she said, "You already know about Lady Tavissa, don't you."

"I know she exists," I said as if I hadn't just learned about her. "I don't know exactly what the relationship is between her organization and yours. Is she trying to cut you out of the deal? Help with the deal? Something else?"

She bit her lip, hesitated, then said, "We aren't sure."

"Huh," I said. "And you were hoping I did?"

She nodded.

"Sorry to disappoint."

"What have you learned of her?"

I dug into my purse, found an imperial, flipped it, caught it, looked at it.

She said, "What—"

"Orb I tell the truth, throne I lie."

She waited.

"I know she was Tsalmoth Heir, left the House in disgrace. Pretty sure she's looking for payback on the current Heir."

Her eyes widened; so that, at least, was something she hadn't known.

"How—"

"No," I said. "Your turn. How skilled is Tavissa as a sorceress?"

She opened her mouth, closed it, and said, "Bide."

Then she was quiet for a long time, like, more than five minutes, which feels like forever when you're just standing there. She was, I figured, asking for detailed instructions.

Eventually she said, "All right. I'm told there is information I can give you."

"Oh, good," I said.

"What was the question you just asked?"

"How skilled is Tavissa as a sorceress?"

"How would we know?"

I waited.

"We speculate," she emphasized that word, "that she has acquired considerable skill in necromancy."

"Yeah," I muttered. "Who would have guessed."

"How did you come by your knowledge about Tavissa's intentions?"

"Dug into her past, put it together. There was a scandal about two hundred years ago. You could have done the same."

She ignored the barb and just nodded.

"Why," I said, "are you the only one talking? Are your friends just here to keep you safe in case us barbaric types get out of hand? They haven't said a word."

They also didn't respond to my pointing that out. She said, "Is that your question?"

"Mmmmm, no," I said. "Never mind. Try this: You said you believe, uh, you *speculate* that Tavissa has some skill in necromancy. Why?"

"Have you heard of the Blackrock uprising?"

"Of course. Zerika's Point, about forty years ago."

"You knew Tavissa was there?"

"Yes."

"We've heard that when her force was defeated, she raised her dead soldiers and had them cover her retreat."

"Oh," I said. "I'd heard she was there; I hadn't heard she was actually involved."

"None of this is certain," she said.

"Isn't raising the dead illegal?"

"Yes. But it's my turn."

"Right. Go ahead."

"Why are you looking for Tavissa?"

"Seriously?"

She waited.

"Because I'm trying to get my eight hundred back, and she's involved in it somehow, and the more I know, the better my chances are."

She nodded. "And why else?"

I started to ask why that wasn't enough, but then I stopped and stared at her. "Well, paint me yellow and call me a lyorn," I said. "Did you have that done to me?"

I felt Cawti looking at me.

"No, but Lady Shireth detected it," said the sorceress.

Cawti spoke into my mind. "*Vlad, is this about . . .*"

"*The demon thing, yeah. They must know about it, and they must suspect Tavissa.*"

"*Well, so did we.*"

"*Our suspicion just got stronger,*" I said.

"My turn again," said the sorceress. "What do you know about Tavissa buying land around Northport a hundred years ago?"

"I know that she did," I said, "because you just told me. Other than that, nothing." I frowned. "You just gave me that for free. You wanted me to know. You want me to find Tavissa for you. Funny, so does my boss. Nice that we all agree on what I should do."

She smiled sweetly. "Your turn to ask a question," she said.

"I hate to admit it," I told her, "but I'm starting to enjoy this. Okay, what is the significance of that thing you just told me, about the land deal."

"I have no idea," she said.

Now it was my turn to give the hard stare.

"I really don't," she said. "It was something we uncovered, and it was big, and we have no idea why she wanted it."

"She bought a bunch of land and, what, that's all you know? You don't know what she did with it?"

"Sold it ten years later, for pretty much exactly what she paid for it."

"Huh. Any indication of ore, or something?"

"No."

"Huh," I said again, though I hate repeating myself. Then I said, "Okay, on our side, I mean, the Right Hand, there's a Council, and they keep, uh, I guess you'd call it a slush fund. A huge—I mean, *huge*—amount of gold that they accumulate and split part of among themselves once in a while, but keep most of around in case of emergencies, and they also use it to give loans for investments in, you know, big things that might profit the whole organization. Here's my question. Do you have something like that?"

"Why?" is what she wanted to know.

"Because, if so, and Tavissa has been contributing to it, we might be able to trace her through that. Put pressure on her accountant or something."

She was quiet again. I gotta say it made me uncomfortable to know that she could do psychic communication with someone and show no signs of it. I tried to remember if Sethra closed her eyes when speaking psychically to someone, but I couldn't recall.

Then she nodded and said, "We're checking on that."

"You didn't answer my question."

"That is correct."

I chuckled.

"I can tell you," she said, "that we are not organized the same as you. There is no 'council' to which we have to answer, or anything like it."

"All right."

"But as for the rest, we'll let you know if we find anything."

That brought up more questions than it answered, but I was going to have to content myself with it. "All right," I said. "Do you have any more questions for me, or is the game over?"

"What exactly was done to you by Tavissa's spell?"

"And that," I said, "is the second time—or maybe the third—you've given me information by pretending it was a question. Why is it you want me to know that? Is it to be sure I'm motivated to find her? I was already motivated; that just makes me suspicious."

"You haven't answered my question," she said.

"Good observation."

"Then I guess we're done."

"I guess we are."

My guests left after saying some things that were polite compared to, I don't know, setting my hair on fire or something.

Once they were safely gone, I called out, "Kragar?"

"Yeah?" he said from the corner.

I glared. "Have you been there all this time?"

"Three of them, three of us," he said.

"Hey now," said Loiosh.

"So, what was that spell she was talking about?" he wanted to know.

"A spell."

"Someone cast a spell on you?"

"Let it go."

"Okay. What now, then?"

I turned to Cawti. "I think locating the source of that spell has just become more important."

"What spell?" said Kragar, just to be annoying.

"But Aliera tried that, yes?" said Cawti.

I nodded. "And used Pathfinder, but got a place in the middle of nowhere, with nothing."

"Maybe we should go there and look?"

"You think a couple of Easterners might see something powerful Dragaeran wizards missed?"

"Yes."

"Me, too. Kragar, find us a sorcerer, a good one, and check this whole place over and make sure our guests didn't accidentally cast a spell that would let them listen in or breach our security."

"Right," he said. "I'll have someone check for accidental spells."

"And arrange a teleport for me."

"When?"

"Time enough for us to get to the western edge of the city and back. Let's say, six hours."

"It won't take that long," said Cawti.

"Food."

"Right."

"Where to?" said Kragar.

"Castle Black," I said. "Again. And get Morrolan a message that I'd appreciate it if the Necromancer were around."

"Who?"

"He'll know."

"Vlad, you shouldn't hang around people who go by honorifics instead of names. They always get you in trouble."

"Who go by what?"

"Epithets?"

"Uh."

"Titles?"

"Just go."

"He's right, you know," said Cawti after he'd left. "I mean, about people who go by titles instead of names."

"Yeah, we have some experience with that, don't we?"

"To the left, it's how we met."

"And, uh, didn't you go by, you know, 'the Dagger'?"

She looped her arm into mine. "Yes, and now look where you are."

"True."

"So, edge of the city, then food, then Castle Black?"

"Whatever we find or don't find in the spot, we're probably going to need to talk to the experts about it."

"Will you also ask them about the other thing? The demon thing?"

"All right."

"Thank you."

"Um. I've been assuming you want to come along, but I should ask—"

"Of course I'm coming."

"I'm going to need to reach Aliera, to find out exactly where that spot is. And then she'll know we don't trust what she found out. And then she'll say bad things to me."

"Disdainful things," agreed Cawti.

"I like that word."

In fact, Aliera was only a little disdainful; if I didn't know better, I'd have said she was pleased to have us look over the area in person even though she'd done it herself.

It only took about four hours in total to get there and back, and we didn't get anything—just a big, empty, rocky area just off Lower Kieron Road. But in spite of how much I've been complaining about all the walking, that was a pleasant time, more of a stroll, since we weren't feeling any time pressure. On the way back we found a nice hostel overlooking the ocean-sea where they went down to the shore, brought in oysters, and served them in a cream sauce. Loiosh was very happy. I got cream sauce on my jerkin from feeding him in my cloak. I think that made him happy too.

The walk back to the office was even slower, on account of having eaten too much. It was a little uncomfortable, too, and I wondered if my trousers were going to survive the experience. I regretted nothing.

Kragar pulled in a guy named Narvane we'd used before, who discovered that, in fact, a couple of spells had been planted that could be used to listen in on what was said. We didn't get fancy; he just removed them, and then I had him do the teleport as well since he was there and I trusted him.

All which cost me an even fifty imperials, and I was now up to nine hundred and twelve and a half.

Cawti and I stepped out of the office onto the street, and Narvane did the teleport, and we felt sick, and we were in the courtyard of Castle Black again. We took our time going inside for the benefit of our insides, then spent a moment exchanging greetings with Lady Teldra. I had mixed feelings about inviting her to the wedding, because I wanted her there, but if I invited her and she didn't want to go, she might not feel it polite to say no. See how complicated things get with polite people? That's why I mostly hang around with jerks.

We took the long, winding stairway, and I noticed another picture I hadn't before—a woman in the colors of a Tiassa holding a sort of scepter that probably meant she was the Heir. I resolved to ask Morrolan about that one, too, but of course I forgot.

Seriously, Sethra? A forgery? I wouldn't have thought Morrolan—

Oh, by a forger, but his own work this time. I get it. Anyway, I like that one: it looks like she thinks it's funny that you'd want to look at her portrait.

So, anyway, yeah, we climbed up the white marble stairway to the library.

Morrolan, Aliera, and the Necromancer. Sethra wasn't there, at least not yet, but there was still enough magical skill and power to handle an invasion from Elde Island or an Easterner's wedding. Wine was served, I talked, they listened. When I stopped talking, they looked at me.

Then Morrolan cleared his throat. "Well," he said, which I guess summed up the situation.

"So the questions are," I said, "first, what happened during the time I don't remember, second, am I right about the missing sorceress and the missing spell, and, third, how do we find her."

"From what you've said," said Morrolan, "I think you're likely to be right about this sorceress having cast the spell. At least, it's a good assumption to start with. The question is, why?"

"I'd say the first question is *what*," said Aliera. "What was the spell supposed to do if Blackwand hadn't interfered? That will give us the why."

"Not necessarily," said Morrolan. He started to say more, but I jumped in with, "I'd like to know in any case," before he and Aliera could get into it with each other.

"Maybe," said Morrolan, I assume just so he wouldn't have to give in to Aliera, "we should start with the first question. That is, what happened to Vlad?"

We were all looking at the Necromancer, who hadn't said a word so far.

For once, she didn't act like the question was too obvious to make sense, or say something incomprehensible. "I think I know," she said. "Vlad, give me your hand."

"It's promised to another," I said. Cawti chuckled, but no one else did; I guess that idiom isn't used among Dragaerans. I held my hand out. She took it and looked at me through those too-full too-empty eyes of hers. I didn't know what exactly she was looking at, and I was just as glad.

"Yes," she said after a moment. "You traveled. You'll have to integrate it."

I stared at her and waited.

She shifted her eyes around, as if wanting to know who would explain things to her. Then she said, "I could help, if you'd like."

"Yes, please," I said.

She took my hand again, then reached out and touched my forehead.

Once when I was a kid, a bunch of Orcas were chasing me up by the East Bank Cliffs, and I ended up jumping off and falling, I don't know, not all the way down, of course, but far enough so they didn't want to follow me. The thing I remember is how my stomach felt as I started to fall—kind of like the rest of me was going down and it figured to hang around the top and catch up later. Well, that's sort of what this felt like, except it was my head, not my stomach. Not an improvement.

I could feel the arms of the chair, and even taste the bitter-sweet coolness of the wine I'd just sipped, but I was somewhere different. I was standing, not sitting, and standing amid sharp stones with bands of yellow, blue, purple, and red; a few green stalks grew between them. Harsh yellow light came from the sky, so bright I couldn't look at it, and it took me a moment to make out anything else. When I glanced back, away from the light, my shadow was clearer and more distinct than I'd ever seen it, which I noticed even before I realized that I was standing on a platform, deliberately smoothed. The platform had even more colors than the rocks around it, and they rose from the ground twisting and weaving and swirling around me. I stood there, not moving, not breathing.

No, I mean, not breathing.

Not breathing, or feeling any need to breathe; not moving, or feeling like I could. It was a lot like what had happened before at Castle Black, though different images, and I wasn't looking in all directions, and the bright light was certainly different.

I was hearing voices, too. I mean, a voice. Someone was speaking, or maybe chanting, in a language I didn't understand. Then I heard that sound, that thing the Necromancer had said was my name, and then whoever it was started speaking a different language, which I realized after a moment was Northwestern, my language, except the worst accent I've ever heard. I was able to decode a few phrases—"eow wool" was "you will" and "eh commund" was "I command" only I didn't know what I would do, or what the command was, and I couldn't even be sure it was directed to me.

Somewhere in there, I realized that the light was two different things: there was the one coming from above, lighting up the area, but then there was also a red-and-gold-and-blue spiral around my body that kept getting in front of my eyes. I noticed that one when it started to get dim and eventually stopped.

That was when I finally managed to see the figure in spite of the other horrid light, but I can't tell you much about it except that it had a head that seemed to have been stepped on by something heavy, no ears I could see, slits for eyes that ran up and down, a wide mouth with no teeth and a long neck.

I still couldn't move, but I watched myself as I drew a stiletto from my boot and shoved it into one of its eyes, and then I was back in the chair.

The Necromancer was just pulling her finger back from my forehead and everyone was looking at me.

"What," I said.

"Did it work?" asked the Necromancer.

"Um. I think so. At least, I got a kind of vision or dream or one of those things I hate."

She nodded. "There were two of you, and you aren't used to integrating the memories. It'll be easier next time."

"Next time?"

"Vlad—" said Morrolan.

"I was summoned," I said. "Like a fucking demon, someone, some *thing* just grabbed me and pulled me in."

"You get used to it," said the Necromancer.

"I'd rather get it cured," I said.

"Is that possible?" asked Aliera.

"No," said the Necromancer.

"So, you're saying it's difficult," I said.

She tilted her head and looked at me like, well, I guess like I looked at her when she said one of those things she says that don't make any kind of normal human sense. See, I was getting all sorts of experience about what it was like to be on the other side of things. Lucky me.

And then I was hit with a sudden thought. I reached down and, slowly, so as not to worry anyone, pulled the stiletto from my boot. It was a good, reliable weapon, made by Kivrath, who always does solid work. About ten inches of blade, with a pommel of polished obsidian and a small, straight crossguard. In my vision, or dream, or whatever it was, it was the one I'd used to kill the thing that had summoned me. Only that one had had a leather-wrapped hilt and was a bit thinner, with a curved crossguard, like the ones Nusir makes. I alternate whose work I carry, and I'd just gotten the one I was holding from Kivrath a few days ago.

Huh.

I returned the blade to my boot.

"What is it, Vladimir?"

"Nothing," I said. "Just . . . nothing."

So, figure that one out, will you? Don't expect me to explain, because I still have no idea how that happened or what it means.

"All right," I said. "One question answered. Let's move on. What was the spell supposed to do to me?"

Now everyone was looking at Morrolan.

I hadn't noticed Blackwand on a table behind him, but he turned and took it, and, when he drew it, well, I've talked about what that thing does to your head, and I don't feel like talking about it again.

I couldn't help but ask, "Are you sure you need to do that?"

"Only if you want your question answered," he said.

Then he raised the weapon, pointed it at me. There was still five or six feet between me and the point, but it didn't seem like nearly enough.

"All right, Aliera," he said. "Go ahead."

"Touch the blade," she told me.

14

THE BIG FEAST

Sometimes I wonder if all of these courtship and wedding traditions came about to make everything so difficult that no one would get married who wasn't really, really sure. But then I remember the big feast. So, at least some of the traditions have other explanations.

Everyone looks forward to the big feast, held the day before the wedding. Noish-pa said that way back, the idea was to welcome all of the guests from out of town. That puzzled me a little, until I remembered that would have been in the East, so there would have been no teleports, so travel would take forever, which made arriving kind of a big deal. Those are the sorts of things you don't think about. I asked him how that worked with the tradition of inviting all guests in person, and he said sometimes you skipped things.

The custom of the feast continued, though, because that's what customs do, which is why they're customs, so we got to plan a feast. Of all the Dragaeran Houses, only the Jhereg comes close to Easterners in thinking how important food is, but that's because we do so much business over a meal. And if the business goes bad, at least you want the food to be decent.

Cawti and I were both Easterners and Jhereg, so, yeah, we wanted the food to be decent. Better than decent if we could manage it, and we weren't going to be cooking this ourselves, so we had to hire someone. I don't know of any kind of people that makes a ritual out of finding a good cook, but there should be one.

Her name was Pietra, and she had a tiny restaurant and a bigger catering service in the far northeastern quarter of South Adrilankha, as far from the smell of the slaughterhouses as you can get, I suppose. We spent *an afternoon sampling some of the options, and had some wonderful arguments about what to choose that were usually settled by saying both.*

I could tell you what we came up with, but who wants to hear about food?

⊰⊱

"Something must be wrong with my hearing," I said. "I almost thought you said—"

"Touch the blade," she repeated.

I looked at her, then at Morrolan. "It's all right," he said. "She won't hurt you."

Not to drag it out for you, but, after a little more convincing—okay, a lot more convincing—I did it. I got up, took a couple of paces forward, right toward the point, and then I put the palm of my hand on the blade like I did that sort of thing all the time.

If you think it was easy, I'll just say you're wrong. Holding it there wasn't easy either; leave it at that.

Aliera stood up—taking her time about it, I think for no reason except to torment me, which I respected—walked over to me, put her palms on each of my temples, and, just when I was bracing for something unpleasant, stepped back and shrugged. "I can't get anything. Necromancer, maybe you can try?"

So I stood there even longer, still having to keep my hand on that blade. The Necromancer didn't even do the thing with the hands, she just walked up to me, peered, nodded, and went back to her seat.

"Yes," she said. "I have it. We should have done that right away."

"Does that mean I can remove my hand now?" I said.

"If you wish," said the Necromancer.

Yeah, I wished.

Some conversation went on that I missed while I returned to my chair and shook for a while. Morrolan, at least, had the decency to put that thing away. Cawti took my hand, and a little later I said, "Okay, start over, all right? I was distracted by sheer terror."

Aliera sniffed; she was of the school that figured bravery meant never being scared, or at least never admitting it. Morrolan, who was a little saner, seemed to understand, and the Necromancer, of course, had no idea what there had been to be afraid of.

She was, however, willing to start over.

"The spell was intended to pull you astrally out of your body and send you somewhere."

"Huh. That's all? Well, that happens all the time. Where?"

"I couldn't tell exactly."

"I'm glad it didn't work, anyway."

"It might have been better if it had," said Morrolan.

"How so?"

"Well, chances are, whatever you were being sent over for, if you'd done it, they'd have brought you back."

"You sure?"

"Not sure, I suppose. But, in any case, Blackwand identified it as a hostile spell—"

"Which it was—"

"And decided to protect you. That put you into a state where, in order to bring you back, you had to, um, undergo certain changes."

"So, wait. It wasn't the spell that made me a demon?"

"Oh, I did that," said the Necromancer. "It was the only way to rescue you."

"Why didn't you tell me that before? No, no. Don't answer that. If you say, 'you didn't ask' I might lose it."

The Necromancer tilted her head at me, but at least didn't answer the question.

I let that all tumble around in my mind; everyone was quiet. I guess they knew how hard thinking is for me.

"Lady Shireth," I said after a moment, "is negotiating with demons. Or with people in a demon world. Or something. She needed someone to go to that plane in order to aid the negotiation, or the exchange of goods."

"Go on," said Morrolan.

"The Verra's tear turned out to be planted in someone's house, someone Shireth intended to use for that, to send over to the other world."

"Unless it was Tavissa," said Cawti. "We're pretty sure she cast the spell."

"Right, but—" I thought it over and chewed my lip as if I could suck some intelligence out of it. "So, is that pretty standard for necromancers, to prepare someone like that before sending them to another world?"

"It is," said the Necromancer. "But it shouldn't be. There's no need. Anyone with reasonable necromantic skill can negotiate with beings from another plane. Of course, there's the language problem, but there would still be the language problem if someone were sent over. And goods, items, can also be exchanged without using a person. But it is a common belief, so a number of people do it."

"Reasonable necromantic skill," I repeated. "Um. Just how much skill would be needed to break through Morrolan's protections and cast that spell on me?"

"The protections wouldn't matter," said the Necromancer. "The spell came under them; he had no protections against necromantic energy."

"I thought necromancy just used sorcerous power."

"Yes, but not in the same way. It is the power of death, of the worlds of the unliving, of the planes."

I glanced at Morrolan, who looked offended. It seems he hadn't known that either. I imagine that was a problem he'd be taking care of soon.

"And the spell itself?"

"Difficult," she said.

"So Tavissa, or Shireth, or whoever did this, is very good."

"Yes," said the Necromancer.

"So, yeah, it was Shireth who did the thing to Fisher with Verra's tear, because she didn't know it was unnecessary, and it was Tavissa who did the spell on me, because she's good, and would have known the other thing was unnecessary. Probably. Maybe."

"I think I followed that," said Aliera.

"And does it hold up?"

She looked at Morrolan and the Necromancer, then said, "I think so."

"Okay, so here's the big question. If I'm right about this, what was Tavissa trying to do when she cast that spell on me? I mean, why? If there's no need to do it to help with the exchange, why *did* she do it?"

No one had any answers.

I shook my head. "Well," I said. "This has been a day. Morrolan learned something he didn't know about necromancy, I learned that it wasn't the spell that turned me into a demon, and we've all had the experience of getting straight, simple answers from the Necromancer. I'm not sure if I can handle any more shocks."

Cawti and Morrolan chuckled, Aliera looked annoyed, the Necromancer looked distracted.

"So," I said. "Necromancer. Could it happen again?"

"What?"

"The spell to send me somewhere. Could she do it again? Or is that what happened earlier?"

"It isn't what happened earlier," she said. "That was a pretty typical summoning."

I decided I didn't want to dwell on "pretty typical summoning," so I said, "All right. But could it?"

"Have you been carrying the stone around with you?"

"No."

"Then she probably can't find you."

"Well, that's good, I guess."

"Where are you keeping it?" said Morrolan.

"My office."

"Is that safe?"

I started to say I had sorcerous protections up, but then remembered that Morrolan had had those, too. I used some words.

"It's probably all right," Aliera pointed out. "It isn't the stone that's important, it was the stone being on you."

"I hope Kragar doesn't pick it up," I said.

"I hope he does," said Aliera with a sweet smile.

"Meanwhile," I said. "Anyone who wants can just summon me?"

"Anyone who can find out your name," said Morrolan.

"How hard is that?"

"Scrying for a name is difficult," said Aliera. "It can be done, but it's hard, and getting the name exactly right can be tricky. It's a bad idea to be off by just a little. Also, well, those who summon demons usually want some particular skill. I don't think you'd be all that, um, in demand."

That hurt my feelings. "What if someone wanted *palaczintok*? I make a mean *palaczinta*."

"Well yes," said Aliera. "Then, certainly."

"Vlad," said Morrolan. "Aliera is right. We summon demons in order to do things we're incapable of doing. I'm sorry if it's offensive, but there isn't anything you can do that would make it worthwhile to summon you. That, by itself, should prevent you from being summoned."

"Should," I repeated.

He shrugged.

"All right," I said. "Another question: That thing you said about getting the name wrong. Think that's what happened to the poor bastard who summoned me?"

"Most likely," said Aliera. "Had your name off, or one of the commands not quite right."

"I still don't like it."

"This may help," said the Necromancer. She leaned forward and lifted her hand, and I felt something like a twinge in the back of my head, only it wasn't exactly physical, and that's the best I can do.

"What—"

"If you get stranded," she said, "I should be able to find you and bring you back. I mean, if you want me to."

"I want you to. Can't miss my wedding. Oh, and you're invited, by the way; I may have forgotten to send you an invitation. So, here's the thing: what if I end up appearing underwater, or in the middle of a fire?"

"That isn't likely," said the Necromancer. "Whoever summons

you has to be there too. Of course, there are the environmental dangers."

"The enviwhatall dangers?"

"Well, not everywhere has the same air."

I looked at Morrolan and Aliera to see if there was a joke I was missing, then I said. "What do you mean?"

"Well, air is different in different places."

"Uh, air is air," I said. "That's what makes it air."

Then the Necromancer looked around, like she wanted support. "That's not exactly true," said Aliera. "Air is made up of, well, lots of different things."

"I thought it was made up of air," I said.

"You must have noticed how the air smells different at the top of Dzur Mountain than it does near the ocean-sea?"

"Well, yeah, but that's just, you know, different scents in it."

"Yes."

"Oh. Right."

"The Necromancer is saying that maybe the air where you could be summoned is fine for whoever summoned you, but toxic for you."

"Oh." I turned back to the Necromancer. "Has that ever happened to you?"

"A few times," she said. "Usually, any being that will summon you is similar enough that you could at least survive for a while, but it has happened."

"What did you do?"

"I died," she said.

I started to object, but then remembered that, when dealing with necromancy, "dead" doesn't necessarily mean what I think of as dead. Fortunately for my career, not too many see it that way. I decided not to push it, because things were difficult enough without adding the headache I'd get trying to figure out what she was saying.

"All right," I said. "So I got summoned, and now I remember it. Yay for that. The idea behind the spell was to drag me to some other world, that might or might not be the one I was summoned to earlier. I'm a demon now because Blackwand saved me from being summoned, which put me in a state where the Necromancer had to turn me into a demon to rescue me. We still aren't sure why there was a spell to send me to another world, and we aren't sure it was Tavissa who did it, and we don't know where she is in any case. Have I missed anything?"

"No, that's about it," said Morrolan.

"Except," said Aliera, "why you got involved in all of this in the first place."

"Jhereg business," I said, because I didn't feel like explaining that this had happened because I'd wanted to recover eight hundred gold.

"All right," she said.

"The one I'm stuck on right now," I said, "is why she was trying to send me somewhere. If she didn't need to do it to complete the hishi deal, then what was it supposed to do?"

"Maybe," said Morrolan. "It was to take the place of what just happened. She tried to send you somewhere, failed, but you became a demon, so she acquired your name, and enlisted those others to summon you."

I tried to ignore how casually he'd thrown out that, "you became a demon."

"Okay, but what was it supposed to do?"

Morrolan shrugged. "There's no way to know. You killed the summoner, so it didn't happen."

"But," I said, "it might happen again."

He nodded.

"So I need to find this Tavissa, make sure she was the one doing that, and make sure she doesn't try it again."

Morrolan and Aliera both nodded at this.

"So, I guess we've covered everything, right?"

"That depends," said Cawti, "on how much Jhereg business you want to talk about in front of Dragonlords."

"Oh, right."

Morrolan and Aliera looked at each other, then back at me.

"What is the crime?" said Aliera.

"Smuggling," I said.

She snorted. "That's just barely even a crime."

"I agree with my cousin," said Morrolan.

There's a first time for everything, I thought but didn't say. I gave them a brief rundown of hishi and its byproduct and some demonic world where that stuff had value.

"Oh," said the Necromancer. "I know that world."

And now we were all looking at her.

I said, "Are there beings there with flat heads and no teeth?"

"No," she said.

"What is the name of the place?" Morrolan wanted to know.

"Frondice," she said. "In one of their old languages it means, 'the world.'"

"How creative," I said. "Which makes me wonder, what does 'Dragaera' mean?"

"Empire," said Morrolan. "Ancient tongue of the Phoenix."

"So we live on the Empire World, and in the Empire Empire?"

"Well, 'Dragaeran Empire' would translate more precisely to Imperial Empire, but pretty much."

"Huh. What did they call the world before there was an empire?"

"Various things that mean 'dirt' or 'ground,'" said Aliera.

"Oh. Anyway, back to the subject. Necromancer, what do you know about this world that wants that greenish gel? What do they do with it?"

"Printing," she said.

"What?"

"It's just one part of the world, one of their cultures. They have a tree whose sap they use for writing, and the gel absorbs the sap and transfers it. They can get more than a hundred uses out of one batch, and then they boil it and get even more. And a pound of the raw gel can turn into hundreds of batches."

"Um," I said. "I'd been thinking, you know, something that they could use to, I don't know, invade us."

"Why would they want to do that?"

I didn't have a good answer to that one.

I felt Cawti looking at me. "What are you thinking, Vladimir?"

"That the business deal is just what it seems to be. An exchange of that gel for gold, just as promised, with nothing sinister about it."

"Which means?"

"I don't know. It means, for the moment at least, we can assume Shireth and her group are telling us the truth. At least part of it."

"Who?" said Aliera.

"The faction of the Left Hand that's been trying to put together the hishi deal, and want me to find Tavissa."

They all sort of looked at each other, and I started to get the idea that I wasn't going to get a lot of help with that.

"I still don't understand," said Aliera, "how it is Tavissa, if that's who it was, was able to conceal the origin of the spell she cast. Did you look at the ground yourself?"

"Yeah," I said. "And like you said, there's nothing there."

She sniffed. "I told you that."

"Do you take my word for everything I say?"

That got me a dismissive look.

"How did you perform the location spell," was what Morrolan wanted to know.

Aliera looked like she was about to say something snippy, then said, "I conjured a map and had Pathfinder point to the spot, then did it again with a narrower map, and a narrower map. Pathfinder was very definite about the location."

"That should have worked," said Morrolan. "Unless—"

"Unless what?" said Aliera.

"Unless nothing," Morrolan amended. "It should have worked."

I think his "unless" had been about to be something like, "unless you screwed up conjuring the map," but he changed his mind about saying that in order to keep blood off the floor of his library, and because, as I understand these things, it wasn't very likely.

"So," I said, "no one has any great ideas for how to find her?"

No one did.

"Or how it is that buying land around Northport, a rebellion at Zerika's Point, and a necromantic business exchange all feed into, I don't know, doing something to the Tsalmoth Heir?"

Blank looks.

I sighed. That was what I'd figured.

"Well," I said, "in any case, thanks to you all for helping me out. I appreciate it."

There were various nods and grunts of acknowledgment.

I stood up. "Morrolan, can we get a teleport back to the office."

"I should have asked Sethra to be here," he muttered.

"Why is that?" I asked innocently. "Not up to the teleport?"

He sniffed. He has very expressive sniffs.

Okay, maybe it was all in my head, but the teleport seemed to take longer than it usually did, and Cawti and I were both sicker than we usually were. Maybe it was because we'd done two teleports so close together, or maybe Morrolan was trying to let me know how much he enjoyed my wit.

When we'd recovered—in the middle of the street in front of my office looking like the fools Dragaerans take Easterners for, and I hate that—we straightened ourselves out, and without a word, started walking toward my flat. I could have stopped in to check that things were going all right, but after a few bumps last year, I felt pretty sure that Kragar would let me know if there was anything that needed my attention.

"We have," Cawti said as we walked, "too many problems."

"Yep. It's complicated."

"So I propose we spend the rest of the evening not thinking about it."

"That may be the best plan in the history of plans. What should we do instead? I mean, in addition to the obvious."

"We could work on our wedding vows."

"Perfect."

So we did.

I mean, we did other things too, but we did work on our vows.

The next morning, we agreed that she was going to talk to Pietra, the caterer, and we'd meet for lunch in South Adrilankha.

I headed back to the office, with Loiosh making suggestions about where this future lunch should take place. We were still half a mile from the office when I discovered that I was on the ground, and then something big and heavy hit me in the back, and then Loiosh screamed into my head. I tried to get up, but, just by luck, I'd landed right in a pool of blood, and my hands slipped on it. Then I noticed the pool getting bigger, which seemed kind of strange.

The world got fuzzy, then became sharp again, then I had four hands, and then only two, and I remember thinking, *this has been happening way too much lately* and after that I don't have any memories until I woke up somewhere unfamiliar, which would have scared me, I think, if my brain had been working a little better.

"Vlad?" I knew that voice.

I was on a bed. I keep waking up in beds. I guess that's a good thing compared to other places I could be waking up, or compared to not waking up. I couldn't see very well. I closed my eyes and opened them a couple of times, but it didn't help.

"Vlad?"

I tried to ask who it was, but couldn't manage to speak.

"It's all right, Vlad. This is Sethra, you're here at Dzur Mountain."

Dzur Mountain? I didn't remember going to Dzur Mountain. Why would I have gone there? Were there chunks of my memory missing? That was a scary thought.

I tried to speak again, but only vague noises came out. I felt Loiosh next to my left ear, but he wasn't saying anything.

"Relax, Vlad. Give it a few minutes."

I felt a hand in mine, then, and Cawti said, "I'm here," and suddenly everything was a lot better. I closed my eyes for a bit and made a careful study of the inside of my eyelids.

Eventually I tried speaking again, and managed, "What—?"

"You died," said Sethra.

"Someone put a shine on you," said Cawti.

I lifted my hand—the one Cawti wasn't holding—looked at it. "Still pretty dull," I said, though it came out as a whisper and I'm not sure they heard it.

Sometime later I sat up and drank some wine, delivered by a strange, shuffling, kind of twitchy fellow named either Chaz or

Tukko, I'm still not sure. The wine wasn't all that good, but it helped. I tried talking again.

"You brought me back, Sethra?"

She nodded.

"Thanks," I said.

Sethra was—no, I can't do this with you sitting here. Could you maybe, get up for a while? Just for—

All right.

Sethra Lavode, enchantress, undead, sorceress, been around for more years than I can count, all scary and shit. There. That'll have to be enough, because, uh, because it'll have to be. I sat there with my wine, still holding Cawti's hand, and said, "What happened?"

"You were killed," she said.

"Yeah, I got that. I meant . . ." I wasn't sure what I meant. Details? I didn't think I wanted them.

She squeezed my hand. "Thoroughly professional," she said. "Dagger into the heart through the back."

"Dagger? I thought it was a club. It felt like a club."

"It was a dagger."

"Huh."

"*Boss?*"

"Hey, buddy."

"*I'm sorry! I—*"

"Hey, relax. *That's why professionals get paid what we do.*"

"*But I didn't even see it coming! I was just—*"

"*I know, and it's fine. You've saved my life enough, okay? And, hey, here I am, which means—*"

"So," I asked Cawti. "No effort to make it permanent?"

"No," she said.

"And no effort to take me somewhere?"

"No."

"Then it isn't about the stuff with the Left Hand," I said.

She frowned. "Then what's it about?"

"Remember what we said about Fisher? That Toronnan must have given permission?"

"But, why would he have wanted you dead?"

"Not dead, warned. To keep peace in the family."

"I'm not seeing it."

"No, there's stuff you don't know about. One moment."

While I may have still been a wreck physically, my mind was working as well as it ever does.

"*That you, Vlad?*"

"*Yeah. Look, Kragar. The new game on Garshos? Shut it down.*"

"*Yeah? Okay.*"

"*Turns out Paquitin cared about it after all.*"

"*Cared about it how much?*"

"*I'll talk to you later. Probably be a few days.*"

"*You okay?*"

"*Mostly. Mind the thing and keep your hand out of the other thing.*"

"*Right.*"

"How are you, Vlad?" Sethra wanted to know.

I sort of took stock. "Weak, but no pain if I don't move. All in all, pretty good. You do good work."

"Tired?"

"Yeah, I guess I am."

"Then we should let you sleep."

"Okay," I said.

I fell asleep holding Cawti's hand. When I woke up, she was asleep next to me.

You know, for someone who'd just been murdered, I felt pretty damn good.

Cawti stirred, and noticed I was awake. I filled her in on who I was pretty sure had just had me knocked on the head, and why, and we talked it over and she agreed I was probably right.

I tried to get up, Cawti told me to take it slow, and she helped me, and I stood and was dizzy for a while. I sat back down on the bed; probably should have sat before trying to stand.

"*Hey, Loiosh. You doing okay?*"

"*I don't know, Boss. I can't believe I didn't see—*"

"*You gotta let that go.*"

"I know, but—"

"Do you remember when I said that you were responsible for making sure nothing bad ever happened to me no matter what?"

"Uh . . ."

"Right. I didn't. Because that would have been stupid. Like I said yesterday, whoever it was, was a pro. That's what they do."

"But I was right there!"

"Would it have been better if you'd been flying overhead?"

He didn't answer.

Cawti was watching me. "Loiosh?" she said.

I nodded.

"Poor guy."

"Hey now. Sympathy this way, please. I'm the one who died."

"I have enough for you both," she said, and kissed me.

Loiosh must have been upset; he didn't even say anything.

I tried standing up again, was dizzy, but managed. There was a kind of robe—deep blue with gold on the cuffs—draped over a chair, and she helped me into it. It felt good against my skin. I wondered how many people I'd have to kill to afford one. Or maybe it would only cost 912 imperials.

I held onto her as we made our way down a hall and into what I guess I'd call a small dining room: there was a table that seated six, and the chairs to go with it, and that was about it. No windows. There weren't many windows in Dzur Mountain.

I needed to eat, but didn't feel like I could, so I ended up having klava and nibbling at some dark bread. Tukko made good klava.

Sethra joined us and asked how I was, and I said I felt weak and got dizzy sometimes and my back hurt if I moved wrong but was doing well and liked the whole being-not-dead thing. She said the pain would be gone within a day or so. I really like magic.

We moved to one of her smaller sitting rooms with a couch where I could stretch out. We started talking about various things, a lot of which I don't remember because I kept falling asleep and waking up again and finding Sethra and Cawti had gone on to something else.

I remember thinking that I was pleased they were getting along so well, and then falling asleep again.

Another time when I woke up they were talking about marriage customs of the various Houses, and laughing about a lot of them, and that time I stayed awake long enough to laugh at them too. Then we talked with Sethra about our marriage plans, and she said yes, we should certainly invite Lady Teldra, so that was one thing settled, anyway.

We went from our wedding to weddings in general, to funny stories about weddings, to funny stories. I hadn't known Sethra could be—

—this is embarrassing with you here.

Fine. But can you at least not look at me while I'm talking about you?

Thank you.

I hadn't known Sethra could be that good a storyteller.

Eventually, I told her about what I was involved in, leaving out the details that would offend someone who didn't have my relaxed attitude about laws. I did tell her that I was trying to find a Jhereg who used to be Tsalmoth, and she asked where she'd been seen last, and I said forty years ago in Zerika's Point.

"Forty years ago would have been during the Blackrock Rebellion," she said.

"Yeah, so I heard."

"It was messy," said Sethra. "Anyone who wasn't involved and was able to leave the area, did. Rebellions are often messy, but that one was especially so."

"You were there?"

"No, by then the Empire preferred to believe I didn't exist, but I still keep in touch with people."

I considered. "Sethra, has there ever been a successful rebellion against the Empire?"

She hesitated, then said, "Well, no."

"Kinda stupid for people to try it then, isn't it?"

I'd expected some sort of wisecrack, but she thought it over. "It's an interesting question. I've studied it."

"*Now look what you've done, Boss.*"

"*Shut up.*"

"Part of the answer is that there has never been a successful rebellion against the Empire. This is because whenever a rebellion becomes too annoying or difficult to put down, the Empire claims it was a negotiation and agrees to whatever is necessary to resolve it."

"Huh. Clever. I gotta try that sometime."

I was pleased that Loiosh had gotten over things enough to throw in a wisecrack. I'd been worried. He was more upset about me kissing the stones than I was.

Sethra did, I don't know, some things later that day. I mean, things that involved furrowing her brow and passing her hands over me while I tensed up waiting for the pain that never came. That's not a complaint. An hour or two later, I noticed I was feeling better, like, not so tired. I felt like with a little more rest, I might even be jaunty again.

We had more conversations with Sethra, a lot of them about how I was feeling, and she eventually said that she was pleased with my progress.

"Of course," she added. "That doesn't change the fact that you're an idiot."

I stood up, drew my weapon, and cut her six times before she could move, and then—

I'm sorry, Sethra. I just had to see the look on your face. I mean, if you're going to be here while I sort of puke my experiences out, you have to expect—

All right, all right.

So, no, I didn't stand up or draw my weapon, I just said something clever, like, "What?"

"Vlad, who is the most powerful sorcerer you know?"

"Uh, that'd be you."

"So, who is the first person you should come to when you have a powerful necromantic event happen, like, you know, becoming a demon?"

"Oh, you heard about that?"

"I hear things," she said.

"So, about that. What do I do?"

"Tell me about it."

"What part exactly?"

"All of it."

15

THE REHEARSAL

The afternoon before the wedding, you get together with everyone in-volved and make sure you know who is going to stand where, and say what when, and then you have food, which doesn't count as one of the feasts.

The more grandiose the wedding, the more rehearsal you need, so we didn't need a lot. About fifteen minutes, and then the food. There was spicy kethna with ginger, and stuffed peppers, and double-fried rice with onions and shooter peas.

I don't like to admit it, but Eastern marriage customs are closer to the Teckla than to any other House. You see a lot of weddings of the ones who live in the City, and there's no question, they celebrate like we do. By which I mean, not a lot of ceremony, but a lot of dancing, a lot of music, a lot of laughing, and crying, and food.

⊰⊱

I told her about it as best I could. She listened, nodding sometimes, only asking a question now and then to keep me going. When I'd run down she said, "Interesting."

"Thanks," I said. "Glad to interest you. What can you tell me?"

"What do you want to know?"

"Lots of things. Let's start with, how do I get out of this?"

"You mean, out of being a demon?"

"Yes."

"You don't."

"What if I ask that different?"

"Sorry."

"And I don't suppose you have any expertise in finding missing Jhereg sorceresses."

"Well, that depends. I might have some ideas."

"Really? I was about to make some kind of sarcastic remark about what good are you. I mean, you know, it being funny because you just brought me back from the, uh, so, yeah, let's hear it."

"What have you tried?"

"As I understand it—and I'm not all that good with this stuff—they found what Morrolan called a 'signature' of the spell, and Aliera traced it with Pathfinder."

"Traced it how?"

"Conjured some sort of mystical map, and had Pathfinder guide her to the spot on the map."

"Seems reasonable. And?"

"They checked the spot in person, and found nothing. I did too, by the way, just to see if human eyes could pick anything out, and there was nothing there."

"Where was it?"

"West of the City, along the coast."

"Was it a flat map?"

"A which?"

"The map Aliera used, did it show a point in two dimensions, or three?"

"Uh, still not—"

"Did it say where it was up and down?"

"Oh. As I understand it, no."

"You know there are all kinds of caves along that part of the coast, right?"

I stared at her, and finally managed, "Damn, Sethra."

"Just a thought," she said. "Here's another: when you were summoned, you might have had a spell cast on you."

"You mean, by the demons?"

"No, by—Um, Vlad, you were the demon. They were the summoners."

"Oh, right. By the summoners?"

"Yes."

"Can you check?"

"Gladly."

She checked, and yeah, I had a spell cast on me, and she did some more checking. "Pre-Empire sorcery," she said at last. "It can be triggered by anyone who can touch amorphia, either personally, or with a device."

"So, in other words, anyone?"

She nodded.

"Triggered," I repeated. "Uh, what will happen when it's triggered?"

"I can't tell exactly. It will give you a compulsion to go somewhere, I'm not sure where, and when you're there, it will do something to all of the amorphia in the area you're in, but it'll take a lot more work to tell exactly what."

"Will it hurt me?"

"It shouldn't. The effect will expand outward from you in all directions, but it shouldn't have any effect on anything that isn't pure amorphia."

"Can you remove it?"

"Yes."

"Then please . . . no, wait. I have an idea."

She might be the only person I know who could hear me say that without it automatically triggering a wisecrack. Well, no, the Necromancer too, I guess.

Yeah, I hang around with some interesting folk.

I felt Cawti looking at me. I glanced over and gave her a smile. "You know, this might actually work," I said.

⊰⊱

Cawti and I ate alone—except for Loiosh, of course—served by Tukko, who grimaced and shuffled and made snuffling sounds. He does a pretty good omelet. As we ate, Cawti said, "Are you going to do anything?"

"About . . . ?"

"Paquitin."

"Oh. Yeah, I'm going to stay out of his way."

"Goodness Vladimir! Wisdom?"

"You get that from getting killed."

"Last time you got killed, you agreed to marry me."

"See?"

I got the feeling that was the right answer.

I spent some time walking around Dzur Mountain, then. I think I had some sort of idea of getting to know the place, but it was too confusing. But I convinced myself that I was healing pretty good.

That led to an argument about whether I was ready to leave. I lost the argument, but it was Sethra, Cawti, and Loiosh against me. I tried to enlist Tukko on my side, but he wasn't having any, so I agreed to stay another couple of nights.

I didn't do much, but Cawti was there with me, and we arranged with Sethra to have the wedding invitations sent out. We had quite a mix. I wondered if that many Dragons and that many Jhereg could be in the same room without killing each other. It was bound to be interesting.

I also gave a lot of thought to finding Tavissa. I knew Sethra was right; she had to be right. Pathfinder had pointed to the right place on the map, it was just, well, lower than that.

I also had to make some decisions: Did I want to tell Shireth what I'd learned, or go in myself? If I went in myself, was I going to go in with weapons out, or with the intention of talking? I did want to talk to her; I wanted to find out what her plan was. I admit to curiosity, okay? But I didn't know if that was going to be possible.

And I wasn't happy about going in without knowing just what she was up to, by which I mean, what was her plan? So yeah, I was worried about going to ask what her plan was before I knew her plan. But I didn't even know if I was better off helping her, or thwarting her.

I like that word, thwart.

I stayed in touch with Kragar, making sure everything was still going okay.

And I paced the halls a lot, trying to figure out what Tavissa was up to. Sethra said the pacing was good because it helped the healing; I didn't find it very useful for figuring things out.

Cawti was walking with me, and we talked about the wedding, and about Tavissa, and sometimes about me being a demon now, only Cawti could tell I didn't enjoy thinking about that, so she didn't press it.

"There's too much we're missing," I said. "There's something that connects the land deal in Northport, the rebellion in Zerika's Point, and the current smuggling deal. And until I know what that is, I'm worried about going in and cornering Tavissa. If I don't know what she's after and how she plans to do it, I don't know how to pry what I need out of her."

"You could always just go in and run a bluff," she said.

I nodded. "Yeah. I might have to do that. It worked with Shireth. Sort of."

"Sort of," she agreed.

"I don't know a lot about land deals, but I know there's money to be made by buying, improving, and selling. And I know there are things where you buy, fake improvements, and sell, and Toronnan was involved in something even more complicated having to do with buying, taking out loans to improve, and surrender of debt. I was protecting his accountant when he did that, but I never understood how it worked."

"How do we know that whatever Tavissa was doing was related to the uprising or to this smuggling operation?"

"Huh. Yeah. We don't. When I see a bunch of weird things, I try to fit them together, but they don't have to fit. The land deal could have been about nothing more than trying to make some quick money, and for whatever reason it failed, and it had nothing to do with—Oh."

"Vladimir?"

I'd stopped walking.

Loiosh was still a bit shaken by what he thought was his screw-up, which is the only reason he wasn't in my head laughing at me while I thought of all sorts of bad names for myself.

"What is it, Vladimir?"

"I'm an idiot," I said aloud.

"No, you aren't. What—"

"Tavissa is a Tsalmoth, not a Yendi."

"I'm not following."

I kissed her. "You were right," I said.

"I like what happens when I'm right," she said. "Care to explain?"

"There was no master plan, there were a bunch of different ones. If I had to guess, the land deal was something she tried to suck Chervik into, and it didn't work, so she dropped it. Remember the coins I found? I'll bet if I looked at them closely, they had Chervik's face on them. She was supposed to be implicated in the rebellion, but that didn't work either. I'll bet a five-day of doing dishes there are a bunch of other efforts that we never heard about. That's what Tsalmoth do—they keep trying until something works."

She considered, then nodded slowly. "That fits."

I nodded. "So her latest idea was to get Chervik implicated in this smuggling thing, and I blew that by taking the stone. Now she's come up with something else, having that spell put on me."

"So then, how do you use that?"

"To get my eight hundred back? I don't know."

"So that's the next thing to figure out."

"Yeah. I have permission from my physicker to leave here tomorrow. Oh, also, thank you."

"For?"

"Staying here with me. I'd have gone off my head otherwise."

She smiled, took my arm, and we continued failing to understand how to get around in Dzur Mountain. Fortunately, Tukko was able to find us and get us back in time to eat. Not that the food was anything special: he just laid out some bread and cheese and meat and some fruits and vegetables and grunted something that I assume meant we should go ahead and eat, so we did.

Sethra joined us for wine later, and we explained what we'd figured out, to which she replied: "Huh."

"So," I said, "now that I have at least an idea of what's going on, I
just need to decide what to do about it."

"Should be easy," said Sethra. It took me a second to figure out
that she was being sarcastic.

We spent a last night there, had some of Tukko's klava, and Sethra
teleported us back home. I thought about maybe signing my name
on that spot of street just outside my office, since I'd been spending
so much time there. I mentioned it to Cawti as we were doubled over
waiting for the effects to pass, and she said it would be better to put
in a couple of nice chairs. See? The practical one.

We finally felt like our legs would hold us, and went in. Melestav
nodded like I hadn't been gone for three days. I went into the office
and watched the door until Kragar appeared.

"What happened, Vlad?"

"Our neighbor turned out to care about us encroaching on his
territory after all. Who knew?"

"How bad?"

"Well, I'm back here, still walking."

"And you've given up on the eight hundred, right?"

"I might have, if that's what got me shined."

"So, what's the plan?"

I looked at Cawti, who was looking back at me.

"Gonna go have a talk with a lady who lives in a cave. At least,
I think she does."

"Will she want to talk?"

"We'll find out."

He shook his head but didn't try to talk me out of it.

"Anything I need to handle here?"

"Nothing that won't wait till you're back, or will matter if you're
dead."

"Such an upbeat guy," said Cawti.

"Okay," I said. "Then here we go."

"Sure you don't want a teleport?" said Kragar, I figure to get in one last wisecrack in case I died. I didn't answer him.

We stopped for the usual "too busy to eat" food: bread and cheese and sausages. I'd get sick of that stuff if I didn't like it so much, and if there weren't so much variety. These sausages were made by a guy named Festir, who had a thing for oregano. The cheese was one Cawti liked, a very sharp Yisten. It was good, but too crumbly. We packed the stuff away and headed west.

It was still before noon when we got to the place we'd been to before, just a road carved out and laid down among the harsh rocks of the coast. We went over to the cliff, about a quarter of a mile off the road, and looked down. It was almost a straight drop of a couple hundred feet. If there's someone who could make that climb, it wasn't me.

"How's your levitation?" said Cawti.

"Good enough," I said. "I can at least manage a slow fall."

She nodded. "I'm ready when you are."

I took her hand to make sure the spell would affect us both and because I wanted to. "Deep breath and hold it," I said, and we stepped off the cliff.

There are several ways to do a levitation spell, but the best way involves fooling the thing you're levitating into thinking it's lighter than it is. That means you've got to sense every particle of it, which means that levitating, say, a knife, is pretty easy. A person is a lot harder, because if you don't keep every bit of it in your attention, bad things will happen either to the person or your head. I've worked on that levitation spell, but I'm not good enough to have any confidence, so I went with one of the sloppier ones that I knew I could pull off: I twisted up the air and made it thick so we drifted down like a marble going through molasses.

I didn't get it as well as I'd have liked, so we fell faster than we should have, but not too much, and that meant we didn't have to hold our breath for very long. Cawti rolled gracefully when we got to the bottom. I didn't, but I didn't hurt myself either.

"So, now we look for a cave entrance," I said.

She nodded, and we started looking.

I'll keep this short: We found five caves within a couple of miles. The deepest of them went back about two hundred feet and stopped, the others were all shallower. We checked each of those for concealed entrances, and we were careful. We used up a lot of day, but none of them were more than caves.

"Well," I said as we finished examining the last one. "That was useful."

"And now we're at the bottom of the cliff. Can you levitate us up, or are we going to have to teleport?"

"Let's sit on a rock and romantically watch the sea for a while."

"I like how you think," she said.

We sat on the rocks and watched the ocean-sea and ate our food, and I got cheese crumbs all over me and Cawti laughed at me. Good times.

As I was brushing myself off, she said, "Any ideas?"

I nodded. "I'm assuming that Tavissa is truly down there, and that you can only reach it by teleporting."

"Vlad, I hope you aren't thinking of teleporting into an area where we can't get a fix."

"Not exactly. Morrolan has this tower, with these weird windows that look out on stuff and then take you there, in theory. I know they can't go just anywhere, but they can go a lot of places. Seems worth it to ask, anyway."

"You've told me about those windows. Didn't you once—"

"Yeah. I don't like to think about it."

"All right. But, not to be indelicate, my love, let's not go to Castle Black right after eating."

"Wise, as always. We'll walk back to town first."

"Levitate up the cliff?"

I stared up it, thought about my sorcerous abilities, and scowled. "Okay," I said. "Second idea."

"Too cold for that."

I nodded. "Good point. Third idea, then."

"Flag down a passing boat?"

"No, that's the fourth idea. The third idea is, start walking along the beach, hopping over rocks, maybe skip some stones, and see if we can find a way up."

"Do you remember us passing a way down?"

"Well, no."

"So, fourth idea?"

"Uh, maybe fifth idea."

"Call for help?"

I nodded.

"Okay. Whose turn is it to help us this time?"

"I don't suppose you want to ask Norathar?"

"Not really."

"Aliera would be a good choice, just because she'd enjoy it so much."

"So she's out."

"Right."

"Morrolan?"

"Same."

"So, Kragar."

"Afraid so."

"*Kragar?*"

"*Need help?*"

"*Yeah, kinda.*"

"*Kinda?*"

"*I'm sort of stuck at the bottom of a cliff. When you laugh inside my head it sounds like someone choking to death. Look, you know that house with those Left Hand sorceresses? See if you can get them a message for me.*"

When I'd finished explaining things to Kragar, I nodded to Cawti.

She said, "By the time he's set something up and gotten someone here, we could probably be able to handle the teleport."

"So, what do we do between now and then?"

"I liked the skipping stones part of your earlier idea."

I'd said that because I'd heard of it; I didn't actually know how to skip stones. But Cawti showed me, and I'd gotten pretty good at it by the time our rescuer arrived.

It was the young sorceress who showed up, levitated us to the top of the cliff, then teleported us to outside their house. We tried to cover up how sick we were while the sorceress gave us a look that managed to hit the sweet spot between puzzled and disgusted.

She ushered me into the same room with the same people, only I picked a different chair just to be contrary.

Once we were seated, Shireth said, "So. Do you have something for us?"

"Yeah, I kinda put it together. Tavissa's been playing you for her own reasons."

"I see."

"But I wouldn't worry about it; she's moved on to another plan already, so you can go ahead with your demonic smuggling."

"You're sure?"

"Quite sure."

"Very well, then. Thank you. I'm afraid this wasn't worth eight hundred imperials, but we can compen—"

"What I'd like," I said, "is a favor."

The young one said, "We just did you one, rescuing you from below a cliff."

Shireth looked at her. She turned a little pale and dropped her eyes.

"What is it you wish, Lord Taltos?"

"Nothing too difficult. A meeting with the Tsalmoth Heir, if you would. Ideally, without a bunch of Phoenix Guards there."

"I expect we can arrange that. Any particular location?"

"Anywhere is fine. If she's more comfortable at her House, I'm all right with that."

"Bide, then."

We sat there in a long, uncomfortable silence, and I wished they'd offered us wine just so I'd have something to do. I was considering getting Spellbreaker out and twirling it for effect when Shireth nodded to me. "Very well. She is expecting you in the next hour."

"Good then," I said. "We'll be on our way, unless there's anything else?"

"It has been a pleasure, Lord Taltos."

My guess is she was lying, but I didn't call her on it.

It took most of the hour to reach the Imperial District. We could have gotten there faster, but we were enjoying the stroll.

This time it was a different Tsalmoth on duty, a woman, older, one of those people whose voice is so soft you have to lean forward, and you think maybe they're doing it on purpose to laugh at you. But we were expected, so up we went, climbing the long, pointless stairway.

She was alone this time, and had dressed—red and silver, ruby headband, laced boots that were useless for anything except looking good, silver paint on her eyebrows, long red gloves, and a cold look. She greeted me with, "Well?"

"Thanks for seeing us," I said, trying to make it casual, like I meant it, instead of formal, like I was mocking her.

She nodded and said, "Okay, get to it."

She didn't offer us a chair.

"Someone's after you," I said.

"What do you mean?"

"I mean, a certain lady who used to be Heir is trying to take you down. I assume for revenge, but she may have other reasons."

It seemed to go home, though she tried to cover it up.

"Why should I believe you?"

"Why shouldn't you?"

"I need more details than that."

"What sort? You know who she is, why she's after you. I can tell you that she was working with the guy who you first tried the fake bribe on two hundred years ago, but he got a little dead along the way."

That got to her. She said, "Did you—"

"No, no. Not me. Or you. He did that on his own. But the previous Heir, well, she's still at it, and she has plans."

"What are they?"

"That's not how it works."

"How does it work?"

"First you pay me, then I tell you how to thwart her."

I got to say "thwart" again. I was happy.

"Pay you how much, Jhereg?"

"Nine hundred and twelve and a half."

"Not a chance," she said.

"I'll settle for eight hundred."

"Get out," she said.

"All right."

We walked out the door. I'd been expecting her to call me back and offer a lesser amount, but she didn't, so we just left.

"Didn't go how you'd planned, Vladimir?"

"I didn't know how it'd go. I mean, I was hoping to get my money and be done with all this, but—"

"Were you?"

"Hmm?"

"Nothing. Where to now?"

I sighed.

"Oh," she said. "Let's find a place to sit first, we've been teleporting too much."

"Don't I know it."

So we found a klava hole and had klava. I also got a biscuit to slip to Loiosh, who was hiding in my cloak. We chatted about the wedding, both of us trying to pretend it was no big deal and neither of us pulling it off.

"Well," I finally said. "One thing I know for sure about it. That eight hundred would come in awfully handy for it."

She chuckled. "I think I'm ready," she said.

We tried a few of the commercial sorcerers who set up near the Palace, and found one who knew Castle Black and didn't charge too much. He just nodded to us, and we nodded back, and he lifted his hands and Adrilankha was gone.

We trudged up the curving marble stairway to the library. I looked for grooves in the steps to see if I'd made any with all the times I'd gone up and down them, but I guess Morrolan had people in to keep the thing repaired.

We sat, we drank wine, Morrolan waited for us to get to the point. He did not have Blackwand with him, so that was good.

He asked how the wedding planning was going, and we told him about the food; he didn't seem to be as excited about it as we were, but that didn't surprise me. We asked him what he'd been doing, and he said something about sorcery that had to do with the nature of the soul, and I think if I'd understood it, it would have had something to do with Morganti weapons, so I was just as glad I didn't.

I'm all for people understanding things, it's just that sometimes I don't want to be one of those people, okay?

We finally got to it, and I explained about where Tavissa was, and how I couldn't get there, and I was about to ask for suggestions when he started laughing.

I'm trying to remember if I'd ever heard Morrolan laugh before. I don't think so, at least, not like this. He didn't make a sound, he just put his head back, closed his eyes, and his shoulders shook. Then he leaned forward and his shoulders shook even more. He even pounded his fists on the arms of his chair. I didn't know if I should be mad, or worried that he was having some kind of attack. I looked at Cawti, who was looking at me, and we shrugged.

We waited.

Finally he settled down; that is, his shoulders were only shaking a little. He wiped his eyes and said, "Oh, I simply cannot wait to tell Aliera that."

"Um," I said. "Just, not until we've left, all right? In fact, maybe we'll visit Candletown until this is over, if that's far enough to be safe."

He laughed some more, though not as much, and finally said, "Well, all right then. What is it you need from me?"

"A way to get there," I said. "Can't teleport because we don't have a fix. So, what about that tower of yours? Can that get us there? I mean, those windows."

"It's in our world. They aren't built for such travel."

"But I saw things—"

"Yes, sometimes. But I can't control them precisely, especially on this world, and especially to a place I don't know."

"Damn. I wonder how much power it would take to blast through that wall?"

"Power isn't the question," he said. "Not bringing the whole place down on your head would be the question."

"Ugh."

He frowned. "There might be a way to get you there."

"Oh? Keep talking."

"Follow me," he said, and stood up. Cawti and I looked at each other, shrugged, and followed.

I'd never been in the basement of Castle Black. I mean, you don't think of a floating castle as having a basement but, I guess, why shouldn't it?

Oh. Because . . .

I cleared my throat. "Morrolan?"

"Yes?"

"When we appear in the courtyard, there's nothing below the castle."

"Yes?"

"But there's a basement?"

I caught a hint of a Kragar-like smirk on his lips, and dropped the subject.

He led us to a narrow stone stairway, and down what seemed like an awfully long way. We turned left down a hallway that was also narrow—we had to follow behind him—until he came to a wooden door, where he clapped.

The door opened, and the Necromancer was there. She gestured for us to go inside. In keeping with the theme of the basement, her room was tiny as well: I've been in jail cells that were bigger. It was utterly bare; not so much as a chair. Just four stone walls and, while I could have stretched out on the floor, it didn't look like Morrolan could have.

"How do you sleep in here?" I said.

She frowned. "As you do."

"I lie down."

"Of course, so do . . . Oh, yes. You are only seeing three dimensions, aren't you?"

I decided to drop that subject, too.

Morrolan said, "Vlad wants to talk to the person who cast the spell on him. My thought was, now that he's demonic, you might be able to send him through a gate."

She nodded. "He'll have to tell me his name," she said. "Or I suppose I could scry for it."

I pronounced it. It was kind of odd that I could say something I'd only heard in my head, and say it so perfectly, and even know it was perfect. But that was something else I didn't feel like thinking about. The Necromancer repeated the word, that is, my name, and I felt a sudden jolt, and then it was like I was cold for a second, then it went away.

"You felt that?" said the Necromancer.

"Yeah."

"Good," she said. "This should be easy enough. Are you ready to go now?"

"Not quite. Um, can you get hold of Aliera? I think she'll want to be in on this."

Morrolan gave me the eyebrows, then nodded, and presently Aliera showed up.

"What is it?" she said.

"If I understand what's going on," I said, "and I admit that's a big *if*, I'm about to go see the woman who managed to fool Pathfinder. Morrolan will explain the details after I've gone."

Her eyes narrowed; then, when Morrolan was unable to suppress his smile, they turned blue.

"My point," I said quickly before things could get ugly, "is that you might feel you owe her something. And then, you know, she also circumvented Morrolan's defenses, so maybe he isn't feeling all that kind toward her?"

He wasn't smiling now. "Go on."

"Okay, Sethra found a spell on me, so I'm pretty sure—"

"What sort of spell?" said Morrolan and Aliera together, then they looked at each other.

"It has to do with amorphia, and I don't understand a lot more than that. But here's what I'm hoping: I go in, I have a conversation with Lady Tavissa. While I'm there, I look around and get a solid fix on the place. Then, depending on the results of our conversation, I either go ahead and do what she wants, or teleport out, or, in the worst case, you, Morrolan, teleport me out while Aliera smashes apart any spells that might prevent that. What do you think?"

Morrolan and Aliera looked at each other, shrugged, nodded.

"All right," I said. I checked my weapons. "I'm ready."

Cawti took a step forward.

"It'll only work on him," said the Necromancer.

Well, bugger.

"You got this, Vladimir?" said Cawti.

"If I'm right, then yes. If I'm not, then I have no idea. Worst that'll happen is she'll kill me, right?"

"Yeah, then I kill her," said Cawti.

"Perfect."

I nodded to the Necromancer. "Go ahead."

She turned her palm over and extended it toward me, her other palm up and extended at a right angle, while she said some words I didn't understand but that contained those sounds I was quickly coming to hate.

My vision tunneled, and I heard something like, I dunno, maybe what waves would sound like if they crashed on metal. And, for just an instant, I had the most intense sensation of smelling new leather, a smell that vanished in the time it took me to identify it. It still seemed I was looking through a tunnel, with a golden light at the end, which then rushed at me and burst all around me.

When I could see again, I was somewhere else.

16

THE WEDDING

Sethra says that in the House of the Jhegaala, the two people being married start at opposite ends of a street or a path, and slowly walk toward each other, while two Old Wise Counselors instruct them on what marriage means, and then when they reach each other they kiss and that's that. We didn't do that, which, after all the walking I'd been doing lately, was just as well. We entered at the same time, from opposite sides of the chapel, and met at the altar, where Father Farkosh talked about what marriage meant and stuff. I don't remember what he said; I was looking at Cawti and thinking about how weak my knees were.

Loiosh, perched on an elaborate sconce off to the side, must have been aware of that, but was kind enough not to say anything.

The priest had us face each other. Cawti was holding a bundle of dried wheat, which she handed to Norathar. I had a bouquet of roses, which I handed to Kragar. If I'd had the attention to spare, I might have thought about how silly he looked holding a bouquet, but that didn't occur to me until just now. Kragar and Norathar gave the bundle and the bouquet to a little girl wearing a tiara of blue flowers, who somberly carried them down the aisle, dropping roses and wheat as she went. She looked familiar; I think she was related to Aliera, but I couldn't remember how.

Once the vegetation path had been created, I took Cawti's left hand in my right; she held my left hand in her right.

Father Farkosh lit a candle, used it to light a stick of incense, then snuffed out the candle and broke it in half. He asked Verra to look with favor on our vows. She didn't show up, and I was just as glad.

Then, at the word from Father Farkosh, I promised Cawti that I would always love her, and always be honest and kind. It felt like each word I said was going into the sky, and down into the bowels of the earth, and would be recorded forever. I don't think my voice was very strong, but Cawti's eyes were shining.

Her voice was strong and clear. When she said that she would love me as long as there was sky overhead and water in the ocean-sea and ground beneath our feet, and when she said she would be honest and kind, it didn't feel like a promise, it felt like a simple statement of fact. My vision blurred, but only with tears, and I didn't even care.

Father Farkosh held out a dull wooden knife, and we reluctantly let go of each other and extended our hands to him. It kind of tickled when he drew the knife over my palm. Cawti and I put our palms together.

The priest announced we were married, and we kissed, and the kiss lasted for as long as the Empire has existed, and I wanted it to last that long again.

We went slowly toward the door, where they'd formed a line to congratulate us. Noish-pa looked so proud and happy I would have burst if I weren't such a tough guy.

⊰⊱

"Boss?"

"I came through okay. I'm in some kind of cavern, except it's been fitted out with chairs, and a bed—I think it's the right place. Oh, and there are people here."

The people were two men in Jhereg colors, who I assumed to be the pretty usual toughs, and four women, also in Jhereg colors, who I assumed to be the sorcerous version of the pretty usual toughs.

They all stood and looked at me, and one of the women took a step forward, so I addressed her.

"Lady Tavissa?" I said.

She was about twenty feet away from me. "Did you bring my stone?" she said. The echo startled me a little.

"You know I didn't." That echo startled me a little too. "Also, it's Shireth's stone, not yours, you just used it because it was convenient. And you don't still need it for anything, do you?"

"I suppose not. How did you get here?"

"Make someone a demon, you permit demonic travel. You know that."

"It wasn't I that made you a demon."

"Close enough," I said.

"Yes, I suppose so."

The cavern was big. The building my flat was in would have fit into it, and it was well-lit, though I couldn't see where the light was coming from.

She took a step toward me and I waited.

"Are you here to kill me?" she said.

A number of answers came to mind. *If I had been, you wouldn't have seen me*, for the tough-guy assassin approach. Or, *I don't do that kind of thing*, for the I-admit-nothing assassin approach, or, *that depends on you*, for the Jhereg boss threat, or, *have you done something to make me want to kill you?* for the old, traditional, answer-a-question-with-a-question-and-see-if-you-get-something approach. After some consideration, I settled on "No."

"Good," she said. "Then I won't have to kill you." See, she was going for the smooth-unconcerned-powerful-sorceress approach.

She kept coming closer, which I took as a good sign; as a sorcerer, she'd have better odds against me by staying further away. She had the pushed-in Tsalmoth nose and the kind of round face. Her mouth was small, with thin lips. She had her hair tied back to show off her Noble's point.

"Lord Taltos," she said.

"A pleasure," I told her.

"And you have questions."

"I do."

"May I offer you wine? It isn't poisoned."

I'd been about to accept until she brought up the idea that it might be poisoned. "No, I'm fine. But please, go ahead." I looked around. "Nice place," I said. "Comfortable, for a cave. And that, um, thing in the middle there, that looks a bit like what I found in a certain storefront in Adrilankha not long ago."

"It's similar," she said. "Not quite the same. It's to place a spell, uh, some distance from here."

"Like in Castle Black?"

"Possibly."

"Or as far away as the duchy of Gillirand?"

"You know a lot," she said. "Please, sit."

There were six chairs, all facing a common point in the middle, and she hadn't indicated which chair she wanted me in, and she couldn't have trapped them all, could she? Well, I suppose she could, but it seemed worth the risk. "Thanks," I said, and sat in one. She sat facing me. The others backed up to give us room. We were all polite and civilized.

"I know what Chervik did to you," I said.

Her eyes narrowed, and she waited.

"What I don't know," I said, "is whether you and Shireth are working together on this, stabbing each other in the back, or both. My money's on both, but I wouldn't put a lot of it there."

She considered me through slitted eyes. "What's your interest?"

"You don't know? Well, that tells me something. My interest is eight hundred gold."

"What are you supposed to do for that?"

"No, no. I loaned it to someone, he died, I want it back."

"What does that have to do with me?"

"That's what I'm trying to figure out."

"Maybe you'd better explain a little."

I shook my head. "I've been doing that too much. Look, I think I've put most of this together. How about you just answer one question for me."

She smiled. "Go ahead."

"How were you planning to get Chervik to bite on the land swindle?"

Her brows went up. "Well," she said. "You are thorough."

"I got good people working for me."

"The idea was to buy her old lands at a good price, implying we had some special and probably illegal use for them. That would have tied her to it."

I nodded. "She didn't bite?"

Tavissa laughed. "Bad timing. She'd just made a real land investment, and didn't have the capital."

"Too bad."

"Yes."

"Was Fisher your friend?"

She wasn't smiling anymore. "You said one question."

"I lied. But I was just going to offer my condolences if he was."

"Thank you," she said.

"Bad break there too."

"Yes."

"And it seems like I sort of messed up that plan when I came into possession of the stone."

"Came into possession," she repeated.

"Let's not get hung up on details."

She shrugged.

"So," I went on, "you have a new plan, because that's what you do. Only this time, it involved me. You pulled me into it. You cast spells that altered me, and you made me a part of your scheme."

"You pulled yourself into it, Lord Taltos, with those details you don't want to get hung up on."

"Um. Okay, well, you just sort of undercut my moral high ground there."

"Sorry."

She didn't seem all that sorry.

"So now," I said, "since I screwed up your last plan—apologies, by the way, that wasn't my intention—what's the next one?"

"I can't think of any reason I should tell you."

"Huh. Okay. I *am* sorry though. I'd never want to get in the way of a good revenge caper."

"If that's a subtle way of asking if my motive is revenge, no, it isn't."

"Reinstatement then."

She nodded. "Not that I'd mind a little payback too, you understand."

"Sure. You spent a great deal of time learning sorcery, didn't you? Did you start out specializing in necromancy, or was that something you did for the Zerika's Point plan?"

"So many questions, so little reason I should answer them."

"In fact, I can give you a reason. I found the spell you had put on me. Well, I should say a friend found it; I'm not all that good."

She reached out her hand, paused, and said, "May I?"

I let Spellbreaker fall into my hand. "If you're only checking, then yes."

She looked at the chain, and her eyes widened. "My goodness."

"Go ahead."

She nodded, reached toward me, then sat back. "The spell is still there."

"Yes, part of it. The effect is still set, and so is the trigger. But wasn't there also a compulsion to make me want to go to the right place?"

She did it again, then said, "I see. Well played."

I bowed my head and put Spellbreaker away.

"So, in order for this to work, I need to convince you to do it willingly, and for that I need to answer your questions."

"It's good we have an understanding."

"All right, Jhereg. What do you want to know?"

"First of all, Shireth."

"She doesn't know I'm using her. Her scheme—the sale of the hishi extract—should still work, so there's no reason for her to be upset, or to know more than she does. What else?"

"How is this thing I'm supposed to do going to help you?"

"It will protect Chervik's land from the effects of the amorphia."

"So? How is that—"

"It's illegal magic, pre-Empire sorcery."

"Oh. Okay, I can see where that would embarrass her. How do you go from there to regaining your title?"

"I have a plan."

"No disrespect intended, but so far your plans haven't turned out well."

"This one might not either. But it's worth a try. Which reminds me, why didn't you go to her? She has the resources of her whole House."

"I did. She wouldn't pay enough for the information."

"I see. Well, permit me to hope that is a mistake she will come to regret."

"Sure. Meanwhile, I guess you'd better lay it out for me."

"Once she is tied to pre-Empire sorcery, I offer the chance to either come clean about how I was removed from my position, or take the consequences."

"Blackmail."

"Persuasion."

"Blackmail."

"Details."

"So, I go there, and this spell goes off that protects the area from the amorphia."

"Right."

"*Morrolan? Do you have a fix on me?*"

"*Pathfinder has it,*" he said. "*We can get you out whenever you want.*"

"To whom were you just speaking?" Tavissa wanted to know.

"I'm assuring my friends that no one has tried to kill me."

She nodded. "So you'll do it?"

"Let's not get ahead of ourselves. I still have questions."

"Go ahead."

"Why plant the spell on me that way? By having me summoned?"

"First of all, when you weren't carrying the stone, I couldn't find you. Next, you have a tendency to surround yourself with powerful people, as witness to the fact that you discovered the spell, and that you're here. If you'd been around them when it was cast, they'd have probably prevented it, as they thwarted my first effort."

I was a little annoyed at her for using my word like that, but I just said, "Makes sense."

"So, what's it going to take for you to go in there and do this?"

"Nine hundred and thirteen imperials. In advance."

"That's an odd number."

"It's what it'll cost."

"Will you take a draft on Harbrough?"

"I use him too. Yeah, that'll be fine."

She went behind her table, dug around, found the necessary items, and I heard the "scratch scratch" sound that I don't like as much as the "clink clink" I'm used to, but it'll do. She blew on the draft, then walked back and gave it to me. It was all in order.

"All right," I said. "How does this work?"

"I teleport you to the area, then the spell goes off, and you go on your way."

"All right." I was just about to say, "I'm ready when you are," but the words wouldn't come out of my mouth.

"Lord Taltos?" she said.

How do I tell you about the next few seconds? I can talk about fights I was in, and times I intimidated someone, and even, sort of, about sorcery, or weird mystical things I had no business being part of. But how do I tell you about that next couple of seconds, the time it took me to draw a breath to tell her to do it, and instead, I had—

Thoughts, that's what I had.

I stood there, about ready to finally get that thing done, and instead I had thoughts, and I don't know how to tell you about thoughts. I know as I stood there, one thing wouldn't go away, and wouldn't be put aside: I was a demon now.

What does it mean to be a demon, anyway? Oh, I know, it means you can "manifest." But what does it actually mean? Does it change who you are, deep down? When Dragaerans talk about demons, they have this kind of curl to their lip—the same one they get when they talk about Easterners, so I guess I should be used to it. But to my people, humans, there's a different sort of edge to it: there's fear, the idea of power that we can't understand, and that isn't good. There's this feeling of something that wants to hurt us, and can do it in ways we don't understand and can't prevent. And

I think even to Dragaerans, there's something in there, something way back, that says demons are evil; that if they weren't evil, they wouldn't be demons.

I don't know what Dragaerans mean by evil. I don't know what humans mean by evil. I don't even know what I mean by evil. I suppose killing people, and sometimes beating them and threatening them for money, would be considered evil, but for me, it's just what I do to get along, to have some little measure of control over my own life. Most people don't have that, you know. But I do; I can make decisions about what I want or don't want that some Teckla, or some day laborer in the Easterner's ghetto just can't, and that's what I want, to have that much freedom.

And now I had that much less.

There were books on demonology—how to summon and control certain demons, the ones who'd been researched. Did that mean I was now going to appear in someone's book, to be passed around?

Did it make me immortal? I'd heard that demons, when they die on their own world, in some sense continue, and can still be summoned and controlled. I could ask the Necromancer about that, only I didn't want to. I wasn't sure I wanted to be immortal, at least, not that way.

I don't like the idea that I can be controlled.

I didn't feel any different. I was still the same Vlad who liked to cook clam sauce for pasta, and liked to kiss Easterners, and liked—may as well admit it—the feeling of power that came from telling Dragaerans what to do, and that came with, sometimes, knowing I was going to be the one to decide their fate, the last person they saw in this life. To them, to those I was paid to kill, I could do them harm, and I could do it in ways they didn't understand and couldn't prevent.

So being a demon shouldn't matter; it shouldn't change anything.

Cawti didn't look at me any different, Loiosh didn't talk to me any different.

But now I had that sound in my head, my name that was my

name at some kind of deeper level than just Vlad; it meant more, and because of it, I could be made to do things.

I could be made to do evil things, even if I did evil things anyway and still didn't know what that meant.

And this piece of paper in my hand was suddenly just one more thing controlling me. It was one thing too many.

I crumpled up the draft and threw it onto the floor. "No," I said. "Sorry, deal's off."

She frowned. "I don't—"

"I don't care," I said. "I don't care about the Verra-be-damned eight hundred, and I don't care that I'm the one who lifted that stone. You did something to me, you took something from me that no one should ever take from anyone. You think about that."

"Morrolan, get me out of here."

He did, but the teleport took too long.

Did she think I was attacking her? I can't see how she'd have thought that. Did she figure I was going to go away, come up with something, then come back and kill her? There wasn't time for her to figure all that; it was so fast.

I still don't know for sure, but my best guess is she didn't think about it—she felt the sorcery, and just reacted. It's not like I've never done something like that.

The teleport took a couple of seconds, and I had time to see her face twist, and time to see her point a finger at me, and time to feel something hit me on the left side below my rib cage.

The library of Castle Black appeared around me, and Aliera said, "You're bleeding. Let me—"

"No," I said. I clapped my hand over my side, pressed, and ignored the wetness. "No."

"Vlad—" said Cawti.

"No. She just attacked me. I'm tired of this. No. I want this done. Now, before she has time to get a block up that Morrolan can't break. Send me back there."

Cawti stood up, her face like stone, and stood next to me. Loiosh landed on my shoulder.

"Boss, you're in no shape—"

"Shut up."

"Do it, Aliera," I said.

"You'll die."

"I don't care. I'm tired of being slashed, cut, ensorcelled. I'm sick of it. Aliera, please. Do it now."

I was so wretched from the after-effects of the first teleport, not to mention the spell I'd been hit with, I hardly noticed the second, except that I saw we were back in the cavern, and then everything thinned and narrowed, and I think I passed out for a second, because I'm not sure how I ended up flat on the ground, or how I stood up again. I was still holding my side.

They could have taken us right then. There were only two of us, or three if you count Loiosh, and Cawti and I were wobbly and barely able to stand. Near as I can tell, they just looked at us, couldn't believe we were a threat, and waited to see what we were doing there. She'd attacked me without thinking when I was no threat, and then, when I *was* a threat, she thought about it and didn't attack.

By the time I was on my feet, Cawti looked steady, and drew her daggers. I removed my hand from my side, hoping I wouldn't bleed out too fast, and let Spellbreaker fall into my hand and drew my rapier.

Tavissa stared at me like I was an idiot, which was only fair. Then she shrugged, turned to her people, and nodded.

We held ourselves still and waited for them to move. Cawti's shoulder against mine felt relaxed and ready. I was light-headed, but I didn't feel inclined to show it. I was also sick, but it was way back, like it didn't matter; maybe having your blood pumping, being in a situation where you're about to die, is a good way to keep from being sick after a teleport. In general, I'd rather be sick.

But I couldn't complain; I'd put myself here.

Time held itself still, waiting for us to attack them, or them to attack us. Instead, something else happened.

I felt a pop of displaced air. I could have looked to see who was there, but I didn't have to: It was Blackwand and it was Pathfinder, and the corrosive, brutal psychic energy of those two weapons were enough to answer all of my questions.

Tavissa took a step back. She was scared, so were the others. Things had more than evened up.

"Vlad," said Morrolan.

"What?"

"Let it go."

"She—"

"I know."

"I can't let—"

"Yes, you can. This is murder, Vlad. And she hasn't earned it."

"She made me a demon."

"Not on purpose."

"Vlad," said Aliera. "He's right. You can't do this."

I turned to Cawti. "What do you think?"

"Whatever your play is," she said. "I've got your back."

"But are they right?"

She hesitated.

"Go ahead," I told her. "Say it."

"Just because you've been hurt," she said, "doesn't mean anyone did anything wrong."

Even weak from the teleport and loss of blood and burning up with the need to put holes in people, that got through.

I took a breath. "You mean, after all of this, we don't even get to kill anybody?"

"Well, it isn't like you were paid for it." She gave me that smile that could make me kill, die, or sometimes, I guess, refrain from killing.

I took another breath, then another, then turned back to Tavissa. "Next time I see you," I said, and then, I think, I passed out before I could finish the threat.

⊰⊱

They brought me back to Castle Black, and I was mercifully unconscious for the teleport. Aliera patched me up again, this time without making any comments. Cawti held my hand.

When Aliera was gone, she said, "I'm sorry you didn't get to kill anyone, Vladimir."

I laughed, and was pleased that laughing didn't hurt.

"You okay marrying a demon?" I said.

"My demon," she said.

"Your demon," I agreed.

17

THE RECEPTION

Aliera told me that the Athyra do everything psychically, the wedding, the reception, all of it, and I believed her until she started laughing. Yeah, she's funny, that one.

Anyway, we don't.

After the wedding, we walked like a parade through the streets of South Adrilankha. People smiled and waved and blew kisses, because weddings are a big thing in that part of town.

Cawti was on my arm, and she was smiling that smile the whole time. I kept looking at her and grinning like an idiot. The Dragons—Morrolan, Aliera, and Norathar—seemed to accept the parade as if it was natural. Kragar, Sticks, and Melestav, as well as the other Jhereg, all seemed uncomfortable about it. Sethra and the Necromancer both seemed unconcerned about the whole thing. Lady Teldra, of course, was perfect, on Noish-pa's arm, waving to everyone we passed and appearing to have the time of her life. What with all the Dragons, the Jhereg, and the Easterners, I don't think South Adrilankha had ever seen anything like it.

We reached the dance hall just off Potter's Market Street, and went in. There were kethna stuffed cabbage rolls in spicy tomato sauce with sour cream, and there was chicken soup with droplets of oil floating in it, and tiny, flaky pastries filled with iced cream and covered with a sauce of chocolate, sugar, and orange liqueur.

There was music of fiddles, and Noish-pa taught Lady Teldra a chardosh, then taught me a Yougrosh. Cawti waltzed with Morrolan, and then Cawti and I did a karikahz alone while our guests threw copper at *our feet, then we did the scarf dance with no music except all our guests clapping.*

You know, here's where I should say some nonsense about how the food and music brought everyone together or something, but, sorry, they didn't. The Dragons mostly stayed with the Dragons, the Jhereg with the Jhereg, and the Easterners with the Easterners. And there were more than a few sour glances between those in one group and those in another. But no one killed anyone, so maybe that, by itself, is a win?

The music started again, and we danced and ate and laughed, and, demon or not, I'd never felt so alive.

⇥⇤

It was a couple of days before I was well enough to leave Castle Black. Kragar had kept the business running all right.

I sent a message to Matiess to confirm that everything was over, and he could safely take possession of his property.

I went back to Three-Dice and sold the Verra's tear for six hundred and ten, now that it was safe, so I at least got back more than I'd invested in recovering it.

I talked to Toronnan to let him know what had happened and to see if I could get him to confirm that he'd given Paquitin permission to knock me on the head, and he did like it was no big deal, and he knew I'd come back on account of who my friends were, and I shouldn't have tried to muscle in, and a bunch of crap like that.

I made up my mind to shove a dagger into his eye someday, but meanwhile I smiled, bowed, and took my leave.

Cawti and I got married and she took up residence in my flat and set in to making it her own, in the best possible ways. We moved a table, and it was as good as I'd thought it would be.

As for Tavissa and Chervik, I don't know. Chervik is still Heir, and I assume Tavissa is still figuring out ways to get at her, and maybe one of these days she'll come up with something. Sethra removed the remnants of the spell, so it's none of my business; she can stay in that cavern and rot as far as I'm concerned.

I returned to Dzur Mountain, and after Sethra had finished removing the spell, she asked if I'd be willing to tell the whole thing into that box, and offered enough gold so I ended up almost even on that eight hundred.

So I sat down to tell the whole thing, yet again, and now I have.

So, the question is, Sethra, can you do something? I know before, you said you couldn't, but—

That's all it would take? If I don't know the name, no one can—

Uh, what do you mean?

Verra? The Demon Goddess? Like, herself, personally? Why would she even—

Okay, I get that. I don't know, it sounds like a good trade-off. I think. Better than—

Oh. Well, how much of my memory would I lose?

That's . . . Okay, yeah. Disturbing.

No, no. If it's a choice between that, and letting some bastard summon me and make me do things, I'm in. Go ahead. Do I need to do anything to prepare?

Yes, now.

I . . . wait.

What were we talking about?

EPILOGUE

That was years ago, and the memories are still returning. I had never forgotten our wedding, but so much of what happened around it had been gone for all this time. And a few remarks Cawti had made that had puzzled me at the time now made sense.

I was in Adrilankha again, or rather, just west of it. Among the things I'd forgotten was just how stupid I'd been. Was I any smarter now? Maybe. I hoped so.

I could have teleported back to the City, of course. Having tossed the Phoenix Stone into the ocean-sea, I had my link to the Orb once again, and could perform sorcery as well as I ever could. But I wanted to walk, to think, to remember.

And if the Left Hand wanted to try me now, out here in the open was fine with me.

So I walked. The walk was not unpleasant, and my mood was— well, I had one, leave it at that.

A little further I stopped, left the road, and walked up to the cliff edge. I looked down at the crashing waves and the rocks below. A few years and many lifetimes ago, Cawti and I had levitated down there looking for a cave we couldn't find, and we'd sat on a rock— there, that one—and talked and skipped stones.

I'd forgotten about that. I'd forgotten about a lot of the things that led up to it, and some of the things that led from it. I'd forgotten that strange sound that was, in some sense I still didn't understand, my name. I remembered that now, too, and I understood what it meant.

I had been angry at the Demon Goddess for messing with my memories, only now it seemed they'd been messed with twice, and neither time was her fault. Once, it was because I was in a place no human mind is able to grasp, and the other time . . .

And Sethra. I wanted so badly to be angry at her, and the Demon Goddess, for what they'd done, but, alas, I also remembered that I had wanted them to do it. And it isn't like I wasn't warned. It really sucks when you have no one to blame but yourself.

Loiosh left me with my thoughts.

I stared at the rock where Cawti and I had skipped stones, and tears burned in my eyes until I got up, turned my back on the ocean-sea, and resumed my walk toward Adrilankha. Maybe I could get carthis there.

ACKNOWLEDGMENTS

My thanks to Alexx Kay for functioning as my external memory, and to Skyler Grey who pretty much saved this one when I had thought all was lost. Will Shetterly, Emma Bull, and Pamela Dean helped with much needed critique, and of course, thanks to my editor Claire Eddy, as well as copy editor Ed Chapman. My humble gratitude to Robert Charles Morgan, who started the ball rolling.

I must also acknowledge here the work of my agent, Kay Mc-Cauley, who passed away around the time I completed this. Beyond how splendid she was as an agent, she was a giant in the field, and a wonderful, delightful, powerful lady who will be badly missed. If I may quote from another of her clients, we will not see her like again.

Turn the page for a sneak peek at
the next Vlad Taltos novel

Available Winter 2024 from Tor Books

PROLOGUE

"Do it smaller," my grandfather had told me over and over. "If your parry causes your opponent's blade to miss you by more than half an inch, it means you've pushed too hard and your riposte will be too slow. In a fight, anything can happen, so end it as quickly as you can, and that means not giving him free chances at you. Do it smaller."

I love how often my grandfather's fencing advice applies to things that have nothing to do with fencing.

But let me start at the beginning, in that little klava hole, talking to Sara, who'd made the mistake of saying, "So, Vlad, what have you been up to?"

She listened without a word until I'd run down, then she said, "I may be able to help."

That was it. Not "That's amazing, Vlad!" or "I can't believe you did that!" or "You could have been killed!" Also, no "So, you got out of the trouble with the Jhereg, but now the Left Hand wants to kill you?" Nothing like that. Just "I may be able to help." I hadn't told her the whole thing because I thought she could help, I just wanted to talk about it, so I was both pleased and surprised by her reply.

"Go on," I said.

"You need to hide from the Left Hand so they can't get rich by killing you, now that you went and, that is, now that you no longer have your sorcery protections."

"Right."

"But you want to be here, in the City."

"Exactly."

"So you need a place with protections from sorcerous detection."

"Right."

"But you can't exactly move in to the Imperial Wing of the Palace."

"Yeah."

"So you're thinking of some individual who is already worried enough about surveillance to keep such protections up all the time."

I nodded. "I know a few, but either the protections aren't strong enough to stand up to the Left Hand, or they're too obvious, like my old office."

"And putting up a new one defeats the purpose; it's like a sign saying, 'Here I am.'"

"Precisely."

"When did you last sleep, Vlad?"

"Night before last."

"So a place to sleep where you can actually relax is getting urgent."

"Yeah."

"Yes," she said. "I can help."

"I'm listening."

"That's the trouble. If I understand you right, you might not be the only one."

"Um. True."

My familiar interrupted into my head. *"Boss? Does this mean Daymar?"*

"Maybe not."

"So," I told Sara. "I need to make sure I'm not found or listened to long enough to get where we're going."

She nodded. "Can you do it?"

"I think so. Or, rather, I think I can arrange it."

"I'll wait to tell you the rest, then."

So, yeah, if you happen to have the most powerful sorceress in the history of the world as a friend, there are times when you go, sure, I can ask her for a favor.

"Vlad. What is it?"

"Greetings, Sethra. I want to ask you for a favor. Is this a bad time?"

"No, it's fine. What can I do for you?"

"Can you make me psychically undetectable long enough for me to get to a safe place? Say, an hour or so?"

She was quiet, then, *"From here?"*

"Yeah."

"You want to walk somewhere, and be sure no one knows you're going there. And you want me to do it from here, while you're there."

"Yeah. Me and one other. I mean, I don't mind if you come here first, but—"

"No, I want to try it from here. I've never done that before. Give me a minute to think about this. I should be able to come up with something."

Sara was looking an inquiry at me. I held up a finger.

We were, by the way, in a little klava joint in the Hook, which is where I ended up after a night of walking through the city, not wanting to stop for fear of being sorcerously evaporated or something. It had nine tables, mostly deuces with a couple of four-tops, and woodwork that needed painting, and the only light was what came through two paper-covered windows in the front. It did, however, have a rear exit. I was tired, but too keyed up to be sleepy. It was late morning, and the place was empty except for us and the staff. I kept them supplied with clinky things and they kept me supplied with klava so everyone was happy.

I love klava so much. The worst part of dying is the idea of an afterlife without klava.

Okay, maybe not the worst.

Presently, I felt the delicate probe of a familiar presence insinuating itself into my mind, and Sethra spoke into my head again.

"Yes," she said. "I can do it. Now?"

"Now?" I said to Sara.

She nodded.

"Yes," I told Sethra.

Then I felt something like a warm blanket settle over my mind, if that makes any sense. Sara looked mildly startled.

"Thank you, Sethra."

"My pleasure; it's a rare treat to do something I've never done before. You'll have to tell me the story sometime."

"Sometime."

"We can talk now," I told Sara. "And move without being detected."

She stood up, picked up her instrument case, slung it over her shoulder, and led me out, preceded by Loiosh and Rocza, who like to be sure about such things. Sara had to hold the door for them as they flew out. Once we started walking, Loiosh returned to my shoulder while Rocza continued circling overhead, for all appearances just another of the jhereg who flew around the city hoping to scavenge someone's leftovers.

Sara immediately turned south, toward the ocean-sea, and took us downhill.

Before I could ask, Sara said, "So, you'll never guess who gets completely paranoid about secrecy."

"Who?"

"Theater companies."

"Really?"

She nodded. "They're absolutely convinced their competitors are going to steal their set ideas, their blocking, their interpretations."

"So, they're nuts?"

She shrugged. "It's happened a few times, so there's at least some reason for it."

"Okay. So, they have good security?"

"Every theater in the City has spells to prevent sorcery, and powerful spells to prevent clairvoyance and any other sort of detection until the show opens, and most of them don't bother to take the spells down after that."

"Huh. Okay, you're right. I wouldn't have expected that. What about psychic communication? Will I be out of touch?"

"As a rule, they leave a channel open for that so the director can supply a line an actor forgets. I'm not sure how that works, but you can reach the Orb, it just won't let you pull in any power for sorcery."

Psychic contact, for most people at least, involves sorcery, at least a little. So there was a mystery there, and maybe indicated a way the Left Hand could find me. Still, it sounded like the best I was going to get. "So," I said, "your idea is for me to hide in a theater?"

She nodded. "Most of them have places backstage where people can sleep, and many of them have extensive basements. Some of them, like the one we're going to, are effectively a block of flats with a theater above them."

"How do I convince them to let me stay?"

"I know some theater people. A lot of musicians do theater work."
For the first time, I had a sinking feeling. "Musicals?"
"Sometimes."
"All right," I said.
By this time, we were climbing again, and I guessed were heading
toward North Hill. We didn't speak for a while, and, yes, we got to
North Hill, and turned onto Fallow Street.
The theater was called the Crying Clown, and there was a big
handbill outside of it. I stopped and read it.

Opening on the 14th of Tsalmoth,
A New Production of Linesca's
SONG OF THE PRESSES
Expanded to Three Days! with Six New Songs
Crafted by our Own LADY SINDRA!
Featuring MONTORRI as Keraasak
and MARSKO as Lethra Savode!

I looked at Sara. "Lethra Savode?" I repeated.
"Liability," she said.
"Um. Okay. In any case, there's one good thing you can say about
a three-day musical."
"It isn't a four-day musical?"
"'Xactly."
She smiled a little. "I like musicals."
"Really?"
"The singing is usually very good, and the lightness lets it come up
under your guard."
"Huh. Okay. I haven't seen that many. There was childhood
trauma involved. And it opens in six days?"
"Yes, the big push to get the word out probably started a week ago,
and dress rehearsals will most likely begin in a couple of days."
We went around to a side door. Sara pulled the clapper, a peeper
opened, closed, and the door opened. An old man, a Chreotha, ig-
nored me and asked Sara, "Substitute?"
"No," she said. "I'm a friend of Kota. Can I see him?"
The old Chreotha grunted and stepped aside.

Sara led us through a labyrinth of corridors broken by open areas that looked like workshops, and eventually up a stair, then through more hallways, until we emerged into the main hall. We went down a last hallway toward what I later learned was called "side seven," that is, the way to get to the stage without passing through the audience. She paused long enough to make sure no one was in the middle of a line or something, and stepped onto the stage. There were several musicians, many of them with instruments I couldn't name, sitting and looking attentive in the lowered area immediately to our left. We took two steps and jumped down into it.

"Hey Sara," said one of them. He looked like he was probably a Jhegaala, and hadn't brushed his hair since the Interregnum. He was holding a violin.

"Kota," she said. "Good to see you."

"Who's the Easterner?" he said.

"A friend."

Kota seemed surprised but only nodded.

"Can you introduce me to the director?" she said.

"Sure. What's it about? I mean, if you feel like telling me."

She looked at me and I shrugged. "In general, sure. If it works, they'll all know eventually."

"My friend here is in a spot of trouble," she told Kota. "I'd like to see if he could use this place to stay out of the way."

"Huh," he said. "All right. Can you wait for the end of rehearsal? We have half an hour until lunch."

We agreed that was no problem, and Sara led me toward a far corner in the side-four section where we'd be out of the way. As we navigated the aisles, I said, "What is *Song of the Presses?*"

"It's about the suppression of another play, *Last Man Printing*, in the Fourteenth Cycle, which was about—"

"Wait," I said. "They're putting on a play about putting on a play?"

She nodded.

"Huh," I said. "That seems kind of—"

I was cut off by a woman sitting right around the middle of the theater, maybe just a bit forward, calling, "Run it from the dramaturge. Keraasak, your line. 'Ah, but you see.'"

A guy, I presume Keraasak, addressed the woman near him in a stage voice. "Ah, but you see, we are not like other companies. We have our own dramaturge."

"You have your own dramaturge?"

"We have our own dramaturge!"

The musicians I'd noticed earlier started playing, and I became frightened. A guy entered from the same place we had, turned to show himself to all six sides, and said, "I am their own dramaturge!" Then, as I was afraid would happen, he started singing.

I am the very model of a Fourteenth Cycle dramaturge
I can tell an epic from a canticle or from a dirge.
In Landza and in Ekrasen I've studied all the references
And if you give me time I will expound upon my preferences.
I can tell you of the change in rhyme and meter from a
        younger age
And why it is you'll always find six sides on every proper
        stage.
I've knowledge of the pay-scales of full actors and apprentices
Along with all the fines for being late upon their entrances.

I know about the costuming of the Eleventh Phoenix Reign
And why the makeup artists nearly always ended up insane.
In short where all the branches of the thespianic arts
        converge
I am the very model of a Fourteenth Cycle dramaturge.

I'm familiar with the history Lord Neering used about
        Northport,
And how to dodge the censors when presenting it before the
        Court.
Producers, they all seek me for my lore of esoterica
And how to turn fine art into the gold returns numerica.
I know which plays will always recompense you monetarily
And which will fail and leave the comp'ny bankrupt most
        unfairily.
I know why complex stagings can be hoist with their own
        petards

And why there's no production of that silly work *The Phoenix
   Guards*.

Then I can say what handbills will attract the most nobility
And know how rigging wire can replace lack of agility.
In short where all the branches of the thespianic arts
   converge
I am the very model of a Fourteenth Cycle dramaturge.

In fact, when I know what is meant by Prop and by Enunciate
And when I know the difference between Punctual and
   Punctuate
When such affairs as openings and callbacks I'm no stranger
   to
When I know what the usher and the lighting color-changer
   do
When I have learned what progress has been made in
   modern set design
When I know more of blocking than an abstinent might
   know of wine
In short, when I know values of reserved and of the common
   seats
You'll say a better dramaturge has never counted gate
   receipts.

Though actors run and cower when they hear that I am on
   the set
And no one has admitted my advice has ever helped him yet,
Still where all the branches of the thespianic arts converge
I am the very model of a Fourteenth Cycle dramaturge.

"Okay," said the woman who was obviously the director. "Good,
but come down left another couple of steps at the beginning of the
second verse, so when you get to the second chorus, you can cross
and—"
   She went on for a while, but I stopped paying attention. Instead, I
turned to Sara, who was looking at me. "Well?" she said.

"I have no words," I said.

She laughed. "If you can withhold your artistic judgments, we might be able to hide you here for as long as you need to settle things."

I nodded. "I'll be strong," I said.

"You always are," she said.

"And thank you," I added.

ABOUT THE AUTHOR

David Dyer-Bennet

Steven Brust is the author of a number of bestselling fantasy novels, including two *New York Times* bestsellers, *Dzur* and *Tiassa*. He lives in Minneapolis, Minnesota.

dreamcafe.com
Twitter: @StevenBrust